THE DEAD OF SUMMER

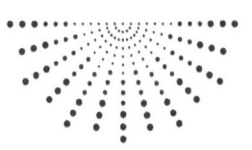

THE DEAD OF SUMMER

A PIPER BLACKWELL MYSTERY #3

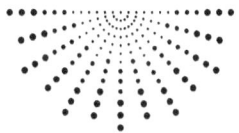

JEAN RABE

Boone Street Press

PRAISE FOR JEAN RABE

Mystery just got a little less cozy in THE DEAD OF WINTER.
New York Times and *USA Today* bestselling author Steven Savile

Jean Rabe delivers a suspenseful morsel that not only celebrates the Yuletide season, but also keeps you up at night with a well-crafted mystery. THE DEAD OF WINTER is chilling indeed!
Raymond Benson, author of The Black Stiletto series, *New York Times* bestselling author of James Bond novels

For years I've admired Jean Rabe's work in the science fiction and fantasy genres, and now, with THE DEAD OF WINTER, she's applying her considerable talents to the field of mysteries. The first in a very promising series with an attractive main character, Piper Blackwell, a female county sheriff who faces obstacles both on and off the job while investigating a puzzling homicide. Very much recommended.
Multiple award-winning and three-time Edgar nominee author Brendan DuBois

THE DEAD OF WINTER was a blast—lots of fun to read! Jean Rabe's characters come to life through the written word, and it takes a real writing talent to accomplish this feat.
Denise Dietz, *USA Today* bestselling author

The Dead of Summer
A Piper Blackwell Mystery

Jean Rabe

Boone Street Press

Boone Street Press
Illinois

Boone Street Press

First Boone Street Press Edition: 2019

Name: Rabe, Jean, author

Title: The Dead of Summer, a Piper Blackwell Mystery / Jean Rabe

Description: First Edition. Boone Street Press

Identifiers: ISBN 13: 978-1-7325267-1-6

LCCN: 9781732526716

Printed in the United States of America

For Rembert

CHAPTER ONE

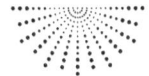

5 P.M. FRIDAY, JUNE 14TH

The gut-punching clang of metal striking metal merged with the screams of fairgoers. Sheriff Piper Blackwell whirled toward the sound, swearing World War III had broken out in Spencer County.

Piper dropped her corn dog and raced into the wall of noise just as a *BOOM* made her think a mortar had exploded. The screams grew louder and a kaleidoscope of colors–the bright summer attire of the agitated crowd–filled her vision.

"Nooooooo!"

"Call an ambulance!"

"Outta my way!"

"Get some pictures!"

"Mary's on that thing! DEAR GOD, my Mary!"

Piper's gaze angled above the heads of the panicked throng as she shoved forward. Fast.

Moving through tiny increments between elbows and shoulders, she pulled out her badge, held it high as if that might buy her more space amid the press of gawkers.

"Sheriff! MOVE!" she bellowed.

1

The fingers of her free hand dipped into a pocket for her cell phone as she rushed toward the metal monstrosity.

"Teegan!" Piper hollered into the device.

"Did ya see the boys flyin'?" This from a big man she stepped around.

"Think they're dead?"

"Dead. Dead. Dead."

"The whole thing's gonna go!"

"DEAR GOD, Mary!"

"There's the sheriff!"

"Where's my kids?"

"Call 9-1-1."

"Somebody call 9-1-1!"

Piper was quite confident everyone was calling 9-1-1, as Teegan was not answering.

"Teegan, pick up the damn phone," Piper willed as she hurtled a fence around the Strawberry-Go-Round, vaulted a bench, and closed on the broken ride, a tilting, towering contrivance called the Cosmic Odyssey. It leaned precariously, resembling a mangled Ferris wheel on steroids. People strapped in on higher levels flailed and shrieked. Riders closer to the ground unbuckled themselves and jumped.

Parents wailed and pushed forward while fair workers tried to hold them back.

"Teegan! Teegan!" Piper yelled.

Finally a reply. "Sheriff."

"Teegan! SOP Mass Casualty Response. County fairgrounds." SOP —Standard Operating Procedure. Piper shivered; she'd practically memorized the department's procedure manual and the CALEA—The Commission on Accreditation for Law Enforcement Agencies—policies for emergencies involving mass casualties. But knowing about it was far removed from putting it all into operation. Piper had never expected it to come into play in rural Indiana.

Piper heard Teegan dispatching ambulances, deputies, and fire engines.

"On it, Sheriff," Teegan said a moment later.

"Vests, radios, follow the deployment plan. Every deputy on duty, send them to the midway. Call Basil. Rockport police for backup. A big ride broke, and we've got injuries, maybe fatalities."

"They're radioing in, Sheriff. Already on their way."

The Cosmic Odyssey consisted of a massive center pole around which three different-sized rings of hang-glider baskets perched at thirty-degree angles to the ground. It was the tallest ride at the fair, and Piper had seen it in operation minutes ago, spinning, rising and dropping, yellow and orange baskets twirling, riders whooping in fear and delight. She now saw mangled metal where two of the baskets had torn loose from the highest ring: top girders were warped, a chunk of the framework had fallen, and it looked like the struts were ready to give out.

A ramp led up to the boarding platform. Piper headed for it, but was jerked back by a burly man.

"My son's up there!" He squeezed Piper's arm in desperation and yelled in her face. "Billie's way at the top."

Piper yanked free. "We'll get him down."

The man made another grab for her, and the woman at his side, red-faced and wailing, reached for her shoulder. Piper evaded them and was up the ramp in two long strides, pocketing her badge, and stretching to catch a dangling teen on a low basket who had unbuckled herself. She steadied the sobbing girl, sent her toward the crowd. Piper would need to run in search of the missing baskets, but the listing ride held a greater deadly potential.

"Bobby! Get my Bobby!"

"They're all gonna die!"

"Mary!"

Screams carried other names, and out of the corner of her eye she saw the swell of people press closer. Other fairgoers had stepped in to help the workers to police the crowd.

"Get all these people down now!" Piper shouted to the ride operator, a shaking tanned man in camo pants and a dayglow-yellow muscle shirt.

"I'm getting them! I'm trying!" He pulled a lever and the lowest ring of baskets descended to the bottom. The Odyssey groaned louder. More earsplitting wails came from riders who fumbled with the catches and released themselves. One of them fell hard nearby and Piper scooped him up, tugging him back toward the ramp and realizing he was too short to have been on the ride according to the height chart. Someone darted in and snatched the boy.

"Mommmmmm!" he cried.

The operator lowered the second ring, and the Cosmic Odyssey complained again. He and Piper frantically pulled one rider off after another, including a sobbing teen with a broken arm.

The shouts from the onlookers were deafening and confusing. Operators from other rides shouldered through the crowd to help.

"These people gotta back way the hell off," one of the operators said. "Vern, this whole thing's gonna buckle."

"GET BACK!" Piper hollered at the crowd. She realized they likely couldn't hear her over their hysterical cries. "This ride could fall. Get back!"

Wearing capris topped by a boat-neck tunic and Birkenstock sandals, Piper didn't look like law enforcement. But most in the crowd grudgingly followed her command and edged away.

Piper assisted two more riders as her phone vibrated and she fumbled it out.

"What?" Piper paused. "Oren? You're here? Already? Where are–?"

She strained to hear him as she and fair workers helped the next batch of hysterical teens out of the baskets.

"I'll get there as soon as I can." Piper needed to be in two places at the same time—with Oren and right here. She spotted the butcher from Rockport's grocery store. "Lou! I could use your help."

He and two other burly men pushed up the ramp and lifted riders out of the hanging baskets.

"I've got this, boss!" One of her deputies, Diego, wiggled through the mob and up the ramp next to Piper. The ramp sagged under all the weight. Apparently Diego—in shorts and a Kentucky Wildcats t-shirt —had been attending opening night of the fair, too. Did she have more deputies in attendance? "Go! I've got this, boss."

"Get 'em down, Diego, get the crowd back. This whole damn thing might topple," Piper warned.

She sprinted away, following Oren's directions, wedging through the horrified gawkers, some of them grabbing at her, screaming about their children, their relatives, their spouses, their friends.

"We're working on it, stay back," she repeated to everyone who tried to slow her. Piper sped on, past something called Crazy Carl's Crooked Coaster, swallowing hard when she found Oren, who had located one of the missing hang-glider baskets. It had landed upside down atop a cotton candy food truck, smashing the roof and shattering its windows. The van doors bulged outward. People swarmed close. Piper ordered them away.

"Get back! Get the hell back!" Piper was too overwhelmed at the sight to be polite. "Give us some space!"

Oren, her chief deputy, was dressed in blue jeans with a khaki polo that resembled his sheriff department uniform shirt. He was trying to keep the gawkers at bay and had clipped his badge on the pocket. Oren was a head taller than everyone else in the cluster. His curly steel-gray hair stuck out from under an Indianapolis Colts ball cap that shaded his lined face. Near him, a man in a garish plaid shirt helped. Piper recognized him as a retired Rockport police officer.

"You heard the sheriff," Oren hollered in a voice considerably louder than Piper's. "Get the hell back!" He waved to a tall, thin man. "Dave. Over here!" And then another. "Bruce! Give us a hand! We need to keep these folks out of here."

Piper registered all the blood. It ran in rivulets down the side of the pink and white cotton candy food truck. A man's arm hung loose where the hang-glider had impacted against the roof. His crushed head was halfway visible.

"Sheila!" Oren boomed. "Over here. Need some help." Piper realized her chief deputy was calling on people he knew to work as a crowd buffer. She could deputize people if necessary, but she didn't have time at the moment.

Were there other riders trapped next to the squashed man? The baskets could each hold three, Piper had noted. There might be two more victims in that awful jumble. No chance of survivors. And where was the second missing basket?

"Give us some room!" Piper directed. She wanted to get back to the Odyssey, where there were living people to help.

"You heard the sheriff. Got ambulances coming. Give 'em space to pull up." This came from one of the men Oren had drafted.

She heard the faint keen of sirens. They warred with the happy, bouncy strains of *Sweet Caroline* spewing from nearby speakers, the constant conversation of the onlookers, and the curious shouts from people who were too far back to see what was going on. Screams still punctuated the racket.

Neil Diamond stopped singing and a voice crackled over the speakers: "The fair is closing. Exit the grounds. The fair is closing. The fair will re-open tomorrow at ten. The fair is closing. Exit the grounds."

Dozens had their cell phones out recording the tragedy, either ignoring the announcement or not able to hear it above everything else.

"We need room for the ambulance crews!" one of Oren's helpers yelled. "Go home!"

"Y'all don't need to be seeing this!" said the man in the plaid shirt. "Don't let your kids see this!"

"Make room for the coroner's wagon!" Oren stepped close to Piper. "I was here with Millie. *Right* here. We were buying some cotton candy–"

The fair is closing. Exit the grounds. The fair is closing. Exit the grounds.

"—and we were almost hit by that thing," Millie finished as she appeared, dragging two stacked sawhorses. Millie, Oren's grand-daughter, was one of Piper's recent deputy hires. "The guy in the ride's dead, no one else was with him. The guy selling the cotton candy's gone, too. There were two who got tossed—"

Piper instantly recalled the comment "Did you see the boys flying?"

"They're somewhere over there." Millie gestured toward the grandstand, and through a gap in the crowd Piper glimpsed a second throng of people gathering. "Another basket is that way. I thought I'd—"

Piper sucked in a breath.

The fair is closing. Exit the grounds. The fair is closing. Exit the grounds.

"I'll take this one," Oren said, nodding his head toward the van. He grabbed the sawhorses. "Thanks, Millie, this'll be a help keeping these folks back." To Piper: "I'll call Annie." Barely audible, she heard him say: "Helluva night to come out to the fair for a concert."

The sirens sounded louder, joined by the beeps of multiple cars. The long honk of a firetruck joined them.

The fair is closing. Exit the grounds. The fair is closing. Exit the grounds. Exit the grounds please.

"Millie, the Cosmic Odyssey." Piper talked rapid-fire. "Help Diego get the rest of the riders off before anything else breaks. Volunteers are helping. Keep the crowd back. If it falls … *when* it falls, people could get flattened."

The howls of the frightened fairgoers continued.

Millie bounded toward the Odyssey, and instinct sent Piper in the opposite direction toward the grandstand, threading her way through anxious, non-stop prattling fairgoers who were milling in stunned curiosity. A woman clutched at her, wailing.

"I think that's my boy!" She pointed at the grandstands and squeezed Piper harder. "My Kurt." The woman stumbled in that direction, but Piper tore away and thrust her at a stranger.

"Hold her back here," Piper said.

She found the second basket in the center of a ring of curious people; two riders in it, also clearly dead, one had been decapitated. Several girls were taking pictures.

"Don't touch anything," she shouted, as she ran past it, seeing more people climbing into the grandstands, toward someone halfway up, facedown straddling a bleacher. "The fair is closing. You all need to leave."

She used her cell. "Oren. The second basket's about a hundred and fifty yards from you at four o'clock, behind a lemonade stand, at least two more bodies ringed by too many people. Send two deputies over there as soon as they show up." Piper knew it wouldn't be long before back up arrived; even more sirens heralded their arrival.

Exit the grounds. The fair is closing. Exit the grounds. The fair is closing. Exit the grounds.

Few people headed to the gates despite the repeating announcement. She needed to get the crowd under control, herded away, but she couldn't do that alone, and knew it wouldn't happen until she had more law enforcement.

She kept talking on her cell. "Millie, get the name of the Odyssey operator. The one in the bright yellow shirt. Hold him for questions. Get pictures. Lots of pictures. See if anyone else is injured. There was a girl with a broken arm. Stay in contact with cell phones. We have more deputies on the way to help, Rockport police. Ambulances."

"Treating this as a crime scene?" Millie returned.

"Yes, for the moment, and—" Piper didn't finish the sentence. She was at the grandstands, hurdling up the steps, hollering at the people to get down. The broken Odyssey was likely an industrial accident, but by protocol would be handled as a crime scene until that was proved.

"Sheriff here! Stay back! Go home." Piper called to the dozen climbing ahead of her. Then she spoke a little too loud into her cell: "Oren, direct the first ambulance crew that gets here to the grandstands. Got one still breathing, about halfway up."

The fair is closing. Exit the grounds. The fair is closing. Exit the grounds.

"I'm a veterinarian," the man hovering over the injured boy announced as Piper climbed higher. "You're right, Sheriff, he's breathing, but I don't know for how long."

Piper scampered across a bleacher plank. "He flew off the ride, right?"

The veterinarian nodded.

"Saw him shot like from a canon," offered a woman on the steps. "Flying like a bird." She craned her neck, trying to get a better look, but stayed back as Piper had commanded.

"Don't touch him," the veterinarian cautioned Piper. "We don't want to move him. You have an ambulance coming?"

"Yeah."

"Figured. I hear sirens. I called 9-1-1, but couldn't get through. Look." He pointed to a spot between the boy's shoulder blades. "See how he's twisted here? Back's broken. See the head? Jaw's broken. The way he hit like this, I'd bet ribs are busted. He has to be bleeding internally, but I don't see any blood, and we're not turning him over to check. Have to wait for a neck brace and back board." He pointed to a woman in bib overalls; she was keeping the gawkers from getting closer. "That's my wife. We can handle this. Check out the other one."

"Other one?"

"Before some Nosey Parker moves him. That one has a better chance. He flew like a bird too." The veterinarian pointed down toward the middle of the track that stretched past the grandstand. Bales of hay were piled up in front of a stage where the concert had been scheduled. A body lay on top of the bales. Piper saw the teen move. A trio of fairgoers closed on him.

"Christ!" She reached for her cell phone once more, sprinting down the bleachers, telling Oren about the second still-living accident victim, and trying futilely to reach Teagan again. It seemed everyone was still calling 9-1-1.

The fair is closing. Exit the grounds. The fair is closing. Exit the grounds.

At the bottom, Piper skidded to a halt at the hay bales and stayed put, ordering the growing number of curious to keep their distance. As she waited for the ambulance, Millie reported that three Rockport police squads had arrived at the Cosmic Odyssey, and two sheriff's department cars were pulling up, one of them heading over to deal with the second basket's contents. Most of the riders were safely on the ground, and there appeared to be only minor injuries, save for the broken arm and a heart attack suffered by a parent of one of the freed riders. Millie reported that a firetruck had pulled close to keep the crowd back from the listing Odyssey.

"We're under control here," Millie said.

Piper shook her head. She couldn't see the Odyssey with the grandstand blocking her view, but she knew things weren't close to under control.

9

"I think the whole thing's gonna drop," Millie added. "Only got two more cars to empty." A pause: "One more now."

Ambulances arrived, their lights bouncing off the concession stands, horns blatting to part the throng. Two pulled onto the track by the grandstand, and Piper waved both arms above her head to the paramedics.

Her eyes watered from the track dust stirred by the crowd's feet. Miraculously, the people stayed back, cell phones out, texting, taking video, and parting reluctantly to let the ambulances through. Her throat tight, she tamped down the adrenalin surge that fueled her pounding heart. She watched the paramedics work while the crowd chattered. One team headed up onto the bleachers, another went for the boy on the hay. The onlookers' voices swirled louder.

"Think he's dead?"

"He's moving."

"Who is he? The boy on the hay?"

"Know him?"

"Nope. His hand's twitching again."

"Someone's gonna sue."

"Get me in the shot."

"Take your own selfie."

"Get a pic of the sheriff."

"Look, his legs are moving."

"Moving? You're seeing things. Did you see how far he flew?"

"Think they're gonna cancel the concert?"

"The fair's closed. There's not gonna be a concert."

"I hope they don't cancel the concert. I got front row tickets."

Listening to them, Piper's stomach twisted.

CHAPTER TWO

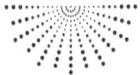

5:40 P.M.

The ambulance crews worked fast. They loaded the two most severely injured survivors and left the fairgrounds. Piper heard a paramedic contact Flight for Life.

A third ambulance prepared to follow, carrying the heart attack victim. Teens with minor injuries had been loaded in a department Explorer and a few parents' cars for trips to the hospital; everyone was going across the river to Owensboro, Kentucky, where the ER had been alerted. Spencer County did not have a hospital.

One ambulance remained, with paramedics ready for any other significant injuries that might be discovered.

"I don't think that boy will make it," the veterinarian said. He walked next to Piper away from the grandstands. "I saw when they braced him, turned him over. Can't be more than thirteen, fourteen. I don't think he has a prayer. So young. Too young."

Piper asked for his business card, saw that he was from Owensboro, voiced her thanks, and jogged toward the cotton candy van. Announcements of the fair closing continued from the loudspeakers. The stubborn rubber-neckers lingered.

Spencer County was small, making Piper wonder if most of the population had turned out for the opening night of the fair, with a

11

chunk of Owensboro's residents in attendance too. She'd noted plenty of Kentucky license plates in the parking field when she'd arrived about an hour ago.

Oren and two deputies had set up a barricade of sawhorses, rope, and hay bales. They wore traffic vests and held radios, and Oren passed a vest to Piper. She was quick to put it on and reach for an extra radio.

"There's the fair manager." Oren nodded toward a barrel-chested man in seersucker pants and a SIC ME ANOTHER t-shirt. "He's staying put until we cut him loose. His staff is trying to herd people out. At least the parents with toddlers have disappeared. Don't need children seeing this shit."

The announcement about the fair closing continued from the speakers.

"I think one of the kids is going to make it," Piper told him. "Landed on hay bales. The other one—" She shook her head.

People, fewer of them and at a distance now, kept recording every awful detail with their cell phones.

Oren pointed to the cotton candy van. Blood still ran down the side. "I'm not touching anything until Annie gets here." Dr. Annie Neufeld was Spencer County's coroner. "She's on her way, was at dinner with friends in Evansville so it'll be a little bit because of the drive. We'll get an ID on the victim then. Manager said the guy who operated the van was Mario Karalis from Virginia. I've got the number for his son."

Piper had obtained the names of the two seriously injured teens before the ambulances took them away. She'd be notifying their families as soon as possible. The woman who'd thought her son Kurt was among the injured reported that he'd been found safe. The identity of the fatalities in the other basket, where two of her deputies had taken a post, would also wait for Dr. Neufeld.

"Still got this?" Piper asked.

Oren nodded and waved her off, and Piper ran toward the Cosmic Odyssey. Three more of her deputies were there. With all the riders out, it looked like the monstrosity tilted even more precariously.

The crowd was perched at a respectable distance, held in check by a string of colorful vinyl flags that had decorated a vendor tent, strips of crime scene tape, and the firetruck. Firemen—Spencer County had an all-volunteer department—also helped to keep people away.

"We're going to take it apart," the fire chief told her, pointing at the ride. "No use it falling."

"I'll need video of you doing that," Piper returned.

"No problem."

Thank God nothing else had broken off the ride and caused even more deaths, Piper thought. Her radio on and linked to the dispatcher, she heard reports coming in from Oren and the others.

The department detective, Basil Meredith, was at the edge of the Odyssey throng. Dressed in jeans and a Chicago Cubs t-shirt with a sheriff department traffic vest over the top, she suspected he had been attending the fair, too.

A glance beyond him confirmed that: his wife and two young children sat on a hay bale, an alligator-shaped balloon on a ribbon clutched in the little girl's hands, all of them facing away from the ride. Piper caught a glimpse of Nang. With one arm he hugged a teenaged girl whose shoulders shook, the other arm was draped across the back of an elderly man with a cane. Maybe the girl had been on the ride, and maybe the man was her grandfather.

Piper had come to the fair with Nang. It was supposed to have been a date. The quick mart owner had entered some of the baking contests and wanted to see if he'd won any ribbons. At five sharp, on their way to the crafts and culinary barn, they'd paused at the corn dog stand because Piper said she was famished. Then the Cosmic Odyssey broke and everything seemed to happen at once.

She gave Nang a sad smile and headed toward Basil, Her head pounding from the buzz of voices. And now the buzz included the local press.

"There's the sheriff."

"Sheriff Blackwell! What happened?"

"Are those kids dead? Sheriff, are they dead?"

"How many are dead?"

"What the hell happened?"

"Spacker! I think Spacker was one of them! Spacker!"

Piper tried to spot who shouted the last bit, but it was all too confusing and the voices competed for her notice. Maybe Spacker was the one smashed on top of the cotton candy van.

The air was dead and dusty, the breeze non-existent, and everything felt close and uncomfortable. The throng seemed to have thinned by half, and in the background she saw people shuffling toward the main exit. But too many were still sticking around, craning their necks or taking pictures, texting, talking. All Piper heard was the susurrus of tones filled with grief, disbelief, and mostly morbid curiosity... and the loudspeaker droning: "The fair is closing. Exit the grounds."

She still couldn't see the woman who'd mentioned "Spacker." Maybe that was a nickname. Piper reached inside a department car parked nearby and used the PA.

"You need to leave the fairgrounds. The fair is closed." She repeated it, satisfied that a few dozen caved to her announcement. "I'm not kidding. Go home. Now!" More acquiesced. "Or I'll charge you all with trespassing." Even more left.

A country concert had been scheduled for tonight. It would have started at seven. The fair rarely had musical acts, but a Rockport native was charting big out of Nashville. According to the newspaper, he was in town for his parents' anniversary and agreed for "old time's sake" to put on a show here, no doubt the reason for the large turnout. Piper had never seen this many people at the fair. Oren, a country music fan, had mentioned the concert earlier in the week. Piper and Nang had bought tickets—thirty dollars each, a bargain to hear someone who was slated for a national tour. Several in the crowd wore t-shirts with the singer's mug splayed on them, and the words: SIC ME ANOTHER in bold type, the title of his first chart-topping hit.

Piper noted that Millie had her cell phone out and was moving among the stragglers, having them email any videos they'd captured of the ride coming apart, and recording their comments. As Piper neared Basil, she saw that he was doing the same.

"You're really with the sheriff's department?" a middle-aged woman asked Basil.

"He's the department detective," Piper said as she stepped up.

Basil was black, and thereby distinct in basically white Spencer County. He was also muscular and handsome and would do well on the cover of GQ. In the county nearly a month, Piper had hired him away from the Chicago Police Department. He lived in Santa Claus, about a half-mile from Oren.

"What did you see? Hear?" Basil held his recorder as he questioned the woman.

"I heard someone yell that it was going too fast, Detective," she replied. "I heard them yell: 'Slow it down. Slow it down.' I got it on my cell phone, the whole thing. I don't know for the life of me why I recorded it. Not like me, you know. Ugh. Good thing you stopped me before I deleted it. Though I'm not sure how to delete stuff. I don't want it on my phone. You look at it and then delete it for me, okay?"

"Yeah, I heard the 'slow it down,' too. Then I heard this *BANG!*" said the man with her. "And screaming. I saw a car fly off, then another one. But first I saw people fly out, two of them. Flying. One must have been tossed more than a hundred yards. Flying. We was gonna get in line for that ride. Now we want to go home. We can go home, right? We don't have to stay here? All those announcements. We should leave. Trespassing? The fair's closed, and—"

Basil took their names and landline number and let them leave. The woman shoved her cell phone at him.

"Get that back to me when you're done," she ordered, "but delete that video of the ride I took. Like I said, I'm not very good at deleting stuff, and I don't want to see that ever, ever, ever again. You delete that for me."

Basil moved on, Piper following. She noticed Nang was escorting the girl and the old man toward the exit.

More people dispersed.

"Pretty good video," Basil told her. "Some were recording their friends on the ride. Some of the kids who were on it have videos, selfie stuff. I've captured a lot. Diego has some. Millie, too. More than enough. And this makes four people who voluntarily surrendered their phones, the best of the images I think. I'll return the phones when we're done. But I won't delete video for that woman."

"I was on that ride!" A gangly teenager edged forward, waving her cell phone. She was so skinny her elbows protruded and her cheekbones stood out. She bobbed her head, tight curls bouncing. "I was on that ride the turn before. It was scary great. I got video of it. Do you want my video too? A guy in my row blew chunks. I got in line to go again when every bad thing happened."

Every bad thing.

A reasonable account, Piper thought. She got the girl's name and number and Basil collected the phone.

Summer, the county fair, it was supposed to be wonderful and exciting, happy, singing along to *Sweet Caroline* and eating too many corn dogs followed by a sugary-sweet Lemon Shakeup.

But tonight, this county fair was far from all of that.

It was indeed *every bad thing.*

Piper joined in collecting statements and used her cell phone to take pictures of the twisted ride and some of the people she talked to. The crowd thinned until only a dozen remained near the Odyssey, and a voice intoned from the loud speakers:

"The fair has closed. Exit the grounds. The fair has closed. The fair will re-open tomorrow, no admission fee. The rides will not run tomorrow. The country concert has been rescheduled for Sunday evening. The fair has closed. Exit the grounds."

Piper looked around for the ride operator, the weathered man in the muscle shirt. She'd told Millie to detain him. She spotted a bench and stood on it for a better vantage, scanning.

There, by the Strawberry-Go-Round, a Tilt-a-Whirl with a fruit theme. He was leaning against one of the cabs.

"Hey!" Piper waved to get his attention.

He saw her, and took off running.

16

CHAPTER THREE

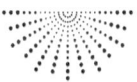

6 P.M.

"What the hell?" Piper sprinted after him.

He glanced over his shoulder, eyes wide as if in terror. Then he lengthened his stride, cutting past Mona's Mirror Maze, slipping around the Champion Chopper Ride ticket booth, and racing out of sight.

The pastel-painted helicopter cabs were a smear of pink and blue as Piper sped by them, and through gaps in the poles that connected everything, she saw the flash of her target's dayglow-yellow shirt.

She sucked in a breath, pulling in the scents of popcorn, something sugary-sweet, and sweat—Piper's shirt was soaked and she imagined her concealed small-of-back holster was outlined from the dampness. A sheriff twenty-four/seven, she always carried a badge and a gun. She hoped she didn't need to use the latter.

"I just want to talk to you!" she hollered. "Stop!"

The man was nearly a foot taller than her, legs longer, and Piper guessed him to be in his late twenties. But she wasn't about to let him get away. Was he fleeing because he'd mishandled the ride and caused the disaster? Was it his fault? An innocent soul wouldn't run.

He whipped to his left and bolted between pens in the petting zoo. His feet churned over a dirt aisle covered with hay. Sheep, pigs, cows,

17

chickens … the disturbed animals made a racket. The scents changed to manure and musk.

"I said stop!" Piper gained on him a little, but hadn't expected him to leap into the pony enclosure and scamper through the fence on the other side. Piper went around it.

"I ain't burnin'! I ain't burnin'!" He ran down a slope away from the fairgrounds and toward a collection of small trailers—the portable homes of people who worked the fair and carnival circuit. It appeared her target was heading to a retro-looking camper that resembled the back half of a VW van soldered onto a big cab Ford. A dozen men and women gathered near one of the largest trailers, beer and soda cans in hand, watching and pointing.

"Vern!" one of them shouted. "Vern!"

"I ain't burnin' in hell!" the man hollered over his shoulder. "I ain't burnin'. I didn't do nothing wrong!"

"Then stop!" Piper shouted.

The man slowed, and he grabbed at his side.

"Stop! I said stop!"

"Vern, you better be listening to her!" a stocky woman yelled.

"Don't be an idjit," another added. "She's some local cop."

Heaving, the man finally acquiesced, held up his hands, and bent over. Piper rushed forward, reached for the cuffs in her pocket, and paused.

"Okay. Okay." He gasped and turned to face her, straightened a little, then brushed the hair off his forehead. "Okay. I stopped. Just let me catch my breath."

His stringy mop reached to just above his shoulders. His muscle shirt was soaked through. Piper noticed he had a thick gold chain around his neck, a crucifix hanging from it. No rings on his fingers, but there were link bracelets on each wrist; one looked like it was a medical ID.

Piper took out her badge and held it up. Maybe he hadn't seen her display it while they worked together at the ride to free the teens. Maybe he didn't know she was the sheriff.

"Sheriff Piper Blackwell. I just want to talk to you."

"Okay. Okay," he panted, gesturing behind him to the retro-camper. "Inside my place?"

The gathered fair workers edged a little closer.

"You arresting him?" It was the stocky woman.

Piper shook her head. *Not yet, at least.*

"Inside my place?" he repeated. "They don't got to watch this." He tipped his head to indicate the gathering.

"No. Let's go back to the Odyssey."

As if on cue the harsh sound of metal scraping against metal shot down the rise, followed by a *clunk, thunk, boom.*

"What's left of the Odyssey," she corrected. Piper hoped the noise had resulted from the fire department dismantling the Odyssey rather than the structure collapsing on its own and damaging other rides on its way down.

Her radio squawked. It was Oren.

"Saw you running into the petting zoo, Sheriff Blackwell. Where are you?"

"I'm at the trailers east of the fairgrounds." She listened a moment. "Annie's making good time, eh? A half hour out? I'm talking to the ride operator, Mr.—"

"Vern."

"Vernon—"

"Vern. That's all you need. Vern. And that's 'cause I'm being polite. I ain't got to tell you my name. You really a sheriff? You ain't old enough to be a sheriff. You ain't dressed like a sheriff. You're too little to be a sheriff."

Oren again: "I'm on my way."

Piper replied. "Yes, Vern, I'm the sheriff."

"You look like you're in high school."

She picked up the sounds of the petting zoo over the radio, knowing Oren was coming closer.

Piper didn't need help with this, hadn't asked Oren to join her. But maybe it wasn't a bad idea. There were ride operators and vendors here who had dutifully cleared out when the announcements

19

persisted about the fair closing. It would be good to have help questioning them.

She studied Vern, revising the age estimate. He probably had at least a decade on her. His hands looked leathery, no doubt from the manual work of a ride operator. His skin was ruddy from being in the sun, traveling from county to county during fair season, the life of a roustabout. He looked fit, lean, but there was the outline of a cigarette pack on the pocket of his shirt. Maybe his habit contributed to his being out of breath and relatively easy to catch. Faintly, she smelled nicotine and Axe.

Piper heard Oren, his footfalls thudding and measured. Not fast, but good for someone his age, she thought.

"Listen, Vern—"

"I know my rights," the man continued. "And I've a right not to give you anythin'."

Piper held up her cell phone and took his picture just as Oren reached her side.

"I've the right to take your photo," she returned. "And to post it to Facebook and Twitter asking for help in identifying the reluctant witness to a mass casualty tragedy."

The man's eyes narrowed. "I didn't do nothing wrong. I ain't burnin' for this. I know my rights."

"You're not a suspect," she said. "But you're a witness. Maybe I'll just talk to the amusement manager or the fair manager. I can get your identification from employment contracts and registration."

Piper let out a deep breath. Really, all she wanted to do was talk to the man, hadn't expected him of any wrongdoing. But his aversion to cooperating was fueling her uncertainties. Had he indeed caused the ride to break apart? "One of the managers will have all those records."

"I suppose you could do that," he cut back. "I ain't givin' you nothin'."

"Look, Vern, I have some questions," Piper pressed. "That's all. Questions. You can cooperate or—"

"Not. Or not cooperate. I know my rights. I said, I didn't do nothin' wrong." He made the sign of the cross and touched his crucifix.

The other fair workers edged even closer. Piper heard the sound of cans being popped open—beer or soda, she wasn't going to look away from Vern. Their whispers were too indistinct to pick anything out. From farther away, she heard the announcement continue: "The fair has closed."

"Vern, I can arrest you, Mirandize you, charge you with interfering with an investigation, fingerprint you, And you'll have to provide the court with a positive ID."

"Ooooooooh. Vern's in trouble," one of the onlookers teased.

"I ain't interfering with any investigation. I didn't do nothin' wrong. You ain't got no call to arrest me for—"

Oren cleared his throat and gave Vern a stare-down. "Sheriff Blackwell, we're required by state law to identify any juvenile that we feel is in danger and deliver that juvenile to their parents. Clearly, these fairgrounds and the rides are dangerous."

"Juvenile?" Vern spat. "Are you sayin' I'm a juvenile? Are you blind? I ain't no—"

The gathering of fair workers tightened.

Oren continued. "Well, I'm not sure that you're not a juvenile because you've not cooperated and told the sheriff your full name, haven't shown any ID that has an age listed. I do believe you just might be a juvenile and—"

"Piss. Juvenile my ass." The man reached into his back pocket, pulled out his wallet, and flipped it open to show his driver's license. "Vern Milgrew. Now will you leave me alone? I didn't do a damn thing to make that ride bust apart."

Piper talked into her radio. "Teegan, I'm speaking to a Mr. Vernon Tyler Milgrew." She quickly noted other details: age thirty-three, address listed as Fairfax, Virginia.

Piper passed the wallet back. Vernon stuffed the wallet into his pocket.

"You gonna arrest me?" He rubbed his hands on his shirt, smearing dirt streaks. "I didn't do nothin' wrong. It wasn't my fault. Ride was inspected. Passed inspection. I don't own it. I just run it. I just buckle 'em in and pull the levers. Been running it for the past five years." He paused. "Shit. I didn't do nothin' wrong."

"Vern's a good guy," one of the onlookers volunteered.

The Spencer County Sheriff's Department had body cameras coming in next week. Piper wished they were already here. It would have been nice for capturing all the awful action at the fair and her conversation with Vernon Tyler Milgrew. She turned the 'record' function of her cell phone on, and let him see what she was doing.

Her radio crackled, carrying the muted conversations between Teegan, Millie, Basil, and Diego.

"Ain't never had any problems with the Odyssey before," Vern said. "Once with the Strawberry-Go-Round some years back at a fair in Illinois. Nothin' major, and I wasn't runnin' it, just watching it when the operator needed a piss break. No kid got hurt. Not hurt bad anyway. Bungee-cord jump in Kansas, a guy hung there for like twenty minutes before they got him down. I wasn't runnin' that one either, just operating the ride next to it. Never anybody died. Nothin' like this." He made a huffing sound. "Oh, hell. This ain't my fault. I ain't burnin' for it." Vern touched the crucifix again.

Piper let him ramble while they retraced their path through the petting zoo and returned to the ride midway. They'd interview the other workers later.

"Let's start at the beginning, Mr. Milgrew," Oren said. "How many riders does the Odyssey hold? How long are the rides? Who can and can't ride it?"

Oren was sixty-five—forty two years older than her, and probably should be the sheriff, Piper had thought on more than a dozen occasions. She wouldn't have considered his tactic to get Vern's full name. Piper had defeated Oren in the fall election, campaigning on her last name. Her father, Paul Blackwell, had been sheriff a long while, stepping down to deal with a bout of cancer; he'd encouraged her to run when she opted not to re-enlist in the Army and came home to help him. She was convinced a significant number of the county residents thought they were voting for him when they'd cast their ballots.

Piper was still growing into the role, and had decided it suited her. She rarely thought anymore about re-upping with Fort Campbell's MP Division. But she couldn't keep the notion away that it might have been better for the county if Oren had won. She was certain Oren thought the same thing.

"I'm careful who I let on that ride," Vern said.

Piper pictured the boy she helped off, certainly too young and small to be allowed.

Vern continued to answer her and Oren's questions as they passed the pastel helicopters and the strawberry-shaped Tilt-a-Whirl. She watched the man shudder and gulp for air when he saw the dismantled Odyssey. Piper pointed him to a bench.

"Crap. Ride's broke. Maybe my job's gone with it," Vern grumbled. "Crap. Hadn't thought about that … no ride, no job. Crap."

"Sit there. Don't go anywhere."

"Okay. Okay."

She gave him a stern look.

"Okay, I said. Okay."

"I'll watch him," Oren volunteered.

Vern shuffled to the bench, sat on one end, and stared at the firetruck next to the dismantled Odyssey. Then he glowered at Oren.

Piper jogged toward Millie and Diego. Nang hung with them. She pulled him aside. They'd come to the fair in his pickup. Hadn't dreamed she'd need her department Explorer and the equipment inside it.

"It's going to be a late night, I think. I'll get a ride to the department, get home from there." She gave him a half-smile. "We'll check on your entries another day, eh? Maybe tomorrow. I'll probably be out here most of the day anyway unless something worse comes up."

"Sure. Or Sunday. We'll come back Sunday for that concert, right? I heard it's going to be at six. An hour earlier than it was supposed to be today." He leaned in and kissed her quickly on the cheek, looking at Millie and Diego out of the corner of his eye. "You call me later?"

"Yeah, it'd be a nice break."

Piper glanced at the bench, saw that Oren had sat down next to

Vern. She stepped up to Millie. "I told you to keep him close, that ride operator."

Millie looked apologetic. "I know. I screwed up. No excuses, really. But everything was just—"

"Chaos," Diego finished.

"This is going to be an awful long night," Piper said. Into her radio: "Teegan, did you run a check on Vernon Tyler Milgrew of Fairfax, Virginia? I want to make sure there are no previous fair incidents connected to him." She believed Vern's story that nothing like this had happened to his ride before. The look in his eyes was convincing. But he had run, and he'd been uncooperative … and that was suspicious.

"Still working on it," Teegan reported. "Actually, Zeke's working on it. He heard all the chatter on the scanner, and the sirens. He came back in to help." Zeke was the day-shift dispatcher.

"Sheriff Blackwell, the fair manager's waiting in what passes for an office," Diego cut in. "Ambulances all left. Last of the crowd's gone. A Rockport squad is posted at the gate to make sure no one comes back in."

"I'll post a department vehicle to relieve them," Piper said. She'd keep a car there until morning when the fair opened because there wasn't a lot to do in Spencer County. Bored teenagers might find a broken amusement ride a great opportunity to score souvenirs. It was something she might have done a half-dozen years ago.

"Basil's taking his wife and kids home, then he'll meet us at the station and we'll start putting the videos and statements together," Diego continued. "I've got a collection of names, including fair workers—none of them are local, most from the northeast, Maine even. Cell phone numbers."

"Moving from town to town, following summer," Piper mused of the fair workers. "Like Vern from Virginia." To Diego: "I also want a list of every civilian who helped us. I'll be sending thank you letters."

"Gonna be a real long night," Diego said.

"Yeah." Piper stared at Vern. "I've a few more questions for the Odyssey operator, and then I'll cut him loose. Tell the fair manager I'll be over soon, Diego."

She took a step toward the bench and her radio squawked. It was Teegan.

"Really?" Piper groaned as she listened to her dispatcher and reached into her pocket for her handcuffs. She approached and gestured for Vern to stand.

Oren stood too, eyebrows crooked up in question.

"Vernon Tyler Milgrew, you have the right to remain silent," she began, knowing she'd repeat the Miranda warning back at the department.

"It was an accident," Vernon protested. "Not my fault. The ride passed inspection. I didn't do nothin'—"

"You're wanted on a felony warrant from Virginia," Piper explained. "Possession of a controlled substance—meth, with intent to distribute."

"Shit," Vernon said, wilting.

"And two is four and four is eight," Oren added softly.

CHAPTER FOUR

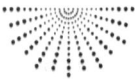

11:30 P.M.

Zeke pulled into the back of the strip mall lot, nosing his 1974 Chevy Nova under a light at an end cap space. Less risk of scratches away from the bevy of cars parked closer to the store.

Serilda sparkled under the mercury vapor light—those parts of her that showed between the rust spots. He touched the hood for luck and eyed the lot. A good number of cars, a few motorcycles; there was a strong turnout for the Loot the Castle pre-release gala at Silver Age Sam's. The crowd gathered in front of Owensboro's only comic and collectible card shop. Zeke guessed there were close to fifty players. There needed to be an even number, divisible by four; that's how the tournament was set up. So forty, forty-four, forty-eight, and fifty-two would work ... the leftovers would have to watch or jump into pick-up games.

Zeke wasn't worried. He'd preregistered and so was guaranteed a place at a table. He would have gotten here a little earlier, but he'd stayed around the sheriff's department, helping Teegan field calls.

"Hey!" He waved and caught Aggie's attention. She was a runt-of-a-girl, just shy of five feet, but she was a fierce Loot the Castle card game competitor and Zeke hoped he didn't end up at her table in the

26

preliminary rounds. He really wanted a chance to win tonight, or at least advance to the final.

"It's the Geek!" Aggie's soprano voice cut across the asphalt. "Zekester Geekster! Four shades of awesome sauce." She ran to meet him. "Wow. New car?"

It was new to him. He nodded proudly.

Aggie walked around it, running her fingers against the door panels.

"I named her Serilda." He'd purchased the vintage auto a few weeks ago from a retired chiropractor in Evansville who'd asked $700 for the "blue beauty" on Craigslist. A more than reasonable price, but Zeke didn't have that much to offer, and apparently no one else had nibbled. He talked the seller down to $300, the amount his uncle had given him for high school graduation.

Said uncle drove him to pick up "Serilda." Zeke had settled on the Teutonic name when perusing a "what to call the baby" website. It meant "a maiden in battle armor," and he figured the car was close to a tank. Fitting. Rear-wheel drive, three-speed manual gearbox, she averaged seventeen to eighteen miles a gallon when the wind was favorable.

Serilda was a gorgeous metallic blue—not the original paint—with nearly three hundred thousand miles on a supplanted V8 engine that Zeke intended to eventually replace with a standard SS six-cylinder. She had relatively new tires and a few large patches of rust that added to her character—including a spot on the front passenger side floorboard that was eaten through to the point he could glance over and watch the street whizzing by. Zeke never let anyone sit up front with him for fear they'd lose their feet. Not that the passenger-side door was useable anyway--the chiropractor had welded it shut because the hinges were mangled.

"Looks like an antique. Give me a ride in it Sunday?" Aggie asked. "Monday?"

Serilda boasted bench seats, and Zeke could cram five thin teenagers in the back if he ignored seatbelt laws. The rusting out trunk was huge, a good "three body trunk" the seller had called it, adding "with the right driver, this baby could beat a Trans-Am off the line."

Zeke planned to fully restore Serilda over the next few years and flip her for at least twenty grand. The sheriff's boyfriend, Nang, ran a quick mart in Fulda and had recently opened a full-service garage. Nang was an automotive whiz and had agreed to help with the restoration at no charge if Zeke purchased all the materials. Zeke was trying to save up for that; if he could just stop spending money on comics and cards, he'd manage. To that end he'd stuffed only thirty dollars in his wallet tonight, not allowing himself to spend a penny more.

Aggie finished her inspection of the car and wrapped him in a bear hug, then tugged him toward the assembly. "So glad you made it. This is my last tournament before I lose my freedom!"

"Freedom? What?" Zeke frowned, clearly confused. Aggie was squeaky clean and no-way would get arrested. Did she mean she'd got a nine-to-five job somewhere? Like him, she'd sworn off college.

She squeezed his hand, pulled out her cell phone, and took a picture of him. "I thought I'd told you. I leave for Camp May next week. One of those spur of the moment decisions. I joined the Coast Guard. Camp May, New Jersey. Basic training. Me in the Coast Guard. Bet you didn't see that coming!"

Zeke couldn't imagine someone so short being in any branch of the military. But his boss, Sheriff Piper Blackwell, wasn't much over five feet, and he knew she'd been decorated for some big-deal-heroic thing she'd done in Iraq or Iran or somesuch with the Screaming Eagles.

"Congrats, Aggie. You'll do amazing and—" Before Zeke could get anything else out, the crowd outside the shop—mostly teenagers and twenty-somethings—chattered to him rapid-fire.

"Zeke the Geek! Were you at the fair?"

"Was there a lot of blood?"

"I heard these new Loot the Castle card packs will have foiled bronze gorgons."

"Only in *some* of the packs, Dun-Dun."

"What about the county fair?"

"How many died, Geekster?"

"Was there blood? A lot of it?"

"When did you shave your soul patch?"

"Sam usually opens a little early. What's the hold up?"

"I saw video on YouTube, the ride falling apart."

"Did you arrest anybody?"

"Was there a lot of blood? What about the blood?"

"I heard some guy was decapitated."

"Hey!" Zeke held up both hands. "Enough."

He'd been hired less than a month ago as a dispatcher for the Spencer County Sheriff's Department, right after high school graduation. Eighteen, he didn't meet the age requirement for a deputy, and he hadn't wanted to pursue a college degree or a stint in the military. But he loved law enforcement, could shoot, and had been to "police camps" in back-to-back summers. He grabbed the dispatcher job when Piper offered it in mid-May and figured he'd ease his way into a deputy slot when he hit twenty-one.

"Dispatcher," Zeke replied. "I'm a dispatcher. I take the calls, dispatch cars. Stuff like that." He took a breath. "And, anyway, I wasn't at the fair."

Aggie snapped another photo of him.

"Did you dispatch—"

"No. I'm on first shift and it didn't happen until—"

"Dinnertime," Aggie said. "I heard that the Ferris wheel shattered at five."

"Yeah, that's about the right time. A couple hours after I'd left work. And it wasn't the Ferris wheel. It was something else. The Cosmic Octopus. Something like that." That was during Teegan's treasured shift. The longtime dispatcher claimed the three-to-eleven and didn't want to budge from it. "I got a scanner at home, and I heard some of it." He didn't add that he was so curious he'd gone back into work and helped Teegan work the 9-1-1 calls. Good experience, he figured.

"So how many died?"

29

Zeke shrugged. He'd heard five, but he didn't know what he could or couldn't say about it. "I guess I'll find out when I go back in Monday."

"Terrorism?" This came from "Dun-Dun" Dunville, the oldest in the group, a fiftyish accountant from Evansville who made the drive here every time there was a booster set pre-release tournament. They were always at midnight.

"Terrorism? In Spencer County?" Zeke swallowed a laugh. "Don't you remember a summer back, the Ohio State Fair had an accident where—"

"Only one person died." Aggie took a few pictures of the crowd, then moved next to Zeke and held her camera out as far as she could and got a picture of both of them. "Made the national news. A bunch injured. It was the Fire Ball. Sent some riders flying, but only one got gacked. Our county fair wouldn't let the Fire Ball set up here after that."

"Heard that's what happened in Spencer County. Just like the Fire Ball." This came from someone Zeke had played Loot the Castle with before, but he couldn't remember her name. "Heard riders went flying, but more than one died. Maybe a dozen. Was it a dozen, Zeke?"

Zeke shrugged and shuffled through the players to the very front, stood square against the glass doors. He smelled cleanser, like the windows had been polished recently, and stopped himself from touching the spotless glass. The store beyond was dark, save for the aisles at the front where the lights from the parking lot reached. He spotted a small Dungeons & Dragons display. Silver Age Sam's was primarily a comics and card game shop, but there was usually a small selection of board games and role-playing games for the serious nerds.

"What's it like working for a sheriff's department?"

"Good," Zeke replied. "It's good. I like it." He liked it a lot, in fact.

More questions swirled, about his job, the accident at the fair, rumors about what cards would be included in the Loot the Castle packs.

Zeke saw the EXIT light above the door in the back of the store. He didn't see anyone moving around. Sam usually opened at least a half-hour early so the players could get settled and chat before he pulled out the decks and collected the entry fees. It was a quarter to midnight now.

"Anybody know why Sam's running late?" Zeke repeated the question, louder, and Aggie answered. She wormed her way up next to him. He noticed she wore lilac cologne. Smelled nice. Aggie always smelled nice. He wished she hadn't joined the Coast Guard.

"He tweeted an hour ago that he'd gone for pancakes with Benzo and Lucky Ducky," she said. "Probably went to Triple P's or Batter Up! Maybe he's eating a lot of pancakes, isn't done chowing yet. Don't worry. He'll show up with minutes to spare. He always does."

"Maybe we should've gone out for pancakes, too."

"Syrup gives me the runs."

Zeke thought he saw the door under that back EXIT sign open and close. Sam owned the place, so he had a reserved parking spot behind the store, always came in through that door. The restroom was back there. Maybe Sam had to make a pit stop before he turned on the store lights. Zeke wanted to make a pit stop, too.

"I think Sam just got here." Zeke waited for the store to open, felt his anticipation rise for the imminent tournament.

"I hope we get paired together first thing," Aggie said.

Zeke really hoped not. Aggie was ruthless, and he didn't want to get knocked out in the preliminary round. He hoped to play all the way to the end ... to three or four a.m.

"Lights. Lights. C'mon. Turn on the lights," Zeke willed. A pause: "He's not turning on any lights."

"Chill," Dun-Dun said. "If anyone gets a bronze gorgon, I'll buy it." Dun-Dun crooked his fingers at his temple, imitating horns. Aggie took his picture.

"I've been standing here a half hour," someone grumbled. "Sam better get his ass moving."

"Chill," Dun-Dun said. "Just chill."

"Patience, grasshopper," someone added.

Zeke tapped his foot and squinted, trying to separate the shadows inside. He swore the back door had opened and closed again, was *certain* of it ... but he couldn't see anyone moving around. Why the hell hadn't Sam turned on the lights? Maybe Sam had gone back out to his car. "I'm gonna go 'round and check on him, see if he needs help carrying anything."

"Chill." Dun-Dun again.

"Patience, praying mantis."

Patience, my ass, Zeke thought, as he looked across the lot and spotted Lucky Ducky's bumper sticker decorated Sonata. He eased out of the gathering, following the sidewalk past closed businesses—a beauty salon, hardware store, candy shop—to the end of the strip mall and then cut around the corner. It was dark here, the lights from the parking lot not stretching far enough. He ran his hand along the brick as he walked toward the back of the complex. Feet slapped the asphalt behind him.

"Wait up, Zekester."

He really wondered how Aggie would cut it in the Coast Guard. Short legs, basic training might be awful on her. She'd probably have to run, and short legs had to pump a hell of a lot faster to keep up. Zeke slowed to accommodate her.

"I'll write you," she said, grabbing his hand. "Letters. On paper. Stamps. The real thing."

"I'll write you back. Stamps." Zeke had known Aggie since junior high, occasionally thought about asking her out on a date, *a real date,* but hadn't wanted to ruin the friendship. Now he wondered if he'd made a mistake. "Wanna go out tomorrow night? Milkshake and pinball?"

"Are we talking a date?"

Zeke waited a beat. "Yeah. A date."

"Awesome." Softer: "About damn time. And I'll get to try out Serilda's ride." She paused: "But could we make it Sunday? Church ice cream social tomorrow. I volunteered to scoop and clean up. My folks are away for a reunion, so I'm working longer at the social to make up for them being gone."

"Sunday. Even better," Zeke replied. Couldn't make it too late, though, he had to be back to work Monday at seven. And he always made sure he was early.

They reached the edge of the building and stepped around the corner. Yellow lights above the back doors illuminated the empty private parking spaces, trash bins, and farther back, behind the comic shop, a sedan that was angled crooked. A tall man in a suit leaned into the driver's window.

Silver Age Sam wasn't tall, didn't drive a sedan, and Zeke had never seen him in a suit.

"A date. Sunday. Milkshakes. That'd be nice." Aggie smiled. "And we could—" She tugged on Zeke's sleeve. "That's not Sam's car. He drives a SUV."

Zeke felt a tingle against the back of his neck. "A white SUV," he said softly. "Calls it Simpson 'cause it looks like the one—"

"O. J. drove when the cops chased him," Aggie finished, taking a picture of it. "Ancient history."

"Yeah, well, Sam's pretty ancient." Zeke slunk closer. "Stay back," he whispered, dropping her hand. "Something's not right."

"Maybe someone's breaking into Sam's shop," Aggie's soprano voice carried, and the man who'd been leaning into the car looked up and she took his picture. "Should we call the cops?"

The tall man hurried around to the passenger side, got in, and the driver revved the engine and pulled away before Zeke closed the distance.

"Dark gray four door, Mazda," Zeke pronounced. He knew cars. "Late model." He went to Sam's back door and tried it. "Locked." But he swore he'd seen the door open and close. Didn't look like anyone had tampered with the lock when he looked at it, no scratch marks like the police usually saw on *Blue Bloods* and *SVU*.

"Should we call the cops?" Aggie asked again. "I got a picture. I probably got the license plate."

"The cops? What for?" Zeke said. "Not illegal to park back here. No evidence of a break-in. No evidence of anything illegal. No reason to call the cops." A beat: "Not yet."

"Creeped me out," Aggie said.

It had creeped Zeke out, too.

After a moment, she said: "Let's go up front, wait with Dun-Dun. Hope you and me get paired for Loot the Castle first thing." She grabbed his hand again and tugged. "Hope Sam shows up soon."

Zeke hoped so too. He really had to pee.

CHAPTER FIVE

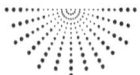

4:45 A.M., SATURDAY, JUNE 15TH

Piper swung her legs over the edge of the bed and dressed in a pair of shorts and a faded Screaming Eagles t-shirt. She fed the dog and cat—Camaro and Marmalade—scratched behind their ears, and watched as they slipped out the dog door and into the orderly landscaped backyard. They could come and go as they pleased while she was at work. The only thing that took away from the yard's *Better Homes & Gardens* image was the six-foot-high heavy-gauge chain-link fence with motion sensors and security cameras on top. The previous owner had been a little paranoid.

Piper watched the dog making his rounds, ritually peeing on the rose bushes and daylilies. Then she put on her Nikes, stuck her cell phone in her pocket, and went out the front,

It had become a ritual ... set up the automatic food dispensers for the animals, run, shower, feed herself, then go into work. Twenty-three and she had a house on a sprawling corner lot, multiple vehicles, pets, and a rigid morning routine. Four years in the military had engendered her to appreciate rigid routines, but it hadn't prepared her for the responsibility of running a sheriff's department, for facing a disaster like last night at the county fair, or for being a home owner who wondered how deep her roots were sinking into Spencer County soil.

Piper stretched and noted the time: 5:15. No wonder Camaro had been so sluggish to get up. This was a little early for the old dog.

She jogged in place on her front step. The new shoes felt good. Three weeks old, they'd molded to her feet and provided just the right amount of cushion. She'd paid ninety dollars for them at a sporting goods store across the river, an indulgence and protection from blisters.

Her department-issued Ford Explorer was parked in front of her extra-deep double-wide garage. There wasn't room for it inside. The garage held her apple red Smart Fortwo, a three-cylinder, turbo-charged five-speed manual with an oatmeal-hued interior. She'd bought the "suggestion of a car" after leaving Fort Campbell because it got excellent gas mileage and she liked the color. The rest of the garage space held a 1935 three-window Chevy coup, a 1922 Franklin convertible, and four vintage motorcycles, everything restored—1953 Ariel Square 4, 1951 Vincent Comet, 1915 Indian 8-valve Board Track Racer Nang estimated the value at eighty grand, and a 1928 Coventry Eagle.

Piper would rather take any one of those other vehicles to work; she didn't like the bulkiness of the Explorer, but it was four-wheel drive and had equipment kits in the back. She took turns driving everything else when she was off-duty, though she had yet to take the Board Track Racer past the end of the driveway. She'd thought about selling some of them, scoring a significant profit, and making room for the Explorer. But the vehicles—and the house—had been a gift, so she would continue to pay insurance, which wasn't awful considering they fit in the "antique" and "classic" categories and were not frequently used.

Piper had moved to Hatfield a month ago after inheriting the four-year-old Cape Cod from a Navy veteran she'd met. She'd later solved his murder. He'd also bequeathed her an elderly cat and an aging Golden Retriever. The teenager charged with the veteran's murder—and at least two other deaths—would go on trial in sixteen months,

36

and Piper would be called to testify. There were dockets, motions, and tests to be sorted through first, and the teen's attorney said he needed the time to prepare. Piper hoped the girl would spend the rest of her life in prison.

Living here in Hatfield, which had been called Fair Fight in the 1800s, proved to be handy, a straight shot over from Rockport where the sheriff's department and attached jail sat. Besides, she liked the privacy of the hint of a town, with a population of just over eight hundred.

The sky was pale, caught in the minutes before dawn; sunrise about a half hour away. Piper's favorite time of day, a taste she'd acquired in the Army, the thin time before the base got noisy with people and vehicles.

She sprinted to the end of the street, seeing only a few lights on in neighboring houses. Oscar was out in a bathrobe, walking a cocker spaniel puppy in his front yard; he waved to her. Two blocks father and she reached the beginning of a small farm field. A young woman sat in a parked VW Bug convertible at the end of the farmhouse's gravel drive. She put on makeup with one hand, and talked on her cell phone with the other. Piper jogged in place, spun around, and took the county road to her right. It circled around and reconnected with her street.

Most of the homes appeared dated, like they'd been built in the twenties, but they were well kept, some of the yards artfully land-scaped. Someone's automatic lawn sprinkler kicked on, delightfully spraying her. The air was clean and cool. She pulled it into her lungs and picked up the pace.

Faster.

She always enjoyed running, had been on the high school track team, and aced the Army's Basic Training Physical Fitness Test on her first attempt. Women aged seventeen to twenty-one... she was eigh-teen when she joined... had to handle a two-mile run in under nine-teen minutes. The time requirement was 19:36 for women aged twenty-two to twenty-six. She was twenty-two when she decided not to re-up.

Piper still averaged under fifteen minutes for her daily two-mile run.

Many mornings she stretched it out to five miles, taking a few turns through the entire community of Hatfield. As much as she loved running, and needed it to relax, she couldn't allow herself the luxury of extra miles today.

Two miles only. Too much to do.

It would have been easier to avoid the workout this morning, but that would ruin her routine and might provide an excuse to miss it tomorrow and the day after that.

At least two miles. Every single day.

Her feet hit the curb in front of a pale blue house in need of new paint and she picked up speed. She felt a faint burn begin in her chest as she came to the end of the next block and wheeled around to start the jog back. Piper reached into her back pocket and retrieved her cell phone, called up some music, and kept going. Wagner's *Ride of the Valkyries* played just loud enough to muffle the sounds of her breath and slapping shoes.

Kill da wabbit, kill da wabbit. The piece reminded her of a vintage Bugs Bunny cartoon in which Elmer Fudd repeatedly sang "Kill da wabbit" in time with the *Valkyries*. *Kill da wabbit, kill da wabbit.* She set her pace in time to the beat and felt the drum strikes travel up and down her spine. The music swelled as she waved to a woman pulling out of a driveway. The woman was new to the neighborhood; Piper would invite her over for dinner some night next week.

Piper felt wired, like she'd just thrown back six cups of coffee. Maybe it was the thought of returning to the fairgrounds and revisiting the site of the disaster. Maybe she'd do three miles instead. That'd be enough. Three. Yeah. She lengthened her stride as the piece ended and another began: Balakirev, a *Mancando* section. Over the whisper of the piano, she heard an engine rev, the woman in the VW off to work. Piper used to run to classic rock, Chicago and Aerosmith, but she didn't want the lyrics to tangle her thoughts. She needed her head clear to think about this case.

Five people had died last night in an accident the likes of which

Spencer County—let alone perhaps all of Indiana—hadn't seen before. It was tragic, unfortunate, and she couldn't begin to imagine what the parents were experiencing. She'd talked to all of them last night, and suspected they'd be filing lawsuits against the county; one father already had made that clear.

Mikhail Glinka's *Kamarinskaya* started when she touched the far end of her block. The burn in her chest was warmer and had spread up her neck. Piper's face was flushed from the mild exertion and her heart rate was up. She felt a sensation in her legs that was not quite an ache but was signaling that her muscles were stretching; it was a good feeling.

She tipped her head back and angled her lower lip out, sending a puff of air up to chase the hank of hair that dangled in front of her eyes. Piper jogged in place in front of her garage, stared at the Ford Explorer.

Yeah, one more mile, a quick shower, then she'd head to the fairgrounds.

She played *Kill da Wabbit* again.

CHAPTER SIX

7:00 A.M.

The amusement rides were at the back of the fairgrounds, not far from the grandstands where she and Nang would attend the rescheduled Sic Me Another country concert tomorrow night. Piper thought the rides placement was designed so people had to walk past all the food vendors and games of chance—enticing them to spend money—before they could reach the rides, where they could spend more money, all in the pursuit of summer fun. The placement also made it easy to cordon off the area with yellow police tape.

Piper sat on top of a picnic table, gaze fixed on the dismantled Odyssey. A crew would arrive around noon to haul away the pieces. The slightly warm breeze felt pleasant. It brought the faint scents of popcorn and cotton candy that lingered from yesterday. She knew those odors would double-down when the fair opened in another three hours.

"Twenty minutes," Basil said. He sat next to her. "Brought the family here twenty minutes before it happened. Shaya'd pulled a green plastic duck out of a tub and won a balloon. She was having a grand time, all twenty minutes of it. But she doesn't want to come back." Shaya was Basil's five-year-old daughter.

"I'd been here about that long, too. Twenty minutes. Just got a corn dog. Never managed to take a bite."

"Corn dogs are not edible."

Piper knew that Basil was health-conscious. Distance runner, amateur boxer, no caffeine, and apparently no corn dogs. Thirty-two years old. Four years Navy. Top of his class at the police academy. He'd spent four and a half years as a patrolman with the Chicago Police Department, then five years as a detective—one with Major Accident Investigation Section and four with Gangs and Narcotics. Commendations and decorations, and he'd been looking for a rural location to move his family when the Spencer County detective position came open. Too many guns, too many murders in the big bad city, he'd said.

Piper considered herself more than lucky to get him, but she wondered how long it would take before he got bored and went elsewhere.

"You warned me this county might be slow," he said, as if reading her mind. "But there was nothing slow about last night. Unfortunately."

He stood and stretched. Basil was six feet tall, lean, his skin a deep sienna and his eyes so dark Piper couldn't easily discern the pupils. His hairstyle was urban, a slow fade, about an inch on top and down the back, shaved close on the sides, complimented with a trimmed Van Dyke. Today he wore chips of turquoise in his ears.

"I've discovered that on and off our county's indeed far from sluggish." Piper yawned.

It had been a long night. They'd downloaded interviews and the collected videos, notified the next of kin of the five fatalities ... four teens from the ride disaster plus the man in the cotton candy van. The teen who had landed on the hay bale was listed in serious condition, in a coma, but apparently would make it. She'd sent almost everyone home a little before midnight and stayed an hour more, reworking schedules, figuring overtime, and writing thank you notes to the civilians who'd pitched in on-site.

Fourteen deputies, fifteen counting her detective-- covering three shifts, each working four days on, two off, rotating. She'd had to do some finessing to make everything even-out and sit within the overtime budget. She'd notified the Virginia State Police about Vernon Milgrew, who was unhappily incarcerated in her jail, repeating: "I didn't do nothin' wrong." Somewhere in there she'd called the Indiana Department of Homeland Security about the Cosmic Odyssey.

Piper yawned again. Her three-hour nap had not been sufficient.

"When are they supposed to get here?" Basil worked a kink out of his neck and palmed his cell phone, scanned some of the pictures of people he'd talked to last night. "When's Chief Deputy Oren—"

"Shouldn't be long, I hope." Piper glanced away from the wreckage and watched a crumpled food wrapper scud across the ground. She hopped off the table and grabbed it. "Text I got said the Homeland Security officer would be at the department by eight, latest. Oren's bringing her. I just wanted us out here early."

"In case she was early."

"Yeah." Piper dropped the wrapper in a nearby waste can. "Yeah. I wanted us out here early. I don't want to miss anything. I want to see what she's looking for." But Piper also wanted to be out early because no one was walking around yet.

While it was quiet.

While she could think.

Five dead to a damn accident at a county fair where everything was supposed to be *Sweet Caroline* happy.

She'd been briefly happy, strolling hand-in-hand with Nang, relishing his company and wondering if they were getting too serious, hovering on the edge of exchanging "I love yous." The music, the colors, the anticipation of the corn dog drizzled with spicy mustard. Piper had been drinking in the county fair atmosphere, smiling. Happy, definitely. *Sweet Caroline* happy. Until hell had broken loose.

Piper's radio crackled and she answered it.

"Oren's pulling in," she relayed to Basil.

"Good thing we came out early," Basil said.

With Oren came Vanessa Wolfe, who immediately passed a business card to Piper, announcing herself as Director of Elevators and

Amusements, a division of the Indiana Department of Homeland Security, based in Indianapolis.

Uttering only a few dozen words, the woman spent the next hour looking through the wreckage while Piper provided details on the fatalities and injuries. Vanessa took video, stills, and gathered metal samples into a kit, and then took close-up pictures of the adjacent rides.

Piper guessed Vanessa was in her late thirties or early forties. She wore steel-toed work shoes, incongruous to her navy suit, the slacks dusty now from the knees down. She looked all-business. Her hair was a severe cut, and her makeup non-existent behind tortoiseshell eyeglasses. Vanessa's right ear had three piercings—all little gold balls. The left ear had one thin hoop with a gold ball dangling just past her jawline. Piper liked the look, noticed a thick wedding band with scrollwork on it resembling the One Ring from the Tolkien films—the only thing approaching whimsy about the woman.

"I want copies of your videos, the interviews," Vanessa said, as she closed her kit. "All of them. You said no body cam footage."

"We don't have the cameras yet."

"Too bad. Those copies? Your deputy can put that together when he takes me back to your office." Vanessa detailed what she was looking for, signs of metal fatigue or clues that the operator did something wrong.

She sighed and ran a hand over her perfectly kept hair. "Sorry if I seem so blunt. I got up at three to get here. I've never dealt with anything so horrific. In all my years with the division, it has been a few broken bones, arms mostly. We only come out to a fair if an injury requires significant treatment. We don't fret over minor stuff … scrapes, sprained ankles. This is … well … this accident has hit the national news now. Brace for reporters swooping in today."

Reporters had started calling the department last night, Piper fielding some of the calls, but putting most of them off with "nothing to report yet" or "we're investigating."

"I'm sure the fair will be happy to sell the reporters cotton candy and lemonade," Piper said.

Vanessa offered a half smile. "I like fairs, Sheriff, the Indiana State Fair especially. But all the noise, people, chaos. Makes it hard to think. This is quiet, nice, right now. That's why I wanted to get here so early. Before the people. Thanks for accommodating me."

"It wasn't nice or quiet last night," Oren said softly. He'd been following Vanessa, intently watching what she photographed and took samples of. " I don't expect a lot of people here today, the rides being closed. They'll be out Sunday for the rescheduled concert. And maybe for the rides if they re-open."

"I think I've gathered all I need right now," Vanessa announced after one more pass around the Odyssey ruins. "Deputy, if you would please take—"

Piper stepped up. "I've got some questions before *Chief* Deputy Rosenberg takes you back to the office."

Vanessa let out a huffing breath. "Questions. Like—"

"I've not been sheriff long," Piper admitted. A little less than six months, and no previous experience with the sheriff's department; but she wasn't going to explain that. "So I'm not sure how this works. What happens next?"

"We've never had an industrial accident at a fair," Oren added. "Not anything close to this, not in the county's history. So this is new to all of us."

"At least someone in your department knew enough to call Homeland Security," Vanessa said.

Only because Piper found a reference to it in the department manual.

"Sheriff Blackwell, there are in the neighborhood of nineteen thousand elevators, escalators, and amusement rides in the state that we regulate yearly. Certified inspectors examine them all ... elevators in schools, nursing homes, hospitals, factories, office and apartment buildings." Vanessa spoke like she was lecturing to a school group. "And in places you might not think of, such as grain storage, steel mills, smoke stacks, TV towers. We take on fairgrounds for the rides —like this one, theme parks, indoor amusement parks in the big hotels. Perfect North Slopes in Lawrenceburg, and the Peaks in Paoli

... the lifts, you know, in ski season. It's pretty amazing what's all given a look, what all falls under my department. We inspect about a thousand amusement rides every year. Part of NAARSO."

Piper raised an eyebrow.

"That's the National Association of Amusement Ride Safety Officials. NAARSO," Vanessa continued. "I have a Level One certification, and in my early years I inspected plenty of them, looking for broken parts, improper maintenance, rigorously tested the seat belts, shoulder harnesses, and lap bars. Every ride is inspected once a year when it comes into the state ... which according to my records in your case was three days ago when this fair started setup. Some states—not ours—accept recent inspections from other states. The rides must prominently display the current permit issued by IDHS."

Piper mentally translated that to Indiana Department of Homeland Security.

"This ride—what's remaining of this ride—has such an up to date sticker. From three days ago."

"So ... what's next?" Piper repeated, wondering if that meant the inspection was not properly done.

Another huffing breath. "I have two investigators coming out this morning—they should be here between nine and ten, along with an insurance company inspector. They're going to look over the pieces before they're carted off, take even more samples. Then they'll re-evaluate the other rides, and determine if this section of your fair can reopen tomorrow. I expect them to be here most of the day, giving another check to everything standing."

"And you'll figure out why this happened?" Piper pressed. "You'll make some sort of ruling soon? That maybe your initial inspection wasn't—"

"As soon as I can. And our inspections are thorough." Vanessa picked up her kit. "Look, I'm going to get copies of what you collected, go through some of it at your office if you don't object. Then I'll go back to Indy and give everything a more comprehensive look, talk to the inspectors who, like I said, will be here in a little

45

while, see what they say. We'll work together, you and me. So, as soon as I can, I'll get you something. But it won't be today or tomorrow."

Piper thought about Vernon "I didn't do nothin' wrong" Milgrew sitting in jail. A Virginia police officer was arriving Tuesday to take him back where he belonged to face assorted meth charges. She hoped Vanessa would make a ruling within that time; otherwise she might have to come up with a reason to keep Vernon longer—just in case he did do something wrong.

"And if you decide it's just an accident? That nobody is at fault?"

"Then the insurance companies get to deal with all the lawsuits and the news reporters have more to write about." Vanessa stared at Piper without blinking. "But if I decide it wasn't an accident, it basically all falls to your department. We have no law enforcement capabilities. Any criminal charges, any arrests, that's all on you, Sheriff Blackwell. And the insurance companies will still get to deal with all the lawsuits. And the reporters will write even more stories."

Vanessa frowned and turned to Oren. "*Chief* Deputy, can you take me to your office now so I can get copies of—"

Oren started walking in the direction of the parking lot, waving his hand in a "come along" gesture.

"I wonder if anybody can sue her office," Basil mused after Vanessa was out of sight. "That ride was inspected three days ago. If her office missed something—"

"—the reporters will have a lot more to put in their stories," Piper finished. "I want to talk to the other operators while we're here. I figure some of them are at their trailers."

"Because the rides aren't running today and there's not a helluva lot to do around the county," Basil said. "Unless they visit the Santa Claus museum or have fishing gear."

"And the bars aren't open yet." Piper took a last look at the pieces of the Odyssey and started toward the workers' lot.

Her radio crackled again, Sylvia D calling. Sylvia was a retired Rockport City police dispatcher who occasionally filled in at the sheriff's department when the regular dispatchers called in sick or went on vacation. "Sheriff Blackwell, there's a problem in Africa."

"Africa?" Basil's perfect eyebrows rose.

"I got Zeke on the line," Sylvia continued. "I'm switching it so you can hear him."

"Sheriff Blackwell! O-M-G, Sheriff Blackwell," Zeke panted. "I'm at Sam's, and he's dead. O-M-G." Zeke talked so loud and fast Piper pulled the radio back from her ear.

"Slow it down, Zeke. Breathe. Who's Sam? And what are you—"

"My dealer." A pause. "Sam's my dealer. He's dead, and—"

"Zeke—"

"Not just dead, like keeled over dead. Or fell and hit his head dead. Or natural causes heart attack dead. He's dead like murdered dead. Awful dead."

"I'll come out, take a look, and call the coroner. Dr. Neufeld is the one who'll make a—"

"It's murder. Don't need a coroner to tell you it's murder. Anybody and their brother could tell you it's—"

"Zeke—"

"I don't see a gun or knife or anything. But I'm not moving stuff to look around. I didn't touch anything. Well, the back door. I touched it, sort of broke it open 'cause I was worried about him. And I touched him, his neck, checking for a pulse. There isn't one, a pulse. I don't think I touched anything else inside, which is a mess by the way, and I don't think it's naturally a mess. I think someone wrecked the place and—"

"Zeke!"

He quieted.

"Zeke, give me an address," Piper stated evenly, hoping to calm him. "And the man's last name."

"Address? Uh, I don't know the address. It's Africa. The green house with the big garage. The only green house. Africa, Sheriff Blackwell. Can you come out? Sam's dead, Sheriff Blackwell. And I don't know his last name. Sam. Everybody knows him as Sam. And there's no Mrs. Sam, or kid Sams. Just him. Only him. If there were other Sams, I think they'd be dead too. Like I said, I was worried about him and—"

"Zeke, go outside and wait for me."

"Sure, Sheriff Blackwell. Sam was a good guy, by the way. My favorite dealer."

"Dealer? Zeke—"

"Oh. My *comic* dealer, you know. He owns … owned … the best and only comic book store in Owensboro. Who'd want to kill Sam? And he hasn't been dead all that long. He felt a little warm. Not as warm as he should be if he was breathing. Not warm like living warm. But a little warm like—"

In the background Piper heard birds squawking, something bubbling. She swore she heard a monkey screech.

"Zeke, go outside right now and wait."

"Going. Going." Piper heard a door open and close. The squawking stopped, or at least Zeke was out of range of it. "Okay. I'm outside. Are you coming right away, Sheriff?"

"Right away, Zeke." She looked at Basil. Did she see a flicker of excitement in his eyes?

"I've handled a lot of murder cases," Basil said. Definitely a flicker.

Piper knew he had dealt with murders; it was one of the reasons he'd left Chicago—too many murders and too many guns.

"Africa? There's really a town called Africa in Spencer County? I don't remember seeing it on the county map. And the map wasn't difficult to memorize," Basil said.

"You won't find it on a recent map. It's south of Rockport, a little west. We'll take County Road 50. Maybe there's still a sign. I think there are a handful of houses left, a couple on stilts, close to the river. We'll look for the green one. We can interview the fair workers later."

CHAPTER SEVEN

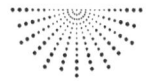

9 A.M.

Piper drove. Basil Googled Africa.

"MCD," he said. "Minor civil division. Three hundred and eighty feet above sea level. One of eight unincorporated towns in Ohio Township. Nothing else about it. No population listed."

"One resident less than yesterday, apparently," Piper said. "Let's ask Sylvia D, and put it on speaker. She's the president of the genealogy club. She'll know something more."

Basil radioed the dispatcher. "What do you have on Africa?"

"The dinkburg you're headed to, not the continent, right?"

"Yeah."

"Just a minute."

Piper heard Sylvia talking to Oren in the background, something about the Buddhist retreat that had recently opened in Fulda. Several of the neighbors had been voicing objections about it to the sheriff's department and the county board; one man in particular had been vocal. She'd ask Oren later about today's grievance.

"Okay, I'm back. Africa. Hope you're not asking me 'cause I'm old. I'm not *that* old. Retired does not mean ancient. And I'm not exactly retired, am I? I've been working plenty of weekends for you. Africa.

49

Africa. Africa. Well, the African American population of Spencer County—"

Piper was pleased that Sylvia D, who at seventy-one indeed fit the senior citizen label, used politically correct terms. Some in the Old Farts club—the genealogy group—employed rude labels for all ethnicities and non-Christian religions.

"—was like zero early in the county's history. Actually two. Two people. Then around 1870 about a thousand African Americans were listed in the census. Bam, all of a sudden settling here after the Civil War. Most moved into Ohio Township, just south of Rockport. The settlement picked up the name Africa. Shameful, but that's what they called it because only African Americans lived there. There was an all-black school down in the lowlands. The river took it a long while back. The river took a lot of things when it swelled. Anyway, people moved out of Africa, and out of the county, maybe because of the river, maybe looking for something better and drier. One dozen houses still stand, ten of them occupied. Our current census shows about two percent African Americans living now in the whole county, but none in Africa. There's an all-black graveyard on higher ground, Sandale Cemetery, near the intersection of 66 and 161. A lot of the stones are worn, but it's an interesting walk-through. I'll ask around at the club next week, see if anyone knows—"

"That's enough," Basil said. "Thanks." He turned toward Piper, his face an unreadable mask. "Have you studied much about black history in this county?"

"Studied? Ha. Basil, I never paid much attention to the county's history beyond what I picked up from members of the genealogy club. But I'm learning more."

"Well, I didn't know anything about Africa or the blacks who settled there. But my wife found a piece at the library about two black men lynched on the grounds of the old county courthouse in 1900. Rowlands and Henderson, don't remember the first names. They were charged with robbery and murder of a barber. Crowd a thousand strong broke into the jail, took them out, and hung them from a tree on the lawn. Then they shot up the bodies."

"Holy shit," Piper said. "Spencer County, eh? Really?"

Basil shrugged and faced forward. "They might have been guilty, but they didn't make it to trial to find out. So if this is really a murder we're going to down this road, at least whoever did it won't get dragged out and hanged." He paused. "I hope."

"Twelve houses," Piper said, changing the subject. "All that's left of Africa."

"Basil?" Sylvia D came back on the radio. "Basil?"

"Yeah."

"Just picked up your wife's new book, *Forever August*. If I leave it on your desk will you have her sign it for me?"

"Certainly."

"Actually, I have four copies. Just have her sign her name in three of them. In the other make sure she writes 'to my dear friend Sylvia D.' I'll leave you a note to that effect."

"Certainly."

Piper caught Basil grinning.

"The cover is just gorgeous, by the way, that sunset and big oak tree, and that handsome guy with his shirt unbuttoned all the—"

"Thanks, Sylvia," Piper said. "We're in Africa now, switching channels. Let's keep this quiet until we discover what's happened."

"Sure, have to get back with Oren anyway. It's about the Buddhists. That elevator inspection lady is still here, in the break room. Oh, and you've a bunch of messages from reporters, all of them wanting information on that awful to-do at the fair last night."

"I'll return the calls later, Sylvia." Piper frowned at the thought of dealing with the press. "Under investigation," is what she'd say to them ... because that was the truth.

"Africa," Basil mumbled. "Wonderful."

Piper shared all the sarcasm he'd wrapped in that one-word assessment. She didn't see a sign for the tiny community; maybe someone had finally removed it. But the dozen decades-old houses along the road—a green one roughly in the middle—told her this was the right place. The bright green mailbox out front had SAM painted on the side in yellow. Zeke's rusty Nova was parked in the driveway

51

near the double garage, leaving plenty of room for her Explorer, and later for the coroner's van. Piper wouldn't call Dr. Neufeld until she'd taken a look.

Zeke waved as she pulled in.

"It's bad, but it doesn't stink," Zeke said. "Not like dead body stink. Not yet. So I know he hasn't been dead long. But I know he's dead. Real dead. Not breathing. Or I would have called an ambulance. And I—"

Piper stared at her off-duty dispatcher. He looked disheveled, bags under his eyes, Loot the Castle t-shirt rumpled, and he smelled less than fresh.

"Stay out here, Zeke. We'll take a look and call the coroner, and then we'll come out and talk to you."

"Yes, Sheriff." Zeke sagged against his trunk. "Okay if I take a nap in my car?"

"Sure. Just stay outside." Piper went back to the Explorer and pulled her kit. Basil retrieved the handheld video camera and a small satchel. At the back door, the knob of which looked crooked in evidence of Zeke breaking in, they put on booties and gloves.

"Like I said, I don't think I touched anything," Zeke called. "Except the door. And except Sam's neck when I checked for a pulse. I sure wanted to clean the place up though, you know, but I stopped myself. The animals ... they're in cages. You don't have to worry about them. They can't bite you or—"

He prattled on, but Piper and Basil went inside, where the squawks and chatter of a pair of parrots drowned Zeke out. Then a monkey started screeching shrilly, and in gaps of that Piper heard cats hissing. She shuddered, recalling a violent cat-hoarder she'd dealt with in early May.

"Sounds like a jungle." Basil started recording. "Sounds like no sane person lived here. Also seems like this place has some serious sound-proofing. Didn't hear a whisper of this racket until we opened the back door." He flipped on the audio. "Appears thoroughly vandalized, in anger or because the burglar was looking for something. Little intact in the kitchen. And Zeke was wrong about the 'it doesn't stink' part. It stinks."

Piper didn't consider it a stench so much as an earthy-musky odor that reminded her of a zoo.

The house had appeared to be a basic ranch on the outside, something built in the nineteen twenties or thirties. Simple. Old-fashioned. Small. The paint peeling in places. The inside warred with all of that. The kitchen was wholly ransacked. But under the mess it appeared state-of-the-art; emerald-green tray ceiling, stainless steel appliances, fancy coffee maker, juicer, cherry cabinets with beveled glass doors. The table was polished wood, bench seats. A tropical rainforest print covered the exposed wall. Exotic plants choked the windowsills, and the pale green tile floor was patterned with darker green vines and broad leaves.

Beautiful in a way—but odd given the house's plain and aged exterior. And it was every bit a vandalized mess. The beveled glass doors stood open, the green dishes and glasses inside smashed—most of that on the green granite counters. Drawers had been opened, their contents spilled; silverware and towels dumped out. The pantry closet's canned food had been tipped over; pancake mix boxes ripped apart, jars of instant coffee upended, large sacks of flour shredded. Cookware was strewn among the jumble. Two footprints were evident in the powdery debris on the floor, and Basil recorded close-ups. Piper slung the evidence kit over her shoulder, pulled out her cell phone, and started taking pictures.

"Those aren't Zeke's," she said of the prints.

"Agreed," Basil returned. "I'd put him at about a size nine or a ten, medium width. He's wearing tennis shoes, and these belong to a larger man. Leather soles, no patterns, got to be an eleven or twelve, double E."

The animals in the other room continued to make a racket. Piper felt a headache blooming behind her eyes. Cages. Zeke said they were in cages. It sounded like a zoo.

Basil stepped around the flour and through an open doorway into what likely had been intended as the house's living room, Piper following. He swept the camera around to capture everything.

One wall held a massive aquarium where stunning fish swam slowly, looking like pieces of colorful lace. Opposite it stood an aviary with four smallish parrots with gray heads, yellow breasts, and green wings, and two larger African Grey parrots. Next to that sat a floor-to-ceiling cage that held a screeching capuchin monkey—three monkeys, Piper noticed, but two of them sat high on a perch and remained silent, hugging each other. Another big cage held a quartet of exotic-looking cats—the source of the hissing and snarls she'd heard. Though small, Piper guessed they weren't a domestic variety. Some of these animals might not be legal to keep, not that she could charge their dead owner with a crime.

A thick green shag carpet, which made Piper think of grass, felt spongy to walk across. A rainforest print similar to the one in the kitchen covered the only visible wall. Elegantly-framed prints of enlarged jungle-themed comic book covers hung on it. An ample green leather easy chair and ottoman sat against a window, the sill jam-packed with tropical plants. Comic book figurines, sadly all of them broken, covered a small table next to the chair. From that seat, the viewer could take in the fish, art, birds, cats, and monkeys.

Zeke's comic book dealer sprawled dead in the chair, wearing a pair of leopard print boxers. He didn't smell like death; the scents of the animals and the blooming tropical plants were too strong to allow that.

"Someone did not like Sam," Piper whispered, observing the body. "Someone did not like him a lot."

CHAPTER EIGHT

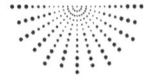

10:30 A.M.

Piper sat on the front step, watching video from the fair on her phone to pass the time. She itched to go back inside, but she wanted to follow proper protocol, and Basil had agreed.

So she'd secured the house while Zeke continued to sleep and Basil went back to the department to fill out a search warrant request—which he claimed to be "like lightning" with—and get it to a judge. A search warrant was required to legally process a scene, to protect against unlawful searches and to prevent any evidence they collected from being challenged in court.

She'd also alerted the coroner, who was on her way back from Evansville, where she was scheduling autopsy times for the county fair victims.

Piper turned off the fair video and switched to the images she'd taken of Samuel Silver—they'd found his last name and address on an envelope, and had needed that information for the search warrant.

She shivered looking at the dead man, fortunate that it was on a small screen, not as gut-tearing as standing over the corpse.

Piper had seen a lot of bodies during her tours in the Middle East. Several of her down-range assignments had involved grisly finds that some nights she couldn't get out of her head. Pieces of people. A few

55

times she'd witnessed the aftermath of torture, too. This was a different kind of grisly because it had happened in her county. Sleepy Spencer County where this should not be possible.

Basil pulled in the driveway and waved the signed warrant as he got out.

"Seventy minutes," Piper said. "You are fast."

"Like lightning," he replied.

Zeke roused and poked his head out the window.

"I'll talk to you when we're done," Piper said.

Zeke retreated back inside the car.

Then she and Basil went in the house, booties and gloves on.

Piper's chest tightened as she looked closer at Samuel Silver and continued to take pictures. She had better understood violence during her military days ... our side vs. their side; perceived right vs. perceived wrong. Not on U.S. soil. Not close to Southern Indiana.

Torture shouldn't happen here.

One of the monkeys continued to screech.

The parrots squawked and the cats hissed. The crescendo of jungle sounds threatened to smother her, and in the back of her mind she saw flashes from down range assignments, glimpses into buildings where foul things had been done to people. Torture happened *there*. She'd dealt with it *there*.

Her detective, a few feet away, had almost ten years more experience in law enforcement than she did. Her chief deputy had forty more years. Only one deputy in her department had less than herself, and that was her recent hire Millie—Oren's granddaughter, who possessed a four-year degree in criminal justice and a master's in communication. Piper had entered the Army straight from high school. An MP trained at Fort Campbell, KY, she was not prepared for this sort of thing in a civilian setting.

Torture happened in the Middle East. Torture and other grisly things.

"Seen some stuff like this in Chicago," Basil said. "But, honestly, not quite this bad. A whole lot of hate was involved here."

Torture happened in big cities, gang violence.

Torture shouldn't happen on a rural road in Africa.

The jungle sounds seemed overwhelming and Piper knew she was hyperventilating. Thankfully, Basil didn't say anything about it.

Get it under control. You're tough. You've seen worse. Truly, she had seen worse.

The down-range assignments in the Middle East had been dangerous; she'd lost friends, nearly been killed a few times. The violence was bullets and bombs, fires, everything, like in the big screen movies that were filled with special effects. It was violence she was more accepting of because it had not happened in a tiny town in Indiana.

Violence in civilian life ... that was something she wondered if she'd ever truly comprehend. She'd handled murders while sheriff—twice so far—but nothing like this.

She wanted to get the son of a bitch who tortured this man. She didn't want to understand this.

The darkness in whoever killed Sam was absolute.

Get it under control. You're tough. You've seen worse.

"White male." Basil spoke clearly so the camera recorded his voice. "Mid-fifties. Five-eight, five-nine approximately, probably one-fifty, one-fifty-five. Appeared to have been fit. Lived alone." He turned off audio and looked at Piper. "One chair in this room, so he lived alone." A pause: "Lived here without *human* company. Look at this place. He was a fruitcake batter served with a side of geek sauce."

Somehow, the monkey screeched even louder. The greys chattered —words coming through—"watcha doin' gorgeous? pshew-pshew, Sam fix me a sammich! Watcha doin' gorgeous gorgeous gorgeous?"

Piper's mouth felt desert-dry, and she tried to work up some saliva. Dizzy, she closed her eyes for just a moment, tried to picture something pleasant—sitting with her dog in her backyard garden. She opened her eyes again and winced, took off a glove and reached out to touch Sam's face with the back of her hand. A hint of warmth. She put the glove back on and carefully touched his arm; rigor was setting in.

"Not dead all that long," she said.

Basil turned the audio back on and continued recording his initial observations: "Lividity just setting in, likely dead four to six hours, closer to the four I think. C.O.D. undetermined pending M.E., but related to the extensive torture inflicted. One sick puppy played with this poor man."

It was clear that Sam's kneecaps had been busted and all of his toes broken, fingers broken, nose broken. Fist-sized bruises covered his face and washboard stomach. Congealed blood on the gag in his mouth, so someone had likely pulled out teeth or his tongue. His thumbs had been cut off and sat amid the shattered superhero figurines on the table. His left ear was missing. No, not missing, Piper spotted the ear amid the long tendrils of shag carpet, next to a discarded pair of jeans and a tropical-print shirt, the edges of loafers peeking out. A patch of his silvery hair had been burned away; Piper swore she could faintly smell the char of the flesh, and small puncture wounds decorated his body. They looked like insect bites.

"A lot of wounds, but not a lot of blood," Piper said.

"Ice pick," Basil noted. "I've seen wounds like this before. Just not so many of them in one body. Probably a hundred or so. Yeah, gotta be that many. Ice pick doesn't leave a lot of blood unless you hit an artery with it. With an ice pick, most of the damage and bleeding are internal, and that happens when you pull the pick out. And someone tasered him, first I suspect."

The honey-glazed donut she'd wolfed down at breakfast was making its presence felt.

"Tasered him twice. No, three times. There and there and there. Bet your coroner hasn't dealt with an ice pick death before."

Piper noticed the twin prod marks on his arm where taser wires had latched on. Another set on his neck.

"To subdue him," she said. "He was tasered to control him."

"Sure. Probably had to more than once because he was fit. He probably shook the first one off and got zapped again. A third time for good measure. Then they went to work on him. Somebody really did not like this man. See where the hair is stripped away at his wrists? Someone duct-taped him to the chair."

The birds continued to chatter. "I love you," one of them said. "Whatcha doin' gorgeous? Pshew-pshew." One of the greys held up a claw when it said that, pointing at its fellow. "Pshew-pshew." Piper realized it was imitating gunfire.

"Ugh. You got me," the other African Grey replied. "Where's my lunch?"

The smaller parrots started whistling; she swore one of them was rendering Garth Brooks' *Friends in Low Places*.

"Did a serious serious serious number on him," Basil continued. "Kept him alive a long while, I'm thinking. But not long enough."

Piper raised an eyebrow.

"They wanted something from him is my guess, tortured him to get it. But Sam here didn't cave. Why else would they toss the place? They were looking for something. If he'd told them where it was, they wouldn't have had to toss the whole place. Or maybe he held out a long while, and there were two doers ... one to use the ice pick while the other tossed the house. Maybe he caved at the end."

"But what the hell were they looking for? In this county, in this itty-bitty city, what would be so valuable that a man was tortured for it?" Piper mused. "And did they eventually find what they were looking for?"

P iper and Basil walked through the rest of the house. No sign of a break-in beyond what Zeke had done to the back door. Not a single window smashed or jimmied. Maybe Sam had invited the killer inside. Neither did they find any surveillance equipment—that might have made things too easy, she considered.

"I don't think I could handle all this green," Basil said. "I'd need a bigger color palette. But my wife would like the bathtub."

The bathroom looked like a rainforest—the jetted tub large and gleaming emerald, the toilet and sink matching, a veil of plants hanging in front of the window effectively served as a curtain. Various shades of green towels lay in a corner; Piper noticed blood on one. The closet and medicine cabinet had been thoroughly tossed and the remnants littered the green-veined marble floor. Beyond over-the-counter pain relievers and sleep aids, it looked like Sam took only two prescriptions—Lisinopril for high blood pressure and another called Istalol, which Piper Googled to discover it was a beta blocker used to treat glaucoma. She took a picture of the label, intending to call Sam's doctor later.

Another wall-sized aquarium stood in the bedroom, which also kept to the jungle theme. It included a king-sized bed covered with a leopard-print quilt, grass-like carpet, plus a tray ceiling from which hung tropical flower-dotted vines. Piper wondered how he had watered them, then saw a sprinkler device and decided it was likely automated. More plants crawled along the windowsill like living strands of thick rope. A second aquarium—massive at six-feet-high— filled the corner with bright red, orange, and blue-yellow fish about the size of her hand.

"Wow, just friggin' wow. Those aquariums, and the fish—"

"I think they're Petrochromis," Basil said. "Pretty sure. An African cichlid. Expensive. Me and my partner worked a robbery at a fish auction at McCormick Place last fall. More than a brick's worth of Petrochromis swiped—"

"A brick?"

"Brick. A hundred thousand dollars. The theft was traced to a Southside gang that trafficked animals. They specialized in big cats. Fish were a sideline. So I know about Petrochromis." A pause: "Petrochromis, and fan-tailed goldfish, in my house those don't have a long lifespan."

"Wow," Piper repeated softly. "Expensive fish. Expensive pets. Those monkeys and parrots, and probably those cats. All of that cost him. So Sam had money. Who knew the comic business was so lucrative."

"And clearly the interior decorating in general wasn't cheap... though I suspect he bought the house for a pittance."

"Sam also had a lot of Hawaiian-style shirts," Piper said. "Don't know if they're expensive. You couldn't pay me to wear one." The chest of drawers had been searched, colorful clothes scattered. The closet was open and most of the clothes were on the floor, everything tropical-casual except one black suit and a white silk shirt. An assortment of tennis shoes and loafers, belts, and baseball hats made up the rest.

Piper saw a small safe in the closet—opened and empty. Maybe what the killer wanted had been in there. The clothes strewn around the safe included an array of Hawaiian-style gaudy prints and cargo shorts, plus a Spiderman t-shirt.

It was a two-bedroom house, but the second bedroom had served as an office. The walls were painted green, but there were no plants, fish, or grass-like carpet, and its contents had been clearly upended, too. File cabinets were tipped over, desk drawers pulled out. Books knocked off the shelf—a mix of titles on tropical fish and comics: *The Marvel Encyclopedia*, *Seduction of the Innocent*, *The Bronze Age of DC Comics*, and *All in Color for a Dime*. A monitor and keyboard remained, but the computer was gone, the cords stretched like dead snakes across the back of a chair. If there'd been a laptop, that was probably gone, too. No landline anywhere. Piper would look close for a cell phone, but she suspected it was with the killer.

"Wonder if they found what they were looking for?" she considered again. "Maybe it was on Mr. Silver's computer. Or in his phone. Or in the safe."

"Something physical, they were looking for. You don't toss a place for a computer file. But they took the computers anyway... maybe because our victim had information about the doer on it. Pictures, addresses. Maybe Sam Silver knew his killer," Basil growled. "Might be hard to tell what's missing. Might never know what the doer was looking for." A pause: "We're going to be here all day, going through this. All night."

"And tomorrow. Probably right up to that concert." Which she really didn't want to miss because it was a date with Nang, and work had kept both of them apart lately. "And the day after that."

"Yeah, you go listen to that goat-roping twang. I'll stick with this. I don't care for country music." She swore Basil's dark eyes glimmered with the intrigue of this case. "Dealt with lots of ugly in Chicago, Sheriff Blackwell, but nothing quite like what was done to that poor bastard in the living room. This is interesting, this house, the dead man. Truly interesting."

"And awful." Maybe Zeke's dealer had settled in Africa because the town's name fit his preoccupation with a jungle motif, Piper thought. Could that preoccupation have been related to the murder?

"Something else odd about this place," Basil added. "Feels unusual. Not a single framed photo on any table, shelf, wall. Just framed comic book art. Even a single dude has a picture of his mother or nephew or something. And I didn't see any bare nails, so photos weren't pulled off the walls. Maybe we'll come across a photo album. But I have a hunch not. I think this guy was ... strange. More than strange."

She hadn't noticed the lack of photos. Piper mentally kicked herself—she should have seen that.

Piper decided that she wasn't close to being in Basil's league, and for the most part she'd let her big-city detective take charge of this investigation. It was why she'd hired him, right? But she'd stay closely involved ... too big, too heinous, too interesting to step back. Her county. She'd stay closely involved and figured Basil would teach her some things.

"We'll need help. And we need to find his relatives. A will. Paper. Some relative is going to have to take the house over. The animals." She sighed and keyed her radio. "Oren?" She waited and continued to study the office mess. There were framed comic book posters in the office. Tarzan, Ka-zar, Rulah, Sheena, Black Panther, Jan of the Jungle, and Congo Bill. She edged to the desk and glanced at the papers on top, found an envelope.

Oren answered.

"You know a lot of people in the county, Oren. Ever deal with a Samuel Silver? In Africa? No? He owns ... *owned* ... a comic book store across the river in Owensboro." She'd have to contact Owensboro, Kentucky, police and work out an arrangement where she could search the comic store, get any records they might have on Samuel Silver.

"Never heard of him? No. I don't read comic books either." Piper tugged on her lip. She knew Nang was fond of graphic novels and had a shelf full of them. Maybe Nang knew Sam. "Yeah, *owned*. Mr. Silver's dead. When you're done with Vanessa Wolfe, get Diego and come out to Africa." She gave him the address she spotted on the envelope. "Mr. Silver was tortured, murdered. The house burglarized, everything horrid and strange. I'm here with Basil. Bring a lot of evidence bags. Really, a lot. Dr. Neufeld is coming to get the body."

Piper wanted to involve Oren both because of his experience and because she didn't want him to feel left out of anything important. No reason to engender hard feelings with the man who'd been with the department a lot more years than she'd been breathing.

"We'll need to handle this *and* the Cosmic Odyssey, divide our resources," she continued. It would have been more convenient for these awful things to have happened weeks apart—or not to have happened at all, but Spencer County hadn't been convenient this year. "I want this Silver murder looked at right now, while it's fresh."

Zeke had been right, Sam had felt a little warm, rigor just setting in. She suspected Basil could be close on the estimate of killed three to six hours ago. "Put Jake on going through county directories to get any records on Samuel Silver. How long he's lived here, where he's from, relatives. Especially relatives. Anything and everything. Maybe Sylvia D's heard of him. As for the fair, Send Millie and Rocco out to the grounds to interview the other ride operators, get some background on Vernon Milgrew, something more personal than his arrest record. Have them check on the Homeland Security people." It wasn't scut work she was passing along; she and Basil had been going to tend to interviewing fair workers before they got the Africa call. "See you in a little while."

"Interesting," Basil repeated as he studied the office. He looked to the hall and turned off the video recorder. "The back door just opened."

Piper glanced at the clock on the wall. "Fourteen minutes. That'd be Dr. Neufeld."

"Didn't hear anyone pull up," Basil said. "Serious sound-proofing, this house."

"So the neighbors wouldn't hear the jungle," Piper said. "So they wouldn't complain." She intended to walk the length of Africa after she visited Silver Age Sam's across the river, talk to the neighbors. "Bet no one heard him scream."

"The monkeys did," Basil said. "And the parrots. But all they'll tell us is Pshew-pshew."

"Pshew-pshew," one of the greys called from the other room. "Fix me a sammich."

The bench was olive green, the paint thick like it had layer upon layer spread on it through the seasons. It sat in the middle of Sam's backyard, which was ringed with a thick hedge on three sides and the garage on the fourth; effectively creating a box that the neighbors couldn't look into. Sound-proofed house, sight-proofed backyard, Sam had been a private person.

And maybe a lonely one, Piper thought.

A half-dozen feet away, a waterfall with a slightly raised goldfish pond bubbled merrily. Piper had a lovely backyard with a high chain-link fence and plenty of flowers and bushes. She thought maybe a goldfish pond would be a nice addition. Another piece of cement to the county, she mused.

She sat next to Zeke, who'd finished the nap in his car. She stared at the waterfall, seeing instead Sam's punctured corpse and hearing in her mind the squawks of the parrots and the screams of the vocal monkey. Piper started a mental list of everything that needed to be done. Securing the crime scene—already managed. Searching the crime scene—taking place now and through at least tomorrow. Latent print processing, recovery of biological evidence, scene diagraming. She hoped Oren would bring a lot of evidence bags; what she had in her kit would not be sufficient.

Basil had made sure that the search warrant he got this morning also covered any safe deposit boxes and other county properties.

But she'd also have to obtain search warrants for his comic book shop in Owensboro across the river, and anything else that he might have owned there. And she'd need to assign deputies to talk to the neighbors along this street if she couldn't get to it fast enough herself. She and Basil and Oren would try to establish a list of suspects. A death investigation was complex, and any prosecution could depend on evidence they would collect from the house and comic shop. Piper had received training in such investigations during her MP schooling at Fort Campbell, though she never faced a murder while stationed at the base. The Middle-East ... there was death, but nothing to really investigate. It was war. Her real training had come in the past six months on this job.

Who offed Samuel Silver? And why?

She keyed her radio.

"Sylvia, on my desk is a rumpled business card. It's for a veterinarian in Owensboro. I'm going to need a veterinarian to come—"

Sylvia D. suggested her own veterinarian in Rockport who had saved her beagle from canine vestibular disease two summers past.

"I know she's a great vet, Sylvia, and much closer. I use her too. But this veterinarian in Owensboro—" He was the one she'd met at the county fair last night and had given her his card. "This guy specializes in exotics. And I've a house full of them here." His card had mentioned: DOGS, CATS, BIRDS, & EXOTICS. "I need the number off that card."

Sylvia provided it, and then whispered,: "Ms. Vanessa Wolfe with the elevator department is snarky."

Piper called the veterinarian and got the receptionist, who made arrangements for Dr. Carlisle to come to Africa to meet with Basil and determine what to do with the animals until Mr. Silver's relatives could be found. They agreed on four-thirty, when scheduled surgeries should be finished: an elderly German shepherd was having seven teeth pulled-- and a French bulldog was having her palate shaved. Piper wondered why some people volunteered information unnecessarily.

"I knew Sam had parrots," Zeke said after Piper finished the call. "Two Africans. He talked about them, has a picture of them hanging up in his comic shop. Never heard him talk about people, really, but he talked about those two parrots like they were his best friends." He made a huffing sound. "Maybe they were. But he sometimes hung out with Benzo and Lucky Ducky. So I guess he liked a couple of people."

Piper made a mental note to look for photos at the comic shop; it might give her a glimpse of friends and relatives.

"Corky and Kesha," Zeke continued. "Took me a minute to remember the birds' names. I didn't know he had more parrots ... cats and monkeys, too." Zeke whistled softly, the sound trailing off in the bubbling of the waterfall. "And fish. That's a honking big tank. Bet it was expensive, maybe special-made. I didn't know Sam was into having so many pets. The fish, though, I think I could get into fish. I bet it would be relaxing, watching them."

Sam had *three* large tanks; Zeke hadn't been in the bedroom to notice the other two. Piper thought about her own pets—a Golden Retriever and a cat, both inherited with the house. She'd become attached to the animals quickly, and to the beautiful home, things locking her to Spencer County. She'd grown up in Rockport, but moved away after high school, joining the Army to "be all she could be." She loved military life; it suited her. But her dad had encouraged her to run for his vacant sheriff seat, and she let herself be talked into it. He was cancer-free and now working as the chief of police in Santa Claus, the largest town in Spencer County. And she was ... sheriff ... and finding the cement getting thicker and thicker.

She sort of liked being sheriff. And being back in the rural county.

But I am taking a break from death and going to that concert tomorrow night with Nang.

The quick stop owner and mechanic and expert Vietnamese chef was part of the cement. She was pretty certain she adored him. A brief step back from the deaths of the Cosmic Odyssey and poor tortured Samuel Silver in Nang's company might give her a clearer head; improve her focus so she could work better. She needed to make a return trip to the fair anyway.

"I can't believe someone would kill Sam," Zeke said. He'd been saying something else, but she'd been too caught up in her thoughts. "Everybody loved Sam."

"No. Very much no." Piper disagreed louder. "Somebody or some-bodies did not like Mr. Silver at all."

"Yeah. I suppose you're right. They cut off his thumbs." Zeke's gaze was fixed on the tips of his tennis shoes. Piper noticed the grass had been recently cut, the lawn looking barefoot-perfect and not a weed to be seen. She wondered if Sam had tended to it himself or hired a service; a look in the garage for the lawn mower might answer that. "Cut off an ear. Man, I can't imagine how bad that must have hurt. I thought everybody loved—"

"You said you came to check on Mr. Silver because you were worried about him." Piper turned her phone on the 'record' function so she could reference the conversation later.

"I figured somebody should check on him." Zeke nodded and made a sound that was a cross between a snort and a laugh. "I didn't know his last name was Silver. I just knew him as Sam. His shop's called Silver Age Sam's. Hadn't realized it was a play on his name. I'd figured he'd named it after silver age comics, you know, the stuff that came out from the mid-fifties to about 1970. Sam liked silver age stuff, carried a lot of it. Some of it was pretty expensive. Too rich for me." Zeke looked up and stared at the waterfall. "I was worried 'cause he didn't show up for the midnight Loot the Castle tournament."

"Some sort of game tournament at his comic shop?"

"Sure, it was a comic book store, sold new and old comics. Sam was really into comics. But his *real* business—the stuff that made the most money—was collectible card games. Loot the Castle's the biggest seller. I know. I've spent too much money on it."

Piper vaguely understood what Zeke was talking about. Some of the guys in her unit had played Loot the Castle and others of its ilk; she'd never been interested. Euchre, bridge, and rummy better suited her.

"Anyway, he'd advertised it a bunch, the pre-release tourney. I signed up for it a week ago and got one of the last slots. I couldn't sign up earlier 'cause I didn't know if I'd be pulling any weekends in June. So we were all waiting outside the store last night." Another snort-laugh.

The way Zeke talked, his mannerisms, his clothes, made Piper realize just how young he was. A kid, really. Graduated from high school a month ago, she'd hired him for his techie skills and enthusiasm about law enforcement. She knew some folks in the county called her a kid behind her back. But she had five years on Zeke, and the military experiences had matured her fast.

Zeke wiped at something on his shirt. "Just standing around, waiting on the sidewalk in front of the store last night. I took off for a few minutes to find a bathroom, but went back. Well, waiting until close to one this morning before we gave up, most of us anyway. Dun-Dun was still there, though. He texted me that he called it quits at two and went home, said he was pissed that he didn't sign up instead for a tourney in Evansville where he might've gotten some special gorgons, said he'd have to shell out on eBay now. There's a shop over in Evansville that has them, you know, the Loot the Castle tourneys. But Sam drew the best players. Competition was top-notch, worth staying up for." He waited a beat. "And, honestly, he had these nice padded chairs. People liked to play at Sam's shop because it was super-comfortable, none of those cheap folding metal chairs that made your butt stiff. Real comfy chairs. His restroom was always clean, and he stocked soda and candy and didn't care if you brought your own snacks. He had lots of customers from as far away as Evansville 'cause his place was so nice. Some hobby shops are real dumps, you know."

Piper stayed silent, listened to the waterfall. After a few moments Zeke started up again.

"I've known Sam a long time, five years, been going to his shop that long. Started in junior high when I'd catch a ride with my older brother. I was always into comics. I discovered the card games by accident, watching people play over there at Sam's place. I joined in on a sealed deck tourney one Saturday afternoon when somebody cancelled, and I had a helluva good time. Been going to the midnight pre-release tourneys since my sophomore year and my driver's license. He usually has ... *had* ... one of those tourneys every four months or so."

"Five years you knew him," Piper said. "But you didn't know his last name."

Zeke shook his head. "Just called him Sam. Everybody called him Sam. Hell, Sheriff Blackwell, I only know the last names of a handful of Loot the Castle players. And in one case, Dun-Dun's, I only know his last name. Lots of first names, nicknames, you know, even Aggie. Her real name's Agnes Tully-Brown, but she hates Agnes. Everyone calls her Aggie." A pause. "Everyone calls me the Geek."

Zeke returned to studying his tennis shoes. After a few more minutes, he went on.

"Never saw a dead body before, Sheriff. Not outside of a funeral home. A plain old dead body would be different, I expect. But this was a friend. And Sam wasn't just dead. He was killed. I can't get that out of my head, the no thumbs, the ear, the ... dead. Is it true somebody was decapitated at the fair last night?"

Yes, Piper thought. Six bodies in two days, all of them dying horribly. But only one of them had been murdered.

"So you came here to check on Mr. Silver because you were worried he didn't—"

"Show. Yeah. Yeah. Worried 'cause he didn't show last night. He'd never *not* shown for one of his tourneys. I went home, caught a few Zs, fell asleep on my couch actually, and woke up to texts from Dun-Dun that he'd been calling Sam and Lucky Ducky and Benzo ... the three of them went out for pancakes before the tourney. Actually, Dun-Dun probably hadn't been calling Benzo. Benzo is anti-tech and doesn't have a cell phone. Dun-Dun said all he got was voicemail for Sam and Lucky Ducky and figured since I was with the sheriff's department I could see if Sam had a heart attack or something or was in an accident and was in the hospital. Dun-Dun wasn't thinking that he should contact the Owensboro police. Anyway, yeah, I was worried."

Piper needed to call the Owensboro police, though the department was right across the river. Maybe she'd drive over there. Talk to them in person, do the required paperwork to get her legal access to the comic store, and then go to Silver Age Sam's. "Sam's shop is in Owensboro, but he lived here."

"Yeah. Yeah. I remember him saying he lived in the jungle in Spencer County because houses were cheaper than in Kentucky. Bought a house and painted it green, he'd said. I did some thinking and figured maybe he meant Africa. Jungle … Africa … you know. Sam really really liked jungle comics, Tarzan, Sheena, stuff like that. He's got an original piece of Hogarth art on the wall of his shop."

"Hogarth? William Hogarth? London's—"

"No. Burne Hogarth. Cartoonist from Chicago. He was known for his Tarzan comic strip work."

"I see. So you went looking for a green house in Africa."

"Yeah. There was only one green house. Yeah." Zeke started worrying at a hangnail. "I saw SAM on the mailbox and knew this was it. Pulled in, looked through the garage window and saw his car. Couldn't get him to answer the door. So I thought maybe Dun-Dun was right about the heart attack. I broke in, found him, and called Sylvia. I would've called you directly, but I knew you were at the fairgrounds. I didn't want to interrupt. Sylvia, she said I should interrupt. She transferred my call to you." He waited another beat. "The fair last night … five died, right? Teenagers? I wonder if I knew any of them, went to high school with them. Do you have their names? Did someone really get their head torn off?"

The back door opened and Basil helped Dr. Neufeld wheel out the gurney with Sam's body on it. Zeke looked away, but Piper got up and met them.

"The autopsies from last night's county fair accident are scheduled to begin Monday, with the Vanderburgh County Coroner's Office assisting to get them finished by the middle of the week," Dr. Neufeld said. "I'm moving this fellow ahead of those kids."

"Thanks," Piper said. She didn't know what else to say.

Basil smoothed a wrinkle out of the plastic covering Samuel Silver. "Tox screening is standard around here, right?"

Dr. Neufeld pulled a face. "Yeah, even in the itty bitty cities," she said. "I'll do a full tox screen, scrape under his fingernails and see if I can get anything, DNA, from his killer. I'll send a blood sample to the state lab, and I'm going to screen the bloodspots on him. Maybe it's not all his blood. Maybe he put up a fight."

The coroner wore jeans, a polo, and a blazer, had brown hair and short, dark circles thick around her eyes. A retired pediatrician who was in her second term, she'd told Piper at the fair she was glad she couldn't run for a third term, wanting to concentrate on the living for a while. She was thinking about re-opening her pediatrics practice.

"Anyway, I'm taking this fellow first. I figure a murder trumps that awful accident last night. And that was some sick S.O.B. who killed this guy."

"Very sick," Piper agreed.

"You catch that sick S.O.B., Sheriff Blackwell," Dr. Neufeld said. "You and Oren." She nodded to Basil. "And Detective Meredith here, too. You all catch the S.O.B." She looked up and shook her head. "Never ever ever seen anything like that in this county before."

CHAPTER NINE

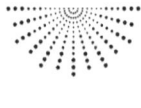

NOON

Piper returned to Zeke.

"So you broke in." Piper pointed to the back door.

She saw him mouth: *Duh.*

"Yeah. When Sam didn't answer. I knew he was in there, his car in the garage, you know. Saw it through that little window." Zeke pointed. "I'm not in trouble for breaking in, right? I've been studying the department manuals in slow times, you know. I read that police, sheriff's deputies and such don't need a warrant or permission to go in a house if they have a reasonable belief that someone inside is seriously injured or—"

"No trouble."

"Saw the mess. And I didn't step in the flour. There's shoe prints in the flour."

"We saw them."

"When Sam was wheeled out, that flour must have been—"

"We got pictures of the flour and the prints in it."

"Found Sam in the chair. All poked to death. Called Sylvia. I am still so so so tired, Sheriff Blackwell, and I know damn well I'm not going to be able to sleep tonight. I keep seeing him. I close my eyes and I see him and hear that monkey screaming. He was a friend,

72

you know. Everybody loved Sam. Except the asshole that killed him."

Piper put a consoling hand against his back. "I'm sorry, Zeke. I can tell you really liked him."

"Yeah. Yeah. Well, I *thought* everyone else did too. What's not to like? The guy sells ... *sold* ... comic books and roleplaying games, board games, cards, has ... had ... Loot the Castle events and real comfortable chairs. How could you not like him?" Zeke twisted the toe of his right foot into the ground. "He wasn't dead long, was he, Sheriff Blackwell? I mean, he still felt warm. If I'd have come over here when I left the shop, he would've still been breathing, right? If I hadn't went home and took a nap ... if I'd come over right away—"

"I don't know." Piper really didn't.

"I *do* know. If I'd come here right away, he'd be breathing."

"I don't know," Piper repeated. "Stop second-guessing stuff, Zeke. Be happy you weren't here when the killer was."

Zeke swallowed hard. "Or maybe I'd be dead too, huh?"

Piper listened to Dr. Neufeld's van pull away, watched Basil return to the back door and put booties on again and go inside.

"Was it all those puncture wounds? All those little holes, you'd think there would have been a lot of blood, right?" Zeke asked. "But there wasn't much blood. Probably internal bleeding. Was that what killed Sam? Punctured his heart? Do you think—"

"We have to wait for the coroner's report."

"How about those kids who were killed last night, not much younger than me, you know. I wonder if there's something after this. You know, after life. If there's really a heaven and—"

"Zeke—"

"I think about that. Stephen Hawkings was an atheist. He died, and if he was right there was nothing for him to—" He sighed. "I just wonder if there's something after, you know."

Piper wondered that too, sometimes. She'd seen a lot of death in her twenty-three years. "Zeke—"

"God, that woman is gonna cut Sam up, isn't she? For the autopsy? The coroner? Slice him open with a saw like on those CSI reruns. But

I suppose that's not any worse what was already been done to him, huh? I just can't believe that—"

"Do you know if Mr. Silver had been in any trouble? Owed someone something?" Piper would have to get a look at his financial records. "Did you ever hear someone threaten him?"

"Never. Never heard—" Zeke stopped fidgeting and straightened. "Wait. Last night me and Aggie went around back. I thought Sam was there, had parked behind the shop. That's where he always parked, back there. I was gonna offer to haul boxes for him, you know, the sets of cards for the tourney. I really wanted to use his bathroom, and it was in the back of the store. But there was a different guy there. And it wasn't Sam's car. It was a dark gray four door, Mazda, late model. I know cars. The guy looked up and saw us, got in the car and they drove away. I checked the back door. It was locked, didn't look like it had been broken into. But earlier I thought someone went in the shop. When I was out front looking in the window I thought I'd seen the back door open under the exit sign. You know, open it and go in. Could have been my imagination." He shrugged. "Do you think those guys that I saw—"

"What did they look like?"

Zeke shrugged. "It was dark, Sheriff Blackwell. The one at the door was dressed dark. White guy, I could tell that. Couldn't tell you anything about the car's driver. Like I said, two guys." He brightened. "But Aggie was taking a lot of pictures last night. I think she took one of the car. Maybe got the guy in a pic. Yeah. I'm pretty sure she did. Maybe we can get the license plate. Maybe those guys were involved with Sam's murder." He rubbed at his chin. "Or maybe they were just looking for Sam. Maybe it was nothing and—"

"Did Sam have relatives around here?"

Zeke shrugged.

"Close friends?"

"Benzo, maybe. But sometimes they didn't get along. Benzo was a little odd." Another shrug. "The parrots. I know he was big on the parrots. Lucky Ducky. He was buds with Lucky Ducky, too."

"Do you have phone numbers for Benzo and Lucky Ducky?"

"For Lucky Ducky," Zeke said, passing over his phone so she could copy the number.

"Employees?"

"I can give you some names. Geeze, the shop's supposed to open at two today. Always opens later than usual after a Loot the Castle tourney. Those things can run until three or four in the morning." He looked at his watch. "That's less than two hours from now. Probably Jinny opening. She's always there weekends. Sam didn't have many employees, a half-dozen full-time, maybe. A half-dozen part-timers. Didn't need many for a shop like that. Jinny's gonna wonder where Sam is. Maybe it's Honora's day. I remember Jinny saying something about a Louisville trip."

"First names, right, of the employees?" Piper thought about calling Owensboro police to get someone over to the store and keep it closed. But she decided it would be better to let it open so she could talk to whatever employees came in.

Zeke sighed. "Yeah. First names. And I can't remember all of them." He rattled off four. "Sheriff Blackwell, I'll get better at names, I promise. Work? I write all that stuff down. First names. Last names. Addresses. Everything like I'm supposed to. Who the hell would've known I'd need Sam's last name? Who the hell would've thought that someone would up and kill him?"

"You mentioned he went out to eat with Benzo and Lucky—"

"—Ducky. Yeah. I even have his address if you want—"

"That'd be helpful."

"You want to make sure they're okay, right? Or ask if they saw something." Zeke paused. "Or that they weren't the ones who killed Sam. But they weren't. They'd never kill anybody."

At least he thought to look for the house in Africa, picking up on the jungle clue. "You're doing fine, Zeke. Basil, me ... and Oren'll be here soon. We'll figure all of this out."

"I want to help."

"You've been a great help already. Seriously."

Zeke sucked in his lower lip and turned his face to meet Piper's stare. "No. I *really* want to help. I know I'm just a dispatcher, but—"

"You can't help with the investigation, Zeke, sorry."

Zeke shook his head. "Let me go to Aggie's and get her cell phone so you can look through the pictures from last night. I can at least do that. I have to tell her about Sam and—"

"You can't do that." Piper stood. Zeke wasn't "just a dispatcher," he was the department tech support guru. In the handful of weeks he'd been with the department he'd proven himself efficient—an excellent hire, and had improved the speed of the computers and added new software. But he wasn't a deputy and he might make inadvertent errors. She couldn't risk sending him for the task. A deputy needed to go to Aggie's and ask for her phone, keep it in sight until the girl agreed to hand it over or so they could copy the pictures off of it. And if Aggie refused, Piper would go to a judge for a seizure warrant ... all the while a deputy keeping the girl's phone in sight. But she wasn't going to explain all of that to Zeke, make him think he couldn't handle the job. "What's her address?"

Zeke grumbled, but supplied it.

Piper keyed the radio. Her deputy Jake could take a break from his records search, so she sent him on the assignment.

She returned her attention to Zeke. "Don't talk about this case, to Aggie, or to any of your Loot the Castle friends. Not to anyone. Not yet." She was going to try to keep that quiet for a little while.

"I get it. You want that all hush-hush while you snoop around." Zeke stood and rocked back and forth. "As much as you can keep anything hush-hush in this county."

Piper fought the smile that threatened. She knew Spencer County was like a big game of telephone; it didn't take long for news to travel from one corner to another. She'd thought about getting Aggie's cell phone herself, but she wanted to get to Owensboro before the comic shop opened.

"Aggie and me, we've got a date tomorrow night. Nothing no big deal, just going out. I don't have to cancel that, do I?"

Piper shook her head. "Just don't talk about this case, the murder."

"I know to keep my mouth shut. It's why I have a job. The previous dispatcher couldn't keep his mouth shut and you fired him."

"And he'd come in late a few times. Listen, Zeke, talking about cases can be a violation of State Certification training and DCI standards. There are liability issues if it gets out, and a risk we lose the ability to run DCI checks for records, DMV, open wanted cases."

"Yeah. Yeah. I know. I read the manual."

"Just cautioning you. Enjoy your date."

"Can I leave now?" Zeke looked to his car. The driveway was double-wide, so Piper knew he could back out around her Explorer.

"Sure. Go home and try to get some real sleep. I'll see you at work Monday." Piper walked to the garage, looked in the little window Zeke had gestured to, and put gloves on. "Don't be late Monday." She saw a white SUV, a Bronco. It looked clean, but an older style. She wasn't very good at guessing the years. The garage door wouldn't lift, so she stepped around to the side door. It opened.

"He called that his Simpson mobile," Zeke said. He'd followed her. "He thought it looked like the car O.J. made his dash in down the highway."

Piper stopped. "That was before you were born, Zeke."

"Before you were born, too, Sheriff."

She edged into the garage and let her eyes adjust to the lower light. Zeke trailed her.

"I thought you were going," she said.

"Yeah. Yeah. I just—"

"Don't touch anything." Piper saw a light switch and turned it on.

The Bronco gleamed like it had been newly washed. An assortment of tools hung along the south wall, more along the north. It was a double-garage but one bay was empty save for a riding lawnmower —green, John Deere. Piper was surprised Mr. Silver's car wasn't green, too.

There were bags of grass seed, fertilizer, mulch—all of the things one might expect to find in a garage. A ladder, buckets, hose, cartons of goldfish food, nets, and other equipment for the pond. She continued her visual inspection as she walked around the Bronco and peered in through the driver's side window. The driver's seat was pushed back, like a tall man had been driving it ... a man taller than

Mr. Silver. She tried the door, and it was unlocked, opened it, and leaned in. Clean, tidy. Something smelled a little funky, and she spotted two take-home boxes on the passenger-side floorboard, PEARL'S PANCAKE PALACE logos pressed into the Styrofoam. Apparently he had indeed gone out for a late dinner at the restaurant and failed to put the leftovers in a refrigerator before he was killed. Whatever was inside had spoiled. Didn't see a cell phone or other electronics; the backseat was clean. She pushed the button and popped the hatchback window, reached over to open the glovebox.

"Holy shit," she heard Zeke say. "Holy holy holy shit."

Piper stopped and extricated herself, looked to Zeke.

Her young dispatcher was standing behind the Bronco, looking into the opened back. His face had gone pasty and his cheeks puffed like he was going to puke. Piper was at his side in a heartbeat. In the back of the Bronco, partially obscured by a black plastic tarp, was a body. The face and left arm visible, as was the bullet hole in the center of the bearded man's forehead.

"That's Lucky Ducky," Zeke said before he bent over and retched.

CHAPTER TEN

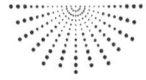

2 P.M.

Millie glanced at her cell phone and called up the digital thermometer: 80 showed on the screen, five degrees warmer than yesterday when she'd come out with Pops for the country concert. Just about right, she thought, for the middle of June.

She envied the fairgoers wearing shorts and t-shirts. The bright colors made the world appear happy, like last night's tragedy never happened. The kids laughed and tugged their parents to games of chance and Lemon Shakeup vendors. She'd get one of those too-sweet lemonades before she left. A girl with pigtails, her hair so blond it looked like spun sugar, stopped in front of her and looked up.

"Darcy!" A woman nearby called. Probably her mother. "Come back here."

The little girl's mouth was in a surprised "O" expression, revealing two missing front teeth. Millie noticed her Hello Kitty dress was stained with something blue, maybe snow-cone drizzle.

"Darcy! Leave the sheriff alone."

The little girl dashed away.

"Sheriff, eh?" Rocco jested. "You're a year too old to be the sheriff of Spencer County."

79

Millie resumed her path through the fair.

Music blared from speakers on poles. Currently playing, a moldy oldie: The Crykle's *Red Rubber Ball.* Smiles everywhere.

The fair wasn't near as crowded as it had been yesterday before the Cosmic Odyssey broke. There was no lure of a concert to make what seemed like the entire county turn out for the occasion. But it was a Saturday afternoon, and so there should be more people. Millie was certain the specter of the Cosmic Odyssey disaster would keep the numbers down throughout the county fair's run—and likely cast a pall over future years, too.

"I would've been out here yesterday, but I waited too late to get concert tickets," Rocco told Millie. "My wife was pissed at me. Ha! I said her fingers weren't broken, she could've got on the website a few weeks ago and bought tickets her own self if she wanted them that damn bad. Good thing we didn't go, though. Would've been a wasted trip, with everything that happened and the concert being rescheduled. I would've ended up working."

"Like I did," Millie said softly.

"Got you some good experience, I'll wager." The man brightened. "Hell, maybe some folks won't come back tomorrow night when he's gonna sing. Maybe there'll be some open spots in the grandstand and I can take her anyway. Maybe we can get in free."

"Maybe, Rocco," Millie said.

"I mean, it shouldn't be up to me all the time, buying something like concert tickets, should it? And I'm not a mind reader. How was I supposed to know she *really* wanted to go? I think she'd only mentioned it two or three times. She hadn't come right out and said 'let's go' you know. Not really."

"Me and Pops are coming back tomorrow night." Millie looked forward to it, a recent convert to country music. "I know Diego has tickets, and he said he couldn't make Sunday, has some weight-lifting thing in the evening. Maybe you should ask about buying his tickets. Maybe he hasn't gotten rid of them yet."

"Anything to make my wife happy." Rocco bobbed his head and

pulled out his cell phone as they walked. "Hold up here a minute." Millie watched his fingers play across the surface, probably texting Diego about the tickets—and no doubt asking for a discount.

Rocco Morse was Millie's partner today. Next to her grandfather, Rocco had the most seniority with the sheriff's department. He was somewhere in his fifties, string bean thin and probably a half-dozen inches shy of six feet—smaller than her. He had a craggy Chuck Norris-like face. Millie figured they were paired so some of his know-how might rub off. During the drive to the fair he regaled her with the saga of January's serial killer, embellishing—she was certain—his role in the investigation.

"Pops? You mean Oren?" Rocco put his phone back in his pocket and resumed their trek. Millie guessed that only folks over fifty were not able to text and walk at the same time.

"Yeah, Oren." Millie watched a severely pregnant woman drag her toddler toward the restrooms. "I've gotta stop calling him Pops in public. Not professional."

"I think it's cute. Pops. I'll have to call him Pops the next time I—"

"Don't," she warned. "Please don't."

Millie hadn't worked the day shift before. Since being hired almost a month ago, she'd been on the three to eleven, knowing it was to avoid the same shift as her grandfather, Chief Deputy Oren Rosenberg. But the accident at the fair had changed schedules and added overtime, and she expected to go back to the middle shift in a few days. Millie who had a bachelor of science in criminal justice had graduated in early May with her master's in communications from the university in Evansville. She'd originally planning to enter law school, but the advertised deputy opening presented an intriguing option. She wasn't giving up on the lawyer-public defender notion, and had signed up for some online courses that would start in August. But she wanted to work in law enforcement for a while first, save some money, and at least partially pay back her grandparents for what they'd given her for college. And if she liked law enforcement well enough, maybe she'd run for sheriff when Piper Blackwell's term was up. She'd recently turned twenty-four, and wondered if the county would be up to electing another young sheriff.

Rocco stopped a dozen yards shy of the rides, which were closed to the public today. The vacant spot where the Cosmic Odyssey had perched looked like a barren patch in an otherwise colorful metal garden. A few of the rides whirred, twirled, rose, and fell, apparently being tested. Most of the eighteen that Millie counted were motionless.

"Here's what we're gonna do." Rocco counted the rides with his index finger. "We split them up. You take the nine to the right. I'll take the nine to the left. We'll meet up in the back and compare notes. Record your conversations with the operators. Get names, contact information." He paused. "Probably already got names and contact information from last night, but it doesn't hurt to double-up, 'specially for something like this. Ask if they remembered anything else about the accident, what they know about Vernon Milgrew. Had he been in trouble, had there been issues with his work? Other mishaps in other states, that sort of stuff. Word is you have a Master's degree, so I maybe don't need to tell you all of this. Just be thorough. We'll compare notes," he repeated. "There's some picnic tables back there. We'll sit and compare and maybe get us a lemonade, one with all the crushed ice in it, and a corn dog, check in with the boss. You know, I read an article on one of those internet news pages last week that said lemonade was something you shouldn't drink after forty. Hell with that, dontcha think? I'm going to have me a lemonade."

"Sure. Lemonades, compare notes." Millie took off to the right, glad to be on her own, not finding Rocco inspiring and definitely not wanting him to rub off. After a week of training, she'd had a car to herself on the three to eleven, no partner; she liked that. Her ideal partner, if she had to have one, would be Basil Meredith. A detective who'd honed his skills in Chicago on various task forces, including gangs and drugs, he'd have a lot to teach her. Rocco? She shook her head and aimed herself at Crazy Carl's Crooked Coaster.

"Millie!"

She stopped and looked past Crazy Carl's. Paul Blackwell waved and rushed toward her. The former Spencer County Sheriff-turned Santa Claus Police Chief was her landlord. Millie lived in a spacious one-bedroom apartment above his big double-garage. The place looked like something out of *That '70s Show*, but rent was only $400 a month, and included utilities ... *and* she got to park in one of the garage bays. Win! Piper had lived there until a month back when she inherited a house. Millie hadn't hesitated to fill the vacancy.

"Hey, Mr. Blackwell."

He was dressed in jeans and a loose polo, with a St. Louis Cardinals ball cap; she spied the bulge of a shoulder holster. Not on duty, but a police chief would carry 24/7, she knew. He had a backpack on, and when he turned, she saw that it was actually one of those "pooch pouches," designed like a baby carrier, but for dogs. An elderly black pug rested in it, oblivious to the noise and softly snoring.

"Wrinkles on duty with you today?" she asked.

He laughed, and the pug opened one eye. "Not exactly. Just came from a vet appointment. Annual shots, got his nails trimmed. My day off, but I'm heading back to the office to look in. I thought I'd stop here first, walk through it, get a feel for what happened."

"Yeah, I have to look it over, too. Interviews and such," she replied. "As for what happened, it was awful. I was here when it broke."

"Helluva thing last night, Millie." Paul Blackwell was an imposing figure. Standing in front of her, he blocked the view of Crazy Carl's operator. Millie hoped he wouldn't chat long. "I just had to come check things out. Can't imagine how horrible that was to work. Talked to Piper on the phone last night about it."

Millie didn't know what to say; it was department policy not to discuss any investigation. She looked around him to Crooked Carl's operator. He was talking to someone dressed business-casual, probably one of the guys from the Department of Homeland Security or a news reporter. "Yeah, it was bad, Mr. Blackwell. Be glad you weren't here."

"Never was much for county fairs," he returned. "Took Piper and her sister when they were kids. Just wanted to come out now. Almost did last night, but Teegan said there were enough units, so I stayed in Santa Claus until about seven. Couldn't stop myself from swinging by now, though, lived in the county too long not to come look." He paused and caught her stare. "I'm not interfering in any investigation, not asking questions, just—"

"Looking around. I get it," Millie said. *Free country,* she almost added, resisting the comment because she liked her landlord and knew he was indeed out here because he was curious. *Free country and anyone can come to the fair.* They just couldn't enjoy the rides today.

"I figured Piper would be out here, or maybe Oren. Piper *should* be, you know. As big a deal as this—"

"Sheriff Blackwell and Detective Meredith were out here early this morning, my grandfather, too, for a little while. They met with Homeland Security before the pieces got hauled away."

"Surprised she's not here still." Paul looked disappointed. Millie wasn't sure if his expression was because he thought Piper should be working the fair investigation or because he'd just wanted to see her.

"They got another call. A homicide," Millie said. "And I don't know anything about it."

"Homicide? Didn't hear anything on the radio. All of 'em out on it, huh? A homicide?"

"Don't know anything," Millie repeated. "Something south of Rockport." That was probably more than she should say, even though he was a police chief. Let Piper tell her dad.

She knew that Basil, Oren, and Sheriff Blackwell were all in Africa. No chatter on the regular channel about it, though she heard the coroner was called. Sylvia D called it a homicide, but she didn't have any name yet. Must be interesting, Millie thought, to have the three main players from the department out there instead of at the fair. She'd have to grill Pops about it tonight.

"So you're here—"

"With Deputy Morse to—"

"Good old, Rocco," Paul cut in. "He's okay."

"We're interviewing ... supposed to be interviewing ... the ride operators and vendors. We couldn't talk to them all last night, everything happening at once. Awful and hectic."

Paul smiled. "So I better let you get to that. And I better get me and Wrinkles over to the office." He tipped his head, stepped past her, and headed toward the fried pickle wagon.

Crazy Carl's was running, the man in business-casual making notes on a clipboard, definitely Homeland Security. The operator's head bobbed in time with the music. Millie would start with him and work her way down. She waited until Homeland Security moved to the next one.

"Passed inspection," the man said as she came up the ramp. "Again."

"That's good," Millie said. "But I'm here to talk about the Cosmic Odyssey."

"I'm pretty sure I talked to somebody from the sheriff's about it last night. Don't really have anything different to say ... other than I bet I won't have many riders from here on out. Not that it really matters, I guess. I get paid no matter how many gets on."

Millie had a list of questions she'd written in a notebook. Pops had told her notebooks made people nervous; she decided not to take it out of her pocket. Instead, she recorded the conversation on her phone and kept eye contact.

"I'm interested in Vernon Milgrew, Mr.—"

"Ben Wojan." He pulled out his wallet and flipped it open, showing his driver's license, then replaced it. Millie thought the gesture odd, as she hadn't been going to ask to see ID. "So you're wanting to know about Vern, right?"

She nodded.

Ben whistled low. "He gonna get charged with it? Those kids' deaths? These rides were inspected. You saw the dude from the State who just left. Second time inspected in a handful of days. We just push the buttons, pull the levers, get 'em off and on." He slowed Crazy Carl's, and then stopped it.

"About Vernon Milgrew," Millie pressed. She figured Rocco would

85

be at the picnic table at the back and finished with his lemonade and corn dog well before she even got there.

"He's been with the circuit some years more than me. I've been doing this almost four, ever since I got laid off from the Proctor plant." Ben was momentarily distracted by a hovering bee. "Look, Vern's not a bad guy. But he's been doing this too long. He's sloppy, lets kids on. Little kids. The Odyssey wasn't built for little kids. Not the *little* ones. It's got a height chart. So's mine, and I pay attention to it. Vern doesn't care who rides his machine. I'm telling you this 'cause his ride got hauled away in pieces during lunch and 'cause we heard he's going back east on a drug charge. Never saw him do drugs, by the way."

"Ever any trouble with the ride, or Vernon Milgrew, at other fairs? Maybe in another state?"

He shook his head. "Careless sometimes, but Vern shouldn't get hung up on any murder charges," Ben went on. "Lazy, you can check that box. Sloppy a little. Check that box, too. Should shower more often. But nothing he did made that thing break apart. He's got two kids of his own with his ex-wife. He likes kids. That wasn't murder. That was an accident."

Millie thanked him and moved on to the Round 'Em Up, her "lawyer brain" churning. She'd watched the videos collected from last night, worked late because she was caught up in everything. She knew lawsuits were coming—regardless of whether Vernon Milgrew did anything wrong, and so far it certainly looked like he hadn't. Was the ride not inspected close enough? People died, people were injured. Maybe the DA's office would charge him with reckless homicide, which would get him up to six years. If it was proven he'd ignored protocol by letting people on who were too short, too young—which could result in serious injury; if he hadn't checked the equipment, he could be liable. But under normal operation, if he had no reason to believe the ride would malfunction, and if he hadn't done anything to cause it to break, she doubted the DA would include a homicide charge. Maybe reckless conduct; she could see that, a Class 4 felony

86

that would get him three years tops ... and that would be provided a jury could be talked into it.

But Vernon Milgrew was going to be sued even if he wasn't charged with anything, Millie expected. Vernon, the county fair, the county, the state, the ride manufacturer—everyone possibly involved. It would be interesting to see how it played out over the next few years.

She moved onto the Tumble Bug. Then Freefall—an aggressive-looking ride that gave her a shiver. Waltzer was next. Red Baron. And then came the Octopus. She'd gotten no more information beyond what Ben had told her, except one operator thought Vernon Milgrew had a problem with child support with an ex-wife "back east." Two operators had videos of the rides being set up, and these were sent to her phone.

She stood in the shade of the Red Baron banner and watched the Octopus. It was an eight-limbed tilting and spinning ride with a cage at each end, all of it painted purple. It looked like each cage could hold four riders. It didn't look like an aggressive ride, but nothing she'd buy a ticket for. Millie doubted she'd step onto anything more adventurous than something like a merry-go-round ever again.

The operator looked to be in his late twenties, maybe early thirties, fit with muscular arms, and well proportioned. He'd be clothes model bait if his head didn't look like a jug, his face flat. His hair was blond and curly, maybe natural, but probably a perm, she thought.

Homeland Security watched the Octopus cages turn, made notes on the clipboard, circled the ride and kneeled to check something with the engine when it stopped. After several minutes, he returned to the operator, briefly spoke, and moved on. Millie wondered if she should have stepped up and eavesdropped. Maybe Rocco was doing that on the other side. She started toward the Octopus just as the operator reached into his front pocket, pulled something out and held it to one nostril, then the other, shook his head and grinned, and replaced the object.

Millie stared and kept her place, waited and watched as he shut down the ride. He polished one of the cabs, then reached into his front pocket, looked around, and held something to his nose once more.

Drugs, Millie thought. Someone taking drugs was operating a carnival ride, and Homeland Security clearly hadn't noticed when they talked to him. She patted the cuffs hanging from her belt, then cautioned herself. Check it out. Make sure he's not taking some prescription allergy inhaler. Check it out.

She walked toward him, inwardly giddy. Maybe it wasn't allergy meds. Millie hadn't made an arrest yet; Pops said her first one would be a drunk driver. DUIs were the number one ticketed offense in the county. Maybe her first arrest would instead by a drug bust at the county fair.

"I'm with the Spencer County Sheriff's Department," Millie said.

"Yeah, I can see that. Out here to ask me about Vernie Mildew, right? Ben texted me you were headed my way."

"Milgrew." Millie figured Ben had texted all the other operators.

"Never spent a lot of time with Vernie. And the Octo is pretty far from the Odyssey. Didn't see it actually break, the Odyssey. But I heard it. I shut this down right away, got my riders off, and—"

"What's in your pocket?" Millie posed. There probably was a better way to do this. He probably didn't have to tell her what he had on him. She might have to take him down to the office.

He didn't hesitate, pulled out a small tube of model glue. Dropped it back in his pocket.

"No drugs, if that's what you're thinking. I'm clean. I don't do drugs."

Millie's mind tumbled over Indiana's laws.

"It's not drugs," he repeated. "It's friggin' glue. Bought it at Hobby Lobby. It's not illegal."

She thought fast. "It is illegal to sniff glue for pleasure, which is what I observed you doing. It carries a fine of up to one thousand dollars."

"Seriously?"

"Any person who inhales or ingests the fumes of glue commits a Class B misdemeanor." She pulled out her handcuffs and rattled off the Miranda warning. She'd repeat it back at the station. Then she'd come back out here—hopefully without Rocco Morse—and finish up her interviews.

The lemonade would wait.

"Seriously?" he repeated.

"Seriously," she answered.

CHAPTER ELEVEN

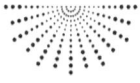

2:30 P.M.

Piper had radioed ahead to the Owensboro Police Department, quickly explaining the case and setting up a meeting with a magistrate to obtain search warrants.

Oren listened to the conversation, a little disappointed that she knew what she was doing. Every day at work he reminded himself that she'd bested him in the fall election, campaigning on her last name. Hell, he was convinced most of the voters figured they were casting their ballots for her father, beloved Sheriff Paul Blackwell. Even he loved Paul Blackwell; they were close friends. Piper hadn't won by much. He mentally kicked himself that he hadn't campaigned harder, had thought his victory was that slam-dunk done-deal. Part of him kept thinking she'd screw up or give up, and that he'd be assigned to finish her term.

He couldn't say that he liked her. But he didn't dislike her anymore.

There was the smallest hint of acceptance and respect.

Twenty-three years old. The whole thing ... *tsutcheppenish*. It was an irritation that had become a second skin he knew he couldn't shed. No, he didn't dislike her, but he didn't like that she was the sheriff— and that latter fact would never change. Too stubborn to retire, too

90

worried about having too much time on his hands, he'd have to keep putting up with the situation. Certainly *tsutcheppenish*.

Piper went on to detail the search warrants she'd be seeking—for the comic book store and for the apartment of Lou Duckworth, aka Lucky Ducky, an Owensboro resident. She also wanted a search warrant for Benzo's place, but did not yet have his real name or address. The warrants would include all computer equipment and phones found at those addresses, bank records and safe deposit boxes to be safe … in case Mr. Silver had accounts in Owensboro. Maybe she'd need more, she told them … but she'd start with this.

And though there was a mutual aid agreement in place among the Spencer County Sheriff's Department, the Owensboro Police Department, and Daviess County Kentucky Sheriff's Department, she also requested a Specific Investigation Agreement revolving around this case … not required, but it would make things more comfortable.

Oren's stomach rumbled. He'd been so busy with the "elevator woman" as Sylvia D called her that he'd missed lunch, and he hadn't stopped on his way to the Silver house. Now it was after two, and he might miss dinner. Maybe he'd find something in a vending machine somewhere. Nothing had looked appealing inside the machines at the Owensboro Police Department.

It hadn't taken long to sign the paperwork, get the search warrants, and be assigned a detective representing the Owensboro Police Department. Oren knew this was in case any arrests needed to be made.

Said detective was Alden Hopper, a forty-something-year-old bald man with a salt-and-pepper goatee. Drenched in aftershave, he sat in the back seat of the Explorer rather than driving his own car. Oren figured Alden wanted to listen to any conversation involving the murders.

There was no question Spencer County had jurisdiction on Samuel Silver. The man was found dead in his house and had been a resident of Africa. For the moment Spencer County also claimed jurisdiction on Lucky Ducky, Piper making a case that the young man was likely killed in Africa with Samuel Silver. But if it turned out the kid had been shot in Owensboro, the jurisdiction issue would be revisited.

"Maybe Duckworth was shot in the pancake parking lot," Alden suggested.

"Maybe not," Oren countered. His stomach growled louder and he wondered if Piper heard it.

Oren had wanted to stay behind and investigate that godawful green house in Africa where the guy had been pin-cushioned to death. He'd gotten there after Annie Neufeld had whisked the first corpse away, but he'd looked at the video Basil captured. Never had seen anything like that in all his decades with the Spencer County Sheriff's Department and the Rockport Police before that. He shivered just thinking about it. But it was so odd and interesting—he'd wanted to keep with the investigation there.

Add the kid shot execution-style, trussed up in the back of the Bronco-- that was interesting and horrible, too. He'd been on the scene when Annie came back for the kid's body, pissed about a return trip because they hadn't noticed both dead men at the same time. She was still at the garage when he and Piper left. Maybe it wasn't so bad, going with Piper now—despite the aftershave reek wafting from the back seat. At least this way he avoided the brunt of the coroner's ire. Annie was in a foul mood today.

And skipping a few meals might help his diet.

They pulled around behind the strip mall to get a look at the back door. Blacktop, they didn't see any tracks, and like Zeke, they didn't note any sign of a break-in. But Oren took fingerprints off the door handle and around the jamb, while Piper threw open the lid of a nearby Dumpster and looked inside.

"Not much here," she said.

"Garbage pick-up in this part of town is Saturday morning," Alden volunteered. "So anything that would have been there from last night is gone."

They'd not found any keys in the initial search of Silver's Africa home, not even for the Bronco, so going in through the back door of the comic shop was out. Piper left their car in the spot behind the store and walked around to the front, retracing Zeke's steps.

"Didn't see a single security camera back there," she said.

Oren hadn't noticed any either, and he'd looked down the entire back of the small strip mall. None of the businesses had them. Old place, probably didn't have much theft problem.

"Maybe out front," she mused. "Maybe some businesses have cameras by their front doors."

Oren doubted it. But indeed there was one in front of Silver Age Sam's—perched near the front door, hidden by an awning, angled down to catch people coming and going.

Oren stayed outside and peered in through the front window, seeing neat rows of shelves and a center table with comic books arranged like records used to be displayed "back in the day." Easy to look through them, he figured. Piper and Alden went inside.

He turned and stared out across the lot and down the front of the strip mall, noting two other surveillance cameras ... one in front of a Dollar General, the other at a hardware store, neither at an angle that would catch the front of Silver Age Sam's, but both of which might still be useful. The sidewalk that stretched across the entire front of the mall was chipped and cracked and decorated with fast food wrappers that hadn't come from this area—Oren had noticed a lack of restaurants in this vicinity. His stomach snarled. A top-heavy woman in hot pink leggings and a black tank top came out of the beauty supply store, carrying a curly brown wig on a mannequin head. An obvious father and son strolled out of the hardware store, each carrying two paper sacks. They headed toward an old red pickup, put the sacks inside the bed, then not worrying about thieves, turned around and went to the Dollar General.

He continued watching, wanting to get a feel for the area. It seemed safe and aged. He'd been to Owensboro more times than he cared to think about, had his father in a nursing home here that called itself a "memory care center." If he'd been by this strip mall on one of his trips, he couldn't recall—not the sort of shops he'd stop at. He saw a thin woman in a yellow sweater—how could she be cold today?—

shuffle toward an Edward Jones office on the far side of the beauty supply place. She wasn't old, fifties maybe, but she leaned on a cane, hadn't gotten out of a car that he'd noticed. Maybe she'd come from a nearby bus stop or been dropped by someone; and if the latter was the case the driver could have been kind and let her off at the door.

Oren sighed, decided he'd go make sure she got to where she was going. But he stopped when a gangly boy toting a backpack ran toward her and gallantly extended his arm. The boy walked slowly with her. Maybe she was more than in her fifties, and maybe the boy was a grandson.

In front of the hardware store two kids rode bicycles that looked too small for them, thick wheeled dirt bikes, one so bright blue it was likely fresh from a store. The other was a burnt orange, caked dirt on the rims, playing cards hooked to the spokes so they clacked. Oren had done that when he was a kid, but he'd used baseball cards— players from 1959 and 60—that would probably have brought a good piece of change had he left them in the pack and sold them now. He remembered using a Yogi Berra card, from when he was a catcher with the Yanks.

Oren shifted his attention to the far corner of the strip mall lot. An older gentleman—Oren chuckled at calling anyone "older" when he, himself, was an "older gentleman"—ambled up an aisle between cars. Oren changed the label to geezer; stoop-shouldered, head forward bringing to mind the image of a pigeon walking, drab olive pants and a striped sport shirt, walking aimlessly. The man turned a corner and started down another aisle, made it to the end, and then turned up another, this one the closest to the comic store. Maybe he suffered from dementia, like Oren's father, couldn't remember what car was his and thereby shouldn't be driving. As he neared the comic shop, Oren got a better look. His sport shirt was partially unbuttoned, revealing a ropy scar likely from some sort of open heart surgery. He wore expensive-looking athletic shoes and had an overlarge Fitbit on his wrist that he occasionally consulted, designer eyeglass frames, and a couple of thick gold rings on one hand.

First impressions could deceive. Oren noted a cadence to the man's walk and that his mouth was working, maybe talking to himself or singing. He was probably told to walk for his health. So he was a well-to-do geezer who was keeping with a fitness routine to give himself a few more years on this earth. Oren immediately thought of the kids killed by the broken ride at the county fair—and Lucky Ducky stuffed in the back of a Bronco. They'd had far too few years.

The people he'd been watching on the lot, none of them were suspicious or out-of-place. Didn't look like this strip mall was the sort of spot for something awful like murder, and it didn't have the feel of a place that would call to a rough crowd.

The geezer raised his head and met Oren's gaze, nodded, providing a closer look at his face.

"Moses on a moped," Oren whispered. The geezer didn't look any older than Oren. Maybe he ought to buy a Fitbit too, but he damn well wasn't going to pace parking lots.

Shaking it off, Oren entered the comic shop and saw Piper and Alden talking to a youngish woman behind the counter. She had unnaturally red hair—just around the shoulders, the rest was blond—and it all clashed with her tight-fitting Green Lantern t-shirt. It took him a minute to notice her eyebrow piercings and neck tattoo. Probably had more tattoos and piercings that he couldn't see from his vantage.

Youth, he thought. *Why spend good money to deface yourself?*

Oren strolled down the center aisle, noting Spiderman, Captain America, the Avengers, Flash, Superman—which he'd avidly read as a kid. He had a fondness for The Man of Steel. He'd read some early Spidermans, too, wished he would have kept them, probably could buy a nice car if he sold them now. Shade the Changing Girl, God Country, Doomsday Clock, Harley Quinn, Trinity, and others he'd never heard of had garish art. Prices printed on the covers: $3.99, $4.99, and graphic novels priced $10 to $30. Hell, he remembered buying Spiderman for fifteen cents. Worse, he could picture the cover of a twelve-cent Iron Man that he'd read until it fell apart.

Because he was a geezer. All the senior citizen discounts applied to him.

Posters on the wall were framed ... one held a large photograph of the parrots from Sam's house, the rest a mix of maps from fantasy and science fiction game worlds and images of Loot the Castle cards. A rack along one wall displayed black t-shirts—*only* black—and they were imprinted with dragons, warriors, wizards, and piles of treasure, all with the Loot the Castle logo underneath.

Was Samuel Silver's death related to the card game? Because some disgruntled customer didn't get the cards he'd wanted or didn't win the game? Oren shook his head. No one would kill for a card game, at least not outside of Las Vegas or New York City.

The customers were mostly kids; he counted a dozen of them perusing the on-sale back-issue comic bins. Three college-age women made their selections from the collectible card games shelf. A man in his fifties thumbed through the Dungeons & Dragons display; Oren wondered if the man looked to buy something for himself or for a child or grandchild. He drifted close to the sales counter and eyed the expensive collectible cards in plastic sleeves. He blinked when he saw the prices. Didn't need many customers if you had a handful who regularly bought this stuff, he decided. No wonder Samuel Silver'd had the money for the interior upgrades to his house, and for the exotic pets.

Another counter had a display of colorful odd-sized dice and miniature soldiers, fantastic creatures, and tanks.

"Oh, what am I gonna do?" the salesgirl sobbed. Oren saw that indeed she had more piercings, a half-dozen in each ear, one in her lower lip, and her tongue had a stud in it. "This has been my favorite job." She sobbed some more, then added "poor Sam."

Piper collected the names, addresses, and phone numbers of Silver Age Sam's employees, one the name and number of a man who quit two months ago and had been disgruntled over "something." Piper rattled off questions, and the pierced girl—her name was Honora Fitzgerald—haltingly supplied answers. Oren listened intently.

"I thought it was weird, you know, Sam not being here when I opened today. I just figured the tourney last night went too long and he was still snoozing. But Dun-Dun called when I was getting in the door, hadn't even turned the lights on, and he said Sam hadn't showed last night. I tried calling Sammy, but it went to voicemail."

Oren saw Piper's eyebrows quirk up. He knew they hadn't—yet—found a phone at the residence. But with a phone number, they could try to locate a cell.

"I called Lucky Ducky, too, and I would have called Benzo, but he doesn't have a phone. Or at least not a number in his file. No fruit, ya know. Nada." Honora reached a finger up and turned the small hoop that threaded through her lower lip. The back of her hand had a rose tattoo on it. "What the hell am I going to do?"

"Close the store, for one," Piper said.

"Can I let them make their purchases first?"

Oren could tell Piper was thinking about that.

"No. Just close up. Please. Now. We have to contact his next of kin, heirs. The store needs to stay closed."

"I already made some sales today. Almost three hundred. Am I supposed to let it just sit in the register?"

"Yes."

"You got the badge." Honora reached in her pocket and pulled out a keychain. "Probably got to hand over my key, huh?" She took it off and slapped it on the counter without waiting for a response, stepped away from the register, and waved her hands in the air. "Best damn job I've ever had. Been a manager here three and a half years. And I'm not the only one with a key. Every full-time employee's got one." Oren saw more tattoos on the undersides of her arms—words, but they were in a script and with her motions he couldn't read them. Again he thought it a shame she'd defaced herself. Thank God his grand-daughter said "no" to tattoos and had only pierced ears.

Honora waved to the customers. "Everyone, time to leave. The store's closing. Sam's—"

"Don't mention—"

"—not coming in today and we have to close up. Next week, too, probably, we'll be closed," Honora added. "Remodeling. Health Department. Whatever. Larry, get moving now!"

The fiftyish man put down the Dungeons & Dragons books,

scowled, and headed for the door. The other customers shuffled out ahead of him, all of them grumbling. Oren thought he should have chatted with them first, learned bits and pieces about Samuel Silver. But a place like this no doubt had a list of regular customers, and that would serve if needed. Depended on whether the murder had anything to do with the comic shop, which he felt certain it did. The comic shop was Sam's income.

It was always about money, wasn't it, murder? Love sometimes, but almost always money. And given the price of some of the comics on display on the wall behind the counter, all "CGC graded" whatever the hell that was and priced in the hundreds ... coupled with those expensive playing cards under glass ... yeah, it was about the money.

Oren loved puzzles; he worked jigsaw puzzles at night in his study. A murder, any involved case, was like a puzzle. Sort the pieces, put them together, and see what picture emerged. Maybe that was the real reason he didn't want to retire—this job was too damn interesting. He had a Superman puzzle in the closet at home, the one-thousand piece variety. The box cover showed the hero flying in the foreground, fist raised to the sky, with a background of old Action Comics covers behind him.

Honora returned behind the counter, leaned on it with a huffing sound, and looked up at Piper, who asked more questions. Piper was recording the conversation, Alden was, too.

The pierced girl didn't hesitate with answers:

- Sam didn't have any enemies.
- Everyone loved Sam.
- Benzo is a regular, practically lives here. Benzo's name is Lloyd Ebersole, not much about him in the store records. Buys some comics, but doesn't collect series. Buys Loot the Castle cards. Doesn't want anyone keeping records on him anyhow.

"Benzo is renegade-Amish," Honora said. "Lucky-Ducky knows

where Benzo lives. Them two are brothers from another mother. Benzo's probably on some of the Loot the Castle players' Christmas card lists, so others might have an addy on him, but we don't. Ask Lucky-D though if it's that big of a deal, he'll get you an address, directions. He gives Benzo rides all the time. Strange, Benzo is. No cell phone. Someone told me he has a landline, but I'm not sure about that. I kind of doubt that. Never saw him with a tablet. Doesn't own a car. Amish-like, you know. Rides a bicycle. Or walks. Or gets rides with Lucky-D. Told me once he achooed tech."

Oren figured she meant eschewed.

Honora continued:

- Sam always paid the rent for the store a few months in advance; paid up through the end of August.
- Only the one disgruntled employee, and no idea what it was over.
- Employees had 401ks and health insurance, including dental, two weeks paid vacation; bonuses at Christmas; $50 Olive Garden cards on birthdays.
- No particularly unruly customers.
- Mostly happy customers, loved the comfy chairs and snack assortment.

A few shoplifters from time-to-time, but not many; Sam never reported them. But if he caught their picture on his surveillance, he tried to hunt them down and make them return the stuff, and put them on a "you're not welcome here" list. Honora retrieved a notebook from under the counter, opened it, and pointed to a "You're Not Welcome Here" header. There were twenty-one names. Piper used her cell phone to take a picture of the list.

"Sam was pretty good at hunting them down," Honora said.

Sam wasn't married, and she didn't think he ever had been. Told her he didn't have kids. He never talked about family, or a significant other, just about his birds. She pointed to a framed picture on the wall of the two greys. "No partner or significant other that I knew of, but

Sam didn't talk much about personal things. He liked to talk about comic books."

The shop did a good business, collector cards mostly, Loot the Castle the big one. Every once in a while they'd sell one of the silver age books for big bucks. He sold on the internet, too, eBay, but Honora said she didn't have to handle that. The eBay sales were mostly from Sam's personal collection.

Sam stocked Dungeons & Dragons and some other roleplaying games, and had an open-play night every other Wednesday—you showed up, you got to play something. "Everyone plays," was Sam's motto. A small display of miniatures and dice complemented the games. Honora said she played D&D sometimes, but mostly steampunk rpgs—role playing games, Call of Cthulhu, and a few board games. She couldn't afford to get hooked on Loot the Castle and the other card games.

The shop did a so-so business in board games, and usually only carried the new ones high on BG-Geek website's recommended list. Wargamers had to go to Evansville or turn to eBay. "Except for Axis & Allies. Sam liked that World War II game so he always made sure there was one in stock."

"As for customers," Honora said, "There's a book with the names of regular comic book buyers, their email addresses, and their standard orders. It's in a computer file, too, includes the names of the people who order cases of Loot the Castle at a whack."

"I'll need that," Piper said.

"Oh, crap, the regs—the regulars—are gonna be coming in Wednesday for the new Marvel and D.C. releases. Not that I'd be able to sort the issues even if we were open. The laptop's gone, with all the pull orders in it. I figured Sam took it home yesterday, the laptop."

"Great," Piper said softly.

"Well, none of this is my worry anymore. Wonder if I can collect unemployment?" Honora opened the cash register and reached into the back of the drawer, coming out with three jump drives. "But maybe the files are backed up on these. Sam never used the Cloud or anything like that, always worried about internet spies."

"The video feed from the surveillance camera?" Piper posed, as she collected the jump drives.

"Feeds into the office. I'll take you back there. Gotta get my purse out of the office. Hey, am I going to get paid? I get paid every two weeks, and I'm supposed to get paid this coming Friday. I should at least get paid for the time I put in."

"We'll work all of this out, heirs, next of kin. It might take a while," Piper returned.

"Crap," Honora said. "Crappity crappity crappity crappity crappity crap."

Piper asked more questions, and Honora answered them politely and thoroughly. Oren's eyes drifted to another display case—it was filled with an assortment of snacks. No vending machine, just counter-service, "Everything $1" the sign said. His stomach growled. Granola bars, mini potato chip cans, candy, peanuts, shiny apples, boxes of raisins, packets of cheese and crackers. A smaller sign read: soda and yogurt in the refrigerator. He spotted the small refrigerator on the back wall near the restrooms. His stomach grumbled again. He selected a raisin granola bar, reached in his pocket, pulled out a dollar and stuck it in the display. He ate the bar in two bites, and made a mental note to buy a box of them next time at the grocery store; they were tasty.

Oren was struck by the organization and cleanliness of the place, nice tables and padded chairs for the customers to sit in while they played games. The community was going to miss this shop, he thought, hoping one of Samuel Silver's relatives or heirs would keep it running … or sell it so someone else could. Spencer County could do with a place like this for the teenagers, put it in Rockport or Santa Claus, might do a reasonable business. Nice place for teenagers to congregate.

"Store's got a landline up by the register," Honora said. "A second one in the office. No store cell phone. He kept his laptop back here. Most all the records were on the computer, but there's some stuff in the file cabinet."

The cabinet had only two drawers.

"Hey, the video surveillance, the little box, the cable. It's gone." Honora scratched her head. "I guess it wasn't here when I opened up. Just didn't think about it. Not something I mess with, you understand."

"We're going to take the paper records with us, sort through them back in the office," Piper told Alden. The search warrant covered that. "And we'll check the video feeds of the other stores in this strip. I've a couple of big evidence boxes in the back of the Ford. And I'm fingerprinting the office, the doors, the—"

"I'll get those evidence boxes," Oren volunteered, looking at his watch. He knew damn well they'd be here another hour or two here. He went out the back door, making sure to turn the deadbolt so it would keep the door from closing completely and he could get back in without walking all the way around. He reached for his cell phone to call his wife, to tell her he wouldn't be home for dinner, probably not until late. His stomach growled angrily. The granola bar hadn't been enough.

Parked crooked behind the beauty supply place a few doors down was a dark gray car with tinted windows. It had been idling. It backed up and drove away, at an inappropriate speed for the narrow lane. It struck Oren a little odd, didn't think someone associated with a beauty supply place would drive a plain, older car, maybe a Mazda, with yellow-gold New Jersey Garden State plates. New Jersey was a long way from Owensboro.

R40 ELE.

Oren repeated it in his head. He'd write it in his notebook when he got back in the Explorer. His stomach grumbled once more.

R40 ELE. Maybe it was important.

CHAPTER TWELVE

4 P.M.

The veterinarian arrived early. Dr. Hunter Carlisle wore blue jeans topped with an olive-green scrub shirt. The faint stubble on his face hinted at the start of a beard rather than he'd skipped shaving, and his wheat-colored hair was just long enough for the man-bun at his nape.. He had bright green eyes, making Basil suspect the doc favored colored contacts.

"Glad you could come, Dr. Carlisle. We need to do something about these animals." Basil handed him a pair of booties and gloves. "Not quite finished processing the scene, so I need you to wear these. I'd prefer you not touch anything unless I say okay." Then he let Dr. Carlisle through the back door. Basil had discovered that the home's front door had been sealed, more evidence of Mr. Silver's oddities.

"Sheriff Blackwell met you at the fair last night, said your card mentioned exotics."

Dr. Carlisle smiled warmly as he followed Basil through the kitchen. "Exotics. Well, to be honest it's not a term I'm fond of, but I put it on my card and in my Yellow Page ad, for marketing. What's exotic? The pets people readily fill their homes with—dogs, cats, ferrets, rabbits, and the like—were once considered exotics. What people call exotics now are just pets that haven't yet achieved the 'common' descriptor. I don't think pot-bellied pigs are considered exotic anymore. I have eight clients with those. A couple who have three kinkajous. An old man in the country has sugar gliders, raises them. They're little possums."

"Oh, *these* are exotic," Basil said. "Ain't never going to be a 'common' descriptor about these." He paused. "The birds maybe. Yeah, I suppose the birds." He paused again. "And the fish. Okay, it's just the monkeys and cats. The monkeys and cats are guaranteed exotics."

Basil entered the living room and pointed to the monkeys, one of which still shrieked. He wondered where it found the energy. It had been making an insufferable racket ever since he'd been here.

Dr. Carlisle stepped closer to the monkey cage. "This is Samuel Silver's home, isn't it? He's brought these monkeys to me. I recognize them." The veterinarian looked around the living room, then back over his shoulder into the kitchen with the debris still on the floor. "Something happened to Mr. Silver."

Basil nodded. "Mr. Silver … he died earlier today."

"Home invasion? Was he killed?"

"We're investigating," Basil said.

"I see." Dr. Carlisle returned his attention to the monkeys, glancing at the cats and African Greys. "The parrots, not exotic. Beautiful, these birds. I treated one of them three or four years ago for intestinal parasites. He'd bring them in once a year for health checks—all of them. The monkeys … Like I said, I've treated them, but they're not exotics either. They're wild animals. Sad that people keep them as pets. They're unhappy in cages. This one, making all the noise, it's upset, bored, frustrated. The two on the perch, they are too. See them hugging, rocking, the one sucking its fingers. They're stressed. Some veterinarians will have nothing to do with monkeys. Mr. Silver's monkeys … these are the only ones I've seen among my clients … I would have rather not treated them. But I didn't turn Mr. Silver away because I love all animals, detective—"

"Detective Basil Meredith."

Dr. Carlisle nodded and went on: "Someone needed to see them from time to time. Monkeys have all the emotions of humans, without any of the inhibitions. They can bite, claw, often out of frustration. People should not keep them as pets. Like I said, they are wild animals. Not illegal to keep these, but it is immoral."

"Why did Mr. Silver bring the monkeys in? What was wrong with them?" Basil was curious; he didn't consider it anything to do with his investigation, but he wanted to know nonetheless.

"Vaccinations and for tuberculosis testing. Monkeys have been known to carry TB, so Sam Silver wanted them checked. Nearly put the one up there on insulin. He was feeding them too much junk food. These monkeys ... you should let me take them. Today. Right now. Please. It would be kind. I know a good animal sanctuary."

Basil shook his head. "We have to find next of kin, heirs, and—"

"Listen ... are these three monkeys going to end up in a little cage somewhere with a relative who couldn't give a rip about them? Will they be set free in the woods because they're difficult to manage, shot for convenience, euthanized? I know a good sanctuary, and you can come up with a legal reason why these animals are going there today."

Basil didn't like the push. However, he liked the veterinarian's passion, and it would get the monkeys out of the house. "You got something with you to put them in?"

"I know Sam Silver does ... did. He'd bring them to my office in plastic gray carriers. If you can't find the carriers, I'll go back to my office and get some."

"And the cats?" Basil watched the veterinarian shudder.

"Wild animals, too. He never brought these in. Monkeys *and* the cats, I would have called someone on him.

"Whatcha doin' Corky bird?" one of the parrots said. "Hey gorgeous."

"Pshew pshew," the other answered, holding up a claw like a gun.

"When's dinner?" the first asked. "Sammy fix me a sammich."

The smaller parrots whistled shrilly.

"These cats." The veterinarian had pulled out his cell phone and was Googling something. "Okay, here they are. Black-footed cat. I was right. Wild. They're not house cats, African, maybe the smallest wild cat species in the world. Their population is decreasing. Rare, endangered. Sam Silver did not come by these legally."

Basil softly growled.

"Pshew pshew pshew," the bird said.

"Maybe they're evidence," Basil said more to himself. He found the cats beautiful, soft appearing, dense-looking tawny gold coats, black and brown spots, a few dark bands. Their eyes were large and amber, the legs white. He saw two dark streaks across their cheeks and dark bars on their forelegs. The tails were short, each with two black rings. The ears were rounded and low-set, not like any house cats he'd seen.

"Well, you can't keep them here. Not without someone to care for them." Dr. Carlisle fixed him with a stern stare. "You called me here—"

"Actually, Sheriff Blackwell called you."

"Whatever. I was called here, and I'm not turning my back on these animals. The monkeys ... immoral, but not illegal. These cats? This is up to the U.S. Department of Fish and Wildlife. I can take them. I have a boarding facility and can keep them until the DFW decides what to do. But they're not remaining here unless you have someone staying here to take care of them."

Basil didn't like Dr. Carlisle's bossiness. "Give me a minute."

"Fix me a sammich," one of the birds called.

Basil stepped into the kitchen, gritting his teeth when one of the monkeys let out an ear-splitting scream. He radioed Piper, told her he wanted the veterinarian to take the monkeys and the cats. Endangered, he told her, rare. He let out a deep breath when she agreed and added the parrots. Basil hadn't found a single photo in the house, nor a birthday or Christmas card. Samuel Silver might not have a relative to claim the animals. And there wasn't a will in the file cabinet; there might be one in a safe deposit box ... looking for one would be on Monday's agenda when the banks opened. A will could detail who got the animals.

He walked back into the living room. "Sheriff Blackwell says you can take all of them. Hang onto the parrots for a while in case they're supposed to go to someone. If no one comes forward, I trust you can get them a home, maybe that sanctuary you mentioned."

Dr. Carlisle nodded.

"And tell me what you know about Mr. Silver. Anything and everything," Basil said. "Absolutely anything and everything."

CHAPTER THIRTEEN

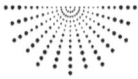

6 P.M.

Barely a seat remained unclaimed in Pearl's Pancake Palace. Most of the diners had tall stacks of pancakes in front of them. There appeared to be only a few scattered orders of eggs. The large open room smelled of coffee, bacon, and maple syrup, and conversations buzzed into a white noise miasma. Piper thought music played beneath it all, or maybe someone nearby had an MP3 player.

Piper had been to Owensboro often, but had never heard of this place. She'd suggested they stop here after they notified "Lucky Ducky" Duckworth's parents of their son's death, and struck out on finding Benzo—Lloyd Ebersole—at his home. Piper had left her card with Benzo's neighbor, and put a note in the mailbox. The Owensboro Police Department was sending an officer over later tonight. If nothing came of that, she'd go back in the morning with Basil and a search warrant. Finding Benzo was crucial. The man was either a suspect or a witness. Hopefully he wasn't another victim.

"Sit where you can find room," a waitress said.

Piper stepped past the waitress and met the manager at the counter, showing her badge and nodding to Oren and Alden. "I'd like to talk to you about three customers you had late last night. Mr. Samuel Silver, a local business owner and two—"

"Well …" The man scratched his head and looked around. He pointed to a vacant booth by the front window. "A table opened up over there."

"About these three men."

"Didn't have any trouble here last night, Sheriff. Nothing in the log anyway, no notes left on the counter. We're a family place. Twenty-four-seven family and—"

"The man's name was Samuel Silver," she repeated. "I have a picture."

"What time was he in?" The man focused on Oren and Alden and pointed to the open booth again. "Really, we haven't had any trouble here in more than a year. If you want to eat—"

"Eleven, around then, they were here and—"

"In that case you'll have to wait an hour. Talk to Ursula when she comes in at seven, the shift changes. We run a seven to three for the late shift. That's until three in the wee. Me, and the rest of my crew, are clocking out soon. Talk to Ursula. She might've seen your Mr. Silver. Probably cashed him out if he was here. Sorry I can't help you."

"So we might as well eat," Piper said to Oren. "I am seriously hungry."

"I'm seriously starving." Oren slid in the booth up against the front window. Alden sat next to him, leaving the opposite bench seat all to Piper, who edged over to the middle. She studied the place—it looked like it had once been an IHOP, but redecorated in pinks, purples with splashes of orange. Castles, knights, dragons, and a bevy of princesses were painted in the gaps between framed posters displaying stacks of pancakes … some of them castle shaped, syrup spilling out the draw-bridges and filling the moats.

The patrons varied from businessmen with briefcases sitting next to their feet and families with giggling children coloring on place-mats, to teens who alternately ate and texted on their phones—not bothering to talk to each other. A youth softball team spread out among several tables and booths.

Looking out the window, Piper noted another breakfast spot, Batter Up! across from Pearl's Pancake Palace, She wondered why the softballers weren't eating at the obvious baseball-themed spot. Ah! Maybe the rival team had staked a claim there. Or maybe it wasn't any good. There weren't many cars in that lot.

She opened the menu and discovered that the names of the dishes matched the theme. All breakfast and reasonably priced: Camelot Cakes, The Spire, Troll Bridge Benedict, Humpty's Three-Egg Fall.

When the waiter came, she ordered The Joust—two Camelot Cakes, two fried eggs, and two pieces of bacon. "With a pot of coffee and a large carafe of orange juice for the table," she added.

"I'll have the Castle-Country Fried Steak and Princess Poached Eggs," Alden said. "Number eleven there, and a side of hash browns with Parmesan cheese sprinkled on top." He looked at Piper. "It's what I usually get. It's always good."

Oren pointed to the middle of the menu. "I want the Dragon Slayer Special, blueberry syrup, no onions in the potatoes, with a side of cinnamon and raisin Texas toast. You can give her my bacon unless you have turkey bacon. Never mind, just give her my bacon."

The food came in a surprisingly short time, and the trio ate quickly. Piper watched Oren shovel it in. She didn't leave a crumb either—not because it was particularly good, she judged it just okay— but because she'd honestly been famished. Then she polished off Oren's bacon strips. The coffee was good, though, and she held it on her tongue and swore there was a hint of raspberry in it, then looked at the clock on the wall. It wasn't quite seven.

Finished, they talked over the coffee.

"That's an odd case you have, Sheriff Blackwell," Alden said. He'd been quiet the entire time they were in the comic shop and after writing the death notification at the Duckworth's. "No sign of break-in at that store, nothing obviously missing. 'Spose it'll take some time to figure that out, though, if something's missing. Motive's got to be money."

"Usually money," Oren said. He was looking out the window to the Batter Up!

"Maaaaaaaaaa!" A toddler tipped over a cup of milk and shrieked from an adjacent table. The diners stopped their conversations to watch. "Maaaaaaaaaaaaaaa!" The mother looked apologetic and stood, picked up the child and headed to the cash register. "Maaaaaaaaaaa!"

"Anything taken from the Silver house, Sheriff?" Alden pressed. "Money? Jewelry?"

Piper shrugged. She didn't want to talk too many particulars of the case. "Still early. I've had a detective going through the house all afternoon. Brutal murder." She conceded that much. "Someone did not like Samuel Silver."

Ursula Higgins came in at seven, and after seeing that her crew members were at their stations, happily agreed to talk to Piper.

She remembered Silver. "And them two odd bodies with him." She grinned, showing her not-quite-invisible braces. "Lucky Ducky and Ben something or other."

"Benzo," Piper supplied.

"Yeah, that's it. Benzo. Name sounded like an indigestion pill. " Ursula smoothed her hands on her skirt. Piper guessed she was in her late-thirties, a little thick through the middle, big eyes magnified by the lenses in her red-rimmed glasses. A friendly-looking woman, no wedding ring, several bangle bracelets. "Benzo and Lucky Ducky. Them two come in often together, usually not so late as last night, though, and always in jeans and t-shirts. Sammy? He comes in with them once in a while, but only late, around ten or eleven. I can check the receipts for you if you want, they're time-stamped. Last night Sammy had the Dragonslayer Special and an extra order of hash browns. Didn't eat it all, shouldn't have tacked on the hash browns. Asked for to-go containers for his monkeys. I figure he meant his kids. Them other two, they ordered The Spire, two dozen silver-dollar pancakes stacked high. Them two always get The Spire, usually with—"

Piper patiently waited until Ursula was finished and then asked some pointed questions.

"No, Sheriff, they didn't cause any trouble, didn't see them talking to anyone while they were here. It was just the three of them. We were pretty empty that late. Maybe had four other tables. I can check the receipts. Anyway, they sat hunched over the food, talking about cards and games and the accident at the county fair across the river. Everyone had been talking about that accident, the kids killed. Nice thing about them three, they didn't pull out their cell phones like everyone else seems to. They just talked to each other."

She paused, grabbed a pot from a server, and refilled their coffee before handing it to another passing server. "Anyway, they ate and left, gave me a ten dollar tip. That was Sammy doing that. When them two odd bodies are by themselves it's a good day if I even get ten percent. And, yeah, we have a surveillance camera, just for the inside of the restaurant. I keep telling Arlo we should get one for outside, the lot, you know. Got the camera about a year or so back when we used to have problems with drunks. We hadn't been open all the time before that, had closed at ten. Better hours then. But at first when we changed to twenty-four-seven we had some drunks, toughs, people who should be in bed. Still get a smattering of drunks once in a while. Tempers get up. The camera was in case we had to call the cops, show 'em who the troublemakers were, record any damage. Came in handy once. It records over itself every day, so we still got video from late last night."

Piper followed her into the manager's office, cup of coffee in hand, leaving Oren and Alden to interview waiters, waitresses, and busboys. She watched the video on a small computer screen at a cramped desk littered with schedules, menus, and stacks of receipts on metal spikes. The video played in black and white showing a still-breathing Samuel Silver. The man smiled, patted Lucky Ducky on the back, and at the end of the meal picked up the tab, and left a ten.

Lucky Ducky—she hadn't gotten a good look at him the way he was stuffed inside the Bronco—was broad shouldered and thin, tattoos on his forearms of dragons and snakes, earplugs in his lobes about the size of a dime. His beard was short and braided at the edges, wearing the same clothes he died in.

Benzo was probably five-eight to five-ten, meaty arms, a long neck, and a nose that looked like it had been broken at some time. He had short hair and a young, smooth face, probably early twenties. Appeared strong, and as he got up to leave, she judged that Benzo carried himself like he had power in his frame, like some of the men in her Army unit had. He wore a Loot the Castle t-shirt, just like one she'd seen on a store patron earlier today. The trio appeared mismatched, bound together by comic books and Loot the Castle cards.

It was just as Ursula said, not a single soul visited them at the table,save the waitress. They'd arrived at a quarter to eleven and left forty-five minutes later.

"So where did they go after here?" Piper mused to herself. "Not back to the comic shop."

She returned to the dining room, where Oren and Alden said they'd come up with nothing useful.

"Let's go across the street," Oren suggested.

"The other pancake place?" Piper replied.

"Yeah." Oren pointed to the video camera inside Pearl's. "Don't have anything that shows the lot. But maybe the one across the street does. Maybe it reaches over here."

Piper drove, seeing two exterior video cameras as she pulled into the lot of Batter Up! From the angle of one, it appeared to aim straight at Pearl's Pancake Palace. She kicked herself for not thinking of this, pissed that it had been up to Oren. She caught his smile when he saw her looking at the camera.

The place smelled of grease. Years of cooking had put a film across the glass covering the posters of ball players from decades past. It didn't look like the dining room had been cleaned in a long while given the dingy tile floor. Piper cringed when something sticky tugged at her shoes. Here a handful of tired-looking middle-aged men made up the clientele, compared to the younger competition across the road.

The manager complied with their request, inviting them into what passed for his office. Here, too, a greasy film covered the computer screen, making the image fuzzy. Piper frowned and wiped the front with a napkin before enlarging the image of the lot across the street. It showed Silver's white Bronco pull in at 10:43. The Batter Up! manager gave her a thumb drive to make a copy, charging her seven dollars for it. Oren tapped an index finger on the screen.

"Run it back," he said. "A little more. Look. See that gray car two over from the Bronco. Pulled in at 10:52. No one got out of the car, too dark to tell how many are in it. But no one gets out."

Piper nodded. "So?"

"See the plate? Make that bigger. Can't make it all out. Maybe we can do better back at the office. But there's an R on the plate. I'd bet my boat that's the same car I saw parked out behind the comic shop this afternoon. Drove off as I was looking at it. Got to be the same car." He tapped the screen again. "Jersey plates. I'll run a search on it. I got the plate from this afternoon. Don't believe in coincidence, not one like that anyway."

"Zeke mentioned seeing a gray car," Piper said.

They continued to watch the video, seeing Sam drive off in his Bronco at 11:44, the gray car following.

"R40 ELE," Oren said. "Can't see the plate, but it's got to be R40 ELE. Interesting."

CHAPTER FOURTEEN

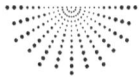

9 P.M.

All the windows rolled down, Piper listened to the county as she drove home, cruising past a few of Rockport's bars—the only places she saw open. Otherwise the downtown was empty, the closed weathered businesses making the place look haunted. When she and her sister were little it had been different, vibrant. She remembered a florist where you could buy a carnation for seventy-five cents. A nearly-faded recollection came to her of a store that sold vacuum cleaners, sewing machines, fabric, and notions … that was back when her mother was still part of the family and would tug the girls in there to look at the Butterick kids' clothing patterns. Her mom used to delight in sewing Piper dresses. The downtown started shuttering almost twenty years ago, people crossing the river to shop in Owensboro or driving to Evansville or, in more recent years, to simply shop online. Maybe Rockport's downtown had starting shutting down before Piper was born.

At least the antique store remained open … on the days when the owner decided to come in.

Teegan had told her a Dollar General was going to take over one of the larger downtown abandoned buildings, and another old building had been bought to turn into apartments.

"So that's something," Piper said.

It usually took fifteen minutes from the sheriff's department to her home in Hatfield. She slowed at the halfway point, looking out across a field sparkling with fireflies. No cars anywhere else, she pulled to the shoulder, shut off the engine, and got out. The houses stood far apart along this part of the road, so there was no light pollution. The fireflies winked, the stars twinkled. Incredible. She stared in awe.

This wasn't the life she'd planned for herself. She'd intended to put in her twenty as an MP with the Screaming Eagles, retire with an Army pension at the age of thirty-eight, and start a second career doing... doing what? She hadn't thought that far out. Maybe put in thirty or forty years instead. Be career Army. Be all she could be.

Piper had been all set to re-up when she heard about her dad's cancer diagnosis, didn't hesitate to set aside the extension papers. She'd resented her dad on some level, for getting sick and making her change the course of her life, but she kept that regret from him. It was her secret. Her commanding officer had told her she'd be welcomed back when "things at home" were taken care of, and so she'd set her mind on returning to Fort Campbell. But then she'd let her dad talk her into the campaign. Willful, she could have said no. But some chunk of her brain was intrigued. She hadn't expected to win.

But that chunk was happy she had.

And despite all the ups, downs, and misgivings of the past five and a half months in office, she had settled into the role. She wanted to keep it—maybe for longer than this one term.

Piper used to think about the Army each morning. Used to. Now she thought about her county and the goings-on there. She looked forward instead to going into work, arresting drunk drivers, and solving cases.

Now she had this huge case. The pin-cushion death of Samuel Silver ... was it solvable? Maybe with her big city detective ferreting out the clues. Basil Meredith had impressed her from the moment she looked at his resume. Overqualified for her small department, but just what the department needed right now.

Samuel Silver.

Piper stared at the fireflies rising, the stars stretching down to the horizon, the motes of light joined into something amazing. As beautiful as it was, it couldn't force from her thoughts the images of Samuel Silver dead in his chair and the teenagers killed at the county fair.

Death made nature's lights less bright.

___

Piper transcribed her scribbled notes into a Word file in her laptop when she got home.

- Lucky Ducky, twenty-eight, had lived in his parents' basement, worked nine to five at an Owensboro factory that manufactured spaghetti sauce, and on Loot the Castle Saturdays sometimes stayed out until late the following Sunday night, when he'd slink in, clean up, grab a few hours of sleep, and head off the next morning to puree tomatoes.
- Though Mrs. Duckworth said they didn't badger him about his whereabouts because of his age, they doubted he ever went anywhere questionable ... not the bars or to Evansville's strip clubs. Never drugs, never saw him drunk. Not his style. Didn't believe he had any enemies. Never had a girlfriend that lasted more than a few dates. His basement room was filled with comic books, computer games, superhero action figures, and stacks of Loot the Castle cards.
- "He was a nerd, like the guys on *The Big Bang Theory*, except without the science-smarts," the father had said.
- Practically inconsolable in their grief, the father admitted they'd told him on more than one occasion to move out and get his own apartment. Father said they'd argued yesterday before Ducky left for his game. Piper had explained that he was found dead with Samuel Silver, didn't mention that he was shot in the head and stuffed inside a Bronco in Africa;

117

all those rotten particulars could wait until the coroner was finished.

Lucky Ducky's car was still in the strip mall parking lot. Piper, Oren, and Alden had searched it before going to Pearl's Pancake Palace, finding fast food wrappers, fast food coupons, empty soda cans, and a satchel full of Loot the Castle cards sorted into what Piper assumed were competition decks. The bumper stickers had screamed nerd: THIS VEHICLE TRAVELS AT WARP 10, VOTE CTHULHU – EVIL FOR THE GREATER GOOD, ROCK PAPER SCISSORS LIZARD SPOCK, I'M A BROWN COAT, GRAB MY MANA, and GAMER FOR LIFE.

P iper hit the "sleep" button on the computer.
    She took Camaro for a brief walk. The old retriever wasn't up to more than a couple of blocks, but he certainly enjoyed hiking his leg on all the mailbox posts. The walk was more so she could unwind, clear her thoughts before she went back to it.

In her kitchen, she cut up some chicken scraps for Camaro and Marmalade, and then settled at the table once more. She re-read the Lucky Ducky notes checked her email to find a note from Nang reminding her about the concert tomorrow night, and one from Jake: *Sheriff Blackwell: Stopped by Agnes Tully-Brown's home twice. No one there. Will go back again tomorrow. Neighbor said the parents are in Fort Wayne for a three-day weekend, will return Tuesday late, said Agnes is out with friends. Got Agnes' cell phone number from Zeke, called and left a message that we want to talk to her.*

Next, Piper scrolled through the reports from her deputies who'd interviewed Silver's neighbors in Africa. She opened a second file and typed in bulleted notes for easy reference, combining the high points from the interviews. She intended to retrace their steps and chat with the neighbors herself.

- Sam was a quiet neighbor

118

- No parties
- Mostly kept to himself
- Couldn't see much of his place because of his hedge and fence
- Rarely saw another car over there
- Always waved when he watered the lawn
- Sometimes snow-blowed other driveways, never took a dollar for it, said he liked the exercise
- Don't think he was married; didn't see any kids there either
- Been living there about twenty years
- No personal Facebook account or Twitter
- Instagram account, latest post is a picture of a plate of pancakes from Friday night
- No email address for Lloyd Ebersole aka Benzo

Samuel Silver had email accounts, both personal and for his store. Honora had provided the password for the latter, and remote accessing it had yielded nothing interesting, though Basil said he'd go through all the messages a third time tomorrow. The personal account? No computers from the store or Silver's residence, no success on guessing a password and logging on remotely. There were ways to get it with a search warrant sent to the email provider, but it wasn't instantaneous.

"Who would want to kill you, Samuel Silver? And draw it out so painfully? And get Lucky Ducky for that matter?" Piper was positive Lucky Ducky had been collateral damage, not the target. She rubbed her thumbs against the space bar. "What about Benzo? Where is Benzo? Is Benzo dead?"

The Owensboro Police hadn't found him or any relatives, neither had Millie and Diego, who she'd sent over almost an hour ago. They were all still looking. Benzo remained a suspect, witness, or victim, and so was a priority. Age twenty-two, and an employee of the same spaghetti sauce factory, he had a sealed juvenile record from Arcola, Illinois, which let her misgivings wander toward the suspect category.

Her cell phone chirped.

"Basil."

"Sheriff, I'm calling it for the night. Coming in early tomorrow to go at it again."

"We need Monday," Piper admitted. "Banks, county records."

"Definitely." Basil audibly yawned. "But we need a motive more."

"Yeah. And for that we need to learn a lot more about Samuel Silver."

"Learn the man, learn the motive," Basil said. "Oren swears it's about money, and I'm not going to argue. Deep down, it's usually always about money. Sometimes love or a hate so dark it makes somebody pull the trigger. But without a single picture of a person hanging up at that house, I don't know if Mr. Silver loved anyone."

"The parrots," Piper said.

"I'll give you that. And that vet?"

"Dr. Carlisle?"

"Yeah. I like him. Glad he's dealing with all the animals. But we gotta feed the fish. That's on us."

In the silence, she heard a phone softly ringing—the dispatcher's. So Basil was at the office.

"I'll put Rocco on fish duty. I heard he has an aquarium. I'm going back to Owensboro in the morning, if Benzo—Lloyd Ebersole—still hasn't turned up," Piper said.

"I'll ride with you. Let's make it early, okay? I want some time to go back over Silver's house. Can't spend all day at it. My wife's birthday, I want to take her out for a nice dinner. I'll catch hell if I don't take her out. Tradition, going to the Calumet Fisheries, a little hole in the wall place that's miraculously still allowed to burn wood to smoke fish. Salmon, sturgeon, sable, rainbow trout—which is her favorite. The place is a dump, and it's famous, everything delicious. Have to find something real good down here."

"Make it someplace fancy," Piper suggested, which meant he'd have to go outside the county.

"Oh yeah, I'll do that. Capers, over in Hartford. Diego recommended it. Said they have rainbow trout."

"Excellent choice."

"G'night, Boss. See you tomorrow."

"Early," she replied. "Let's say meet at the office at seven. If Benzo's not around I'll have to get a search warrant and we'll go in." Because she hadn't included that in her request today. She'd figured she could just go over to Benzo's place, knock, and he'd open the door. Too bad he wasn't living in his parents' basement like Lucky Ducky had been, which would have made it easier. "I think I'll get a search warrant regardless, just to be safe."

Piper had told Oren to stay home Sunday, that maybe she'd see him at the concert tomorrow night. He didn't argue, other than to say call if something came up regarding the murder case.

She stood and stretched, worked a kink out of her neck, and decided to get a cup of coffee and go through all the notes again. Marmalade rubbed across her ankles.

Her phone chirped again.

"Really? What now?"

She gave up on the coffee notion, sat again, and answered it.

"Punkin?"

"Hey, Dad."

She'd intended to stop by his house on her way home, but she'd spent longer at the pancake places than she'd intended and had wanted to take her dog for a walk.

"I bet you're still in uniform, Punkin."

"I bet you are too."

He chuckled. Her dad had a nice laugh.

"Long day," she said.

"Same here, but not near as eventful as yours. Mine was a semi-tipped into a ditch, with a dash of fender benders in the mix. Yours was—"

"Grisly." Piper watched the screen saver start in on the laptop, a waterfall followed by a desert sunset, followed by a snowy mountainside.

"That's a mild word. Punkin, for that thing at the county fair. Oh, God. People should not die that young. And then a murder on top of it."

Two, she almost said. Two murders. Her dad probably hadn't yet heard about Lucky Ducky, though she was certain he'd hear soon enough. Piper blew out a breath, fluttering the curls on her forehead.

"Anything I can help with?" In the background a dog barked, her dad's old pug.

"I dunno. Maybe. Probably eventually. But not at the moment. I need Monday to come so I can get to records."

"Weekends can slog an investigation," he replied.

"But I have a helluva detective leading the murder case. He'd applied for your job. Did you know that? I am very lucky you were offered the top cop spot in Santa Claus. Otherwise I wouldn't have landed him and he'd be running the Santa Claus department." She let out another long breath.

"So where you sitting with the fair?"

"We're reviewing cell phone video and interviews. Again and again. Got a state agency examining pieces of the ride, and the earliest I'm going to hear from them is Tuesday. But Tuesday a State Police officer is coming to pick up Vernon Milgrew—"

"The ride operator?"

"Yeah. He's wanted on a felony warrant from Virginia. The charge is meth, possession with intent to distribute."

Paul whistled. "Makes you wonder about the background of the other operators, eh?"

"Millie arrested one for glue sniffing this afternoon."

Paul laughed again.

"Every time I go to check on Mr. Milgrew he moans that he shouldn't go to hell because he didn't break the ride." She gave a hint of a smile. "I'll be glad when he's out of here. The usual cell occupants are drunks, and they're mostly quiet and sleep it off. Quiet is not in Mr. Milgrew's vocabulary."

"You like the job, don't you, Punkin? Despite the bad stuff."

Or maybe because of it?

Unfortunate and malicious acts kept her busy. Piper waited a few beats before answering. "I don't like that five people died at the county fair, and that Samuel Silver was ... killed ... in his living room. I don't like that I've both incidents on my plate at the same time ... happening within a handful of hours of each other. But, yeah, I like the job. And you know that."

Piper imagined that her dad was grinning at that comment. She thought he looked handsome when he smiled. His face was careworn, and though at fifty-five he could easily pass for a man of sixty-five, she chalked that up to his going through cancer and its treatments twice, and suffering a heart attack at the beginning of the year.

"The job suits you," he said. "I felt guilty, you know, Punkin, you coming back here last year to help me mend. I felt guilty because I knew how much you loved the Army."

I loved you more than the Screaming Eagles.

"Then I talked you into this sheriff's campaign. I wanted you to win, but I didn't think you would. Never confessed that to you before. Honestly, as many years as Oren's been around, all the people who know him ... I didn't think you could beat him. I'd hoped, but I didn't think it would happen."

"It was the last name, Dad. *Blackwell.* People thought they were re-electing you."

"Nah, they knew different. Most of 'em, I'm sure of it. Maybe they thought Oren was too old. Glad he stayed with you, though, didn't retire."

"Yet. Retire yet. He makes noises about it once in a while."

"You still don't like him, do you, Punkin?"

"I like him just fine, Dad. But it's itchy working with him some-times. And I don't think ... no, I *know* ... that he doesn't like me."

"You're wrong. I think he really likes you. Well ... he likes you okay."

"I'd say tolerate. He tolerates me. Doesn't respect me."

"I'll concede that part." Piper heard a soft snore. "Wrinkles sleeping?"

"He does that a lot."

"My old dog, too, Dad."

"Oren wanted the job. And you know that. We've been over the subject. It's a dead horse I'm done beating."

And maybe Oren should have gotten the job, she thought for the hundredth time, *way the hell more qualified than me.*

Practically every deputy in her department had more qualifications. But she was determined, indeed liked being sheriff, and would make it work. Piper mused about Oren wanting the video checked from Batter Up! She wouldn't have thought to go across the street for the video, and so she wouldn't have noticed Silver's Bronco being followed. She wondered if the search came back yet on the license plate.

"R40 ELE," she said.

"What?"

"Nothing. Just ... oh, I think I'm going to call it a night."

"I don't see you often enough, Punkin. I liked it when you lived above the garage. Nice that you've got a big house of your own. Hell, I envy you that house, a cedar closet as big as my spare bedroom. But I miss breakfast and coffee with you."

"I miss it too," she admitted. "Let's plan a cookout. Friday would be good, you think?"

"Invite Nang, okay?"

"Because he'll likely bring some food with him?"

"I'm that transparent, Punkin? You know I do like the man. Maybe he can fix some spring rolls or something."

And I'm afraid I like him too much.

"We'll have Millie over, too, if you don't have her on nights next week. She's a fine tenant. Painted the whole apartment, is ripping up that shag carpet—"

"That awful orange stuff."

"It was there when I bought this place. There's hardwood flooring under it. Did you know that? She's refinishing it. I'm crediting her some months' worth of rent for all the work. She's grumbling about the color of the appliances—but they work. I am not going to replace appliances just because they are avocado green." He paused. "I think all that grumbling, though, all the work she's doing ... I think that means she plans to stick around a while. Hope so. I like her."

"She's only been a deputy a month, but I like her too," Piper said.

"Thorough. Sincere and eager. But I'm not so sure she'll be here all that long. Two degrees, and taking online law classes later this summer. She's ambitious."

"I hope she sticks," Paul said. "Oren's granddaughter, this department is in her blood. G'night."

She checked email one more time.

Something had come back on the license plate. It was from a red Ford Focus, 2014, a car registered as a delivery vehicle for Big Tony's Pizzeria in Hoboken, New Jersey. The car had been reported stolen four days ago. She sent a reply that the plates—not the Ford—had been seen in Spencer County, Indiana. The plates were now affixed to a gray four-door, believed a late-model Mazda.

CHAPTER FIFTEEN

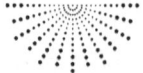

8 A.M. SUNDAY, JUNE 16TH

Benzo—Lloyd Ebersole—rented a three-bedroom, beat-down house on Rockham Road. He had one nearby neighbor. The few other houses in the block, also rentals, were empty while the property management company renovated them. It looked like Benzo's house also needed some serious upgrades.. It had a carport with a sagging roof, a bicycle double-chained to a post underneath, and a shed in the side yard, or rather what was left of a shed.

Piper had managed to finagle a search warrant a half hour ago and met a representative from the property company who had a key. He let her and Basil in, said he'd be sitting on the front porch and would lock up when they were finished.

"You'd think a young single man wouldn't need a three-bedroom house," Piper said as she entered the kitchen. "But at three hundred and forty a month it's cheaper than a lot of smaller places or apartments."

The place smelled like apples, and she spotted one of those air fresheners on the counter: Cinnamon Apple Berry Delight, the label read.

"There's a reason it's only three hundred and forty." Basil stepped past her and stood near an out-of-date kitchen table, half of which

126

was covered with inch-high plastic figures in various stages of being painted. Most science-fiction themed, but there a few wizards were in the mix. He pointed to the walls, paint chipping, and then the ceiling, stained where the roof had leaked. The floor was uneven, corners of tile pieces curled up. "Place is a dump, but a clean one. Looks like Mr. Ebersole is relatively tidy."

"Twenty-two," she said, "doesn't have a lot of resources for a nice place. But this run-down house has an upbeat feel to it. Hobbies on display. No alcohol in the fridge. Lots of fruit." She opened a cabinet and found a set of four plates, four cups, and four saucers, Dollar Store brand probably.

"You're, what ... twenty-three?"

"Yeah, for a few more months. I saved my money and lived above my dad's garage for a while. And, like Lloyd, I don't ... didn't ... have a lot of stuff. Didn't need stuff." But she'd been acquiring more ... her house, vehicles, furniture, all the books and movies her benefactor had left behind. She had plenty of stuff now.

Basil took out his cell phone, set it to record. "Should've brought a real camera."

"We did bring a camera. In the car, and—"

"Nah, don't bother. This is good." He continued a visual sweep of the kitchen, and then walked into the living room. Piper followed him, noting that he panned the cell phone to take in everything. "We'll get what we need with this. Not a lot of furniture. Tidy, for the most part."

The living room had more peeling paint and the nap showed through on the carpet in places, a couple of chairs placed over the worst spots. There were posters of Spiderman, Batman, and Lord of the Rings characters on the walls, along with hand-painted illustrations—circles with star, tulip, and bird designs that reminded Piper of quilt patterns. The furnishings looked like St. Vincent DePaul's would turn them down. But Basil was right ... everything was clean, every surface dusted.

One bedroom was wholly empty. Another had three folding tables,

127

the plastic ones like you could find at Walmart. They held comic book boxes, labels on the ends.

The final room had a twin bed, a nightstand stacked with fantasy and science fiction novels, and a closet filled with jeans, t-shirts, plus a few nice polos and sweaters.

"Lloyd Ebersole, a simple life," Basil said. "Obsessed with comic books and science fiction, a geek or nerd. Gamer. I know the terms are not interchangeable. Geek. I'd say a geek. Harmless, friendly according to the man across the street, held the spaghetti sauce job for the past four years, since high school graduation most likely. No car. No evidence of a computer. The symbols in the living room are Amish, so maybe he came from an Amish family."

"Manager at the comic store called him renegade Amish or almost-Amish," Piper said.

"So maybe he was born Amish and left the community. Could explain the lack of computers, cell phones, and other tech. No television." He nodded toward the lone telephone in the house, an old wall model. "Could be why a computer search hasn't come up with the parents. Can't always trace Amish. At least not easily."

Piper looked in the nightstand drawer, seeing a thick King James Bible, New International Version. "Neighbor said he hasn't seen him since Friday, early evening," she supplied from Diego's notes. "Said he rode his bike home from work, waved, and disappeared in the house."

"And probably got a ride with Lucky Ducky to the card game tournament," Basil said. He turned off the record function and put the cell phone back in his pocket.

"His juvenile record, I have to wait until the courts are open tomorrow to try and get it unsealed."

"Sure, we can get the records. But we've no need to do that, Sheriff," Basil said. "Whatever he did when he was younger ... it has nothing to do with Sam Silver's death. Lloyd Ebersole did not kill Sam Silver or Lucky Ducky Duckworth; they were all friends. I'm still calling money the motive for the Silver murder, and Lloyd didn't seem to have a lot of interest in money—beyond using it to buy comics. You can see that. A basic soul with a geek heart."

Piper studied Basil, who continued to look at the bedroom walls. It was like he was seeing something far beyond this rental house.

"Gonna have to locate his parents, though. Or siblings if there are any. Owensboro police can do that." He turned and gave a head shake. "He's dead, you know, Lloyd Ebersole, Benzo. Whoever killed Sam Silver and Duckworth also killed Lloyd. Maybe Lloyd wouldn't fit in the Bronco's trunk. Maybe he was killed first and dumped. Or killed last and dumped. But he's dead. And maybe we'll have to find Sam Silver's killer to find where Lloyd's body is."

"Because no witnesses," Piper said. "But I hope you're wrong. I hope Lloyd—Benzo—is still breathing."

"I'm not wrong. But Silver was the target. And whoever offed Silver wasn't going to leave any other eyes open."

They locked the door and handed the key over.

"Call us," Piper told the landlord, "if Lloyd—or anyone else—comes back to this house."

"If I see 'em," the man returned.

Piper gave him her card, went across the street to the neighbor, and said the same thing.

"I'm going to take another pass through the Silver house," Basil said as they approached the Ford.

"I should go back to the office, review all the notes again and the video," Piper said. And she wanted to spend some hours on the fair disaster. "But I'm going with you—at least for a while. I'm as curious as hell who Samuel Silver was."

"Ain't that the hundred dollar question," Basil said.

CHAPTER SIXTEEN

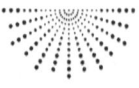

11 A.M.

Basil stood in Samuel Silver's front yard, staring at the house. Piper wondered if he noticed the assortment of flowers, or if the groupings and tidiness were lost on him.

Admittedly during her hours here yesterday she'd not paid attention to the plantings. The geraniums in a long bed under the front window were mixed, pink, white, two red ones, all about a foot tall and twice again that wide. Healthy looking, no weeds. Behind them stretched a scattering of Black-eyed Susans. The flowers didn't complement each other. Maybe someone planted them for him. Maybe he got them on sale or he'd not given a rip what he'd put out front. It was clear he'd spent his outdoor time in the backyard next to the pretty pond. The plantings there were more elaborate.

They walked to the garage and raised the door, Piper following Basil and taking note of what drew his interest. The Bronco had been moved to the sheriff's department parking lot and myriad samples had been taken from the trunk, every surface fingerprinted.

Another visual study of the garage contents.

Piper was jealous of some of the tools and the riding lawnmower. It all seemed high quality and well maintained. Silver had not been miserly with any of his implements. The garage floor had some sort of sealant on it to prevent oil stains from soaking into the concrete. It was pretty obvious Silver only had the one car, and he'd always parked it on the left side of the garage, leaving him plenty of room to take the riding lawnmower in and out without moving the car. She thought about the vehicles in her oversized garage. Vintage, insurance reasonable—especially since she didn't have a mortgage to compete for the money. Adding a shed to the property might be a good idea, something to store a lawnmower in so it didn't have to argue with premium garage space.

She watched Basil pace the garage interior, retrace his steps, and take pictures with his cell phone. Grass seed, fertilizer, organic weed killer listed as bio-safe. Nothing that shouldn't be in a garage. Nothing hidden behind anything.

Piper took pictures, too, of the garage door, the side door, and the rafters, which held a snow shovel, fishing poles, and a small brown suitcase.

"Interesting," Basil said.

"The suitcase?"

"Yeah. Didn't notice it yesterday. It's why you always come back. The first day at the scene, you're processing the death. You're so focused on the body and any immediate clues. It's why I always come back. Pick up what I missed the first time."

Piper doubted he missed much.

He put his cell phone in his pocket and plucked the ladder from the wall, propped it up so he could get to the case. "The Bronco was parked right underneath it. Maybe what the killer was looking for is right up here. Because we both agree the killer wanted something, right?"

Maybe whoever drove the Bronco into the garage didn't look up and therefore didn't notice the suitcase, Piper thought. She crossed her fingers that it held whatever the killer had wanted. She could not shake the thought that indeed Samuel Silver was killed because of something he possessed. But neither could she fathom that the killer had not claimed the prize. Nobody could have taken the torture dished out on Mr. Silver and not talked.

What would be worth killing a man over?

"Heavy for its size," Basil pronounced as he brought it down. He'd put on gloves. "I didn't see anything else interesting up in the rafters, and the fishing poles and shovel had a lot of dirt and dust on them, like they hadn't been used in years, more likely decades." He brought the case down, took it out onto the driveway, and opened it. "Hell, that's an antique."

Inside was an old manual typewriter, the ribbon dried and curled, and breaking when he touched it.

Piper pointed to a sticker on the edge: $4.

"Garage sale special. Odd thing to buy, at least these days." Basil returned it to the garage rafters and closed the door. "Could print it, but it's covered with dust. Like the poles, it's been up there for years. Not relevant to the murder."

"Maybe belonged to the previous owner."

"A good bet. Makes sense. Seeing how there's a snow shovel propped against the back wall, a lot nicer than the shovel in the rafters." He made a circuit of the backyard, stopping and staring into the goldfish pond. "This is nice," he said. "I have a big backyard. Maybe I need to do something like this in it. Be pretty. It'd teach the kids how to keep fish and plants. Might talk to Meredith, see what she thinks."

"Funny," Piper mused. "Yesterday I was wondering the same thing, putting a pond in my backyard."

"You should do it." Basil smiled. "You don't need to check with anyone for their approval on the project. This county doesn't even make you put up a fence if you have a pond."

Piper figured Basil had schooled himself quickly on county laws.

They went inside the house. The place remained a mess, would stay this way until they cleared the scene and a crew came in to clean it. Piper knew that would be days away. Besides, they had to find a relative or an heir, and they needed Monday for that—banks and the courthouse.

They searched through every cabinet, just like yesterday, but this time noticing little things like an impressive collection of spices that suggested Sam Silver liked to cook. There was an assortment of teas and coffees, no coffee cups, but a half-dozen ceramic mugs. Each mug was different: Superman, Tarzan, Dance Like A Monkey, Kessel Run Special, Hard Work Beats Talent, and a prophetic Life is Short and so Am I. The half-dozen wine glasses were crystal. The silverware was real silver, and at the back of the drawer were small jars of silver polish.

"He liked nice things," Piper said. "Expensive things, given the fish and the exotic pets, the way the interior of the house was fitted. Expensive."

"Couldn't have told that from the outside." Basil moved into the living room. "Sam Silver did not want to stand out in Africa. Hell, he didn't want to stand out in the county. Picking a tiny place to live like this. Oh, I think he liked the name—Africa—fit with his jungle motif. But an itty bitty spot on the road like Africa? A great place to hide. Who would come here? Who would drive by?"

Piper was glad the monkeys and birds were gone. She could think today. The muskiness of their odors lingered. The house might have to be fumigated to get rid of the funk.

"He wasn't hiding in Owensboro. Nice comic shop. Ad in the Yellow Pages. Zeke said the shop had a Facebook page so it could promote the tourneys." Piper fixed her gaze on the chair where Sam Silver had died. "Lived here twenty years, but only had the comic shop in Owensboro for a dozen. Need to find out what he did, where he worked, for those eight years between."

"Monday for records," Basil growled softly. "Helluva thing, a murder case on a weekend when offices are closed."

"Owensboro," Piper mused. "He probably worked somewhere over there, then decided he was done working for someone and would start his own business. He was definitely not hiding there."

"Yeah, I'll give you that. He wasn't hiding in Owensboro. But I think he was hiding here. Just a feeling." Basil paced. "Usually I can get a read on a victim by his surroundings. But this man … weird, just weird. No photos of relatives. No social media beyond the store's Facebook page."

Piper also found that odd. Everyone was into social media now, even the eighty-year-olds in the genealogy club her dad had joined.

"Neighbors say no regular visitors. Friendly, but distant. Helpful, but standoffish. A commoner on the outside, lavish on the inside. Money, but not obvious to anyone driving by. Clothes? No one helped him pick anything out. Bet he had to mail order those garish Hawaiian print shirts. I'll wager you cannot find them on the rack around here. And speaking of shirts—" Basil went to the bedroom.

He went to the closet and starting looking at clothes sizes. Checked every shirt and pair of pants, then checked the shoes. "All his," Basil pronounced. "All the same size and style. He wasn't gaining or losing weight, so no indication of illness. Don't see any garments that look out of place to hint that a significant other sometimes stayed here. Nothing in any of the pockets."

Piper put on gloves and checked the clothes that had been strewn around when the killer had searched the room. "Same size." She hadn't thought to check that; Basil was teaching her more than a few things. "Wait, there's a false bottom in this drawer." Tapping it, she heard a hollow sound, guessed the space to be about an inch. She finessed it open, releasing a hint of cedar scent. There was nothing in the opening, but it would make a good place to store documents or small valuables.

"Might have been something in there," she said. "Maybe what they were looking for."

Basil took out a flashlight and showed it around in the drawer. "I'm going to print the catch and the bottom. No discoloration to suggest what size of object was kept in here, if anything."

Piper checked the rest of the drawers, then the space under the bedroom fish tanks, finding no other hidden compartments. She returned to the living room, an idea itching at the back of her brain. If Sam Silver had a secret place in a dresser, maybe there were more. She looked through the cabinet under the massive fish tank, and tapped the bottom—no hollow spots. Next the cat, monkey, and bird cages.

Bingo.

They all had pull out drawers at the bottom so they could be cleaned and fresh paper put down. But the drawer under the parrot cage was thick, and tapping revealed a hollow space beneath the tray that caught the seed husks and bird droppings.

"Basil!" She knelt, fiddled with it a while before finding a catch, sending seed husks flying when it popped open. "Oh my."

"Oh my indeed," Basil said, standing over her.

He aimed the camera and started recording.

It was an assortment of weapons fitted inside foam cut-out shapes.

"Luger," he said. "A toggle-lock pistol."

"Desert Eagle," Piper said. "You have to be an experienced shooter to use this, and in good shape. Fifty-caliber, can be a case of overkill."

"An old one," Basil said. "That's a Colt Model 1911. Holds seven rounds, forty-five caliber."

"You know guns," Piper said.

"The city has a big big problem with guns. Deal with gangs, got to learn about guns."

"I know this one. My dad used to have one like it. Smith and Wesson, forty-four magnum. Double-action, not for beginners. Gotta have good arm strength. Clint Eastwood made it famous in his Dirty Harry movies."

"That'd be ... what ... 1970, 71?"

"Before we were born. Yeah, somewhere in there. Harry claimed it was the most powerful handgun in the world. And he wasn't lying ... at the time."

"My turn." Basil pointed with his free hand. "That one's a Browning Auto-5. Big, so I'd say the 16 gauge model, semi-automatic. Looks like it's been overhauled with some custom parts to give it more punch. But the original part of it looks old. Mint, but old, maybe from the thirties."

"And this one?"

"That's a Ruger."

Piper nodded. "I thought so."

"Detachable magazine, one of the easiest rifles to shoot. Good thing the bird cage was big, otherwise this beauty would not fit under it." He whistled softly. "Doesn't have a lot of serious firepower, certainly not compared to some of these other guns. But with the scope, all you need is one well-placed shot."

There were three more guns, which Basil identified while Piper took pictures on her cell phone and Googled the knives.

Beretta 92. 9 mm caliber, double-action, slide, ambidextrous safety catch.

Glock semi-automatic pistol, made for seventeen rounds of 9mm ammo.

Sig Saur P226, customized to .357 to give it more bite.

Piper said, "According to the internet, this is a Fairbairn-Sykes fighting knife, a seven-inch blade, used by British commandos back to World War II. And these are—"

"Butterfly knives," Basil cut in. "Seen butterflies up close. They are more about flash than killing because the blades are short. Typically used by someone looking to be intimidating. You twirl it, show off that flash of swirling silvery metal. If you're not an expert with one you can slice your hand up pretty bad."

"So those two are about the cool factor."

"Yeah," he replied. "The swagger. The bigger one's a Bali-Song, the other a Kimura. Toys for gangs."

Piper stepped back. "I doubt Samuel Silver was in a gang."

"I don't know. He was into something. He had the body, the hands to use those guns, and he was clearly hiding them, maybe hiding himself in Africa. Who's gonna look under parrot poop for weapons?"

"I wonder if his killer was after the weapons. I doubt they're worth all that much."

Basil shrugged. "Great condition, they're worth something. The Colt is old, a hundred years, collectible. But if the doer was after the guns, had tortured Sam to find them, I'd think Sam would have given them up. You could replace any of these by hitting a couple of gun shows."

"And here's ammo boxes," Piper said, finding a secret compartment under the bottom of the cat cage. "Lots of ammo. But the boxes are all yellowed, nothing bought recently. That's for certain."

"So a dude living in Africa has no pictures of relatives, has a hidden cache of guns and ammo, and spent his money on exotic animals and expensive fish. What the hell."

"We'll take back each piece," Piper said.

"Print each one," Basil said. "Then test them, ballistics."

"Because—" Piper was curious why ballistic tests, as Samuel Silver had been ice-picked, not shot. And it didn't look like these guns had been touched in a long while.

"S-O-P," Basil said. "Doesn't matter if they weren't used or handled. Anytime weapons are discovered in proximity to a homicide you test them, print them. In the city—"

Piper translated that to Chicago.

"—I had to submit everything to the FBI for comparisons. But in the city we had a lot of gun issues, questions."

"I question why Mr. Silver had a lot of guns." Piper stood as she heard the back door opening.

"Sheriff Blackwell? Sheriff, you here?"

She recognized the voice. "In the living room, Rocco. Booties and gloves!"

"Yes, ma'am."

She heard the back door shut, some fumbling. She took more pictures of the weapons.

"Sam Silver was an odd man," Basil said. "And maybe, given the guns, a dangerous one."

"Certainly a complicated fellow," Piper added. "I'm looking forward to tomorrow, when the offices and banks open."

She watched as Basil took pictures of the guns as each one was bagged and tagged. "Doesn't matter if he had permits for these. Dead men can't get charged for—"

"I drew fish duty," Rocco announced as he walked in. "And house patrol. I got a couple of tanks at home, thought I should do this. Hey,," his eyes widened, "that's a lot of guns."

"And an unusual place to store them," Piper said. To Basil: "They are valuable, but, yeah, you can probably buy most of these. The Sig Saur, my commanding officer had one of those, a personal weapon.

I'm still wondering if Mr. Silver was he killed because of something to do with the weapons."

"This, all of this, is interesting as hell." Basil whistled. "Too bad I have to take my wife to dinner tonight."

"Let's bag the ammo, too," Piper said. "I'll haul everything back to the department with me."

Rocco edged closer. "Wow. Just ... wow."

"I could work through the night on this," Basil said.

"You need to take your wife to dinner," Piper countered.

"Yeah, I know. And you've got goat-roping music. A break helps clear your head."

Piper brushed sunflower seed husks off her pants and turned to her deputy.

"Rocco, we're going to keep these fish alive so a relative or heir can assume ownership. They seem to be quite valuable."

Rocco looked away from the guns. "I like fish, Sheriff. You don't want to be overfeeding tropicals. Builds up on the bottom. Clogs the circulation and fouls the water. That's an impressive tank. Easily five hundred gallons." Rocco shook his head. "Big money. This place is dumpy on the outside, but that tank, your vic didn't get it for less than six or seven thousand. Hell, my wife had kittens when I bought a full reef set-up, a hundred gallons. She'd have a heart attack I try to put in something like this. Beautiful. Just beautiful."

Piper nodded. "I'm not much up on fish. But I am impressed with these. Two more tanks in the bedroom. Gloves until we clear this place. When you're done feeding them, I want a ride back to the department—with all these guns. And when you come back to feed them tomorrow, gently go through the gravel and decorations on the bottom, just in case something's hidden there."

She gave Basil the keys to her Ford. "Drop the keys in my desk when you're done for the day here. I'll pick it up in the morning. Enjoy dinner tonight."

"I will do that," Basil said. "And you enjoy your concert."

"Yeah, well, I'm going 'cause I want to take another walk around the fair." Goat-roping. Piper chuckled. Goat-roping music. Sitting next to Nang, listening to tunes about pickup trucks, beer, and dogs would help chase away the horrific images of Samuel Silver, Lucky Ducky, and the dead teens.

Or at least keep them at bay for a few hours.

But as much as she looked forward to the company and the concert, she wanted to stay here. Basil was right: this case was as interesting as hell.

CHAPTER SEVENTEEN

5 P.M.

The sweet, crispy cornmeal breading tasted tangy with the mustard. Heaven. Piper counted Basil wrong. Corn dogs were indeed edible. She got a second corn dog and bought a Lemon Shakeup in the premium refill cup so she could return for more.

She'd walked the fairgrounds twice, talked with the manager and the ride operators again, recording the conversations, and discovered that Vernon Milgrew had been temporarily laid off from the ride circuit two years ago because he'd let children board that didn't meet the height requirements. Somehow he'd gotten back on the circuit a few months later. Friday's disaster had nothing to do with how tall the riders were, but Piper found the tidbit nevertheless curious.

"We've got time for the craft barn before the concert," she suggested.

"Only because we have assigned seats." Nang nodded toward the back of the fair, where a line had formed for general admission to the grandstand.

Piper was in her uniform, Nang having picked her up at the department. She'd been alternating between reading the interviews of Samuel Silver's neighbors and watching video of the fair accident.

She'd intended to go home and change into casual summer attire before coming out here, but she'd lost track of the time, and so had remained in her uniform.

The lemonade tasted like heaven, too.

Despite the line for the concert, the fair overall wasn't near as crowded as it had been Friday night, which made it easier for her exploration, and she'd heard from her deputies that attendance was thin yesterday, too. The horror of the Cosmic Odyssey tragedy hung like a heavy dome over all. People appeared to be enjoying themselves now, however. Children tugged parents to the games of chance and food vendors. But a glance at the rides showed that not everything operated—an apparent lack of riders—and those attractions that spun merrily were not close to full. As she watched, she counted only four of the seats occupied on the Ferris wheel. Beneath the summer music that blared from the loudspeakers, Piper could still hear the screams from the Odyssey and the sirens that followed.

"Surprised you're keeping this date with me," Nang said.

"I feel a little guilty about it," Piper admitted. "I've got a lot going on. Maybe I should be at work. I really should be at work. But I thought some hours away would let me look at everything fresh. And I wanted to walk around the fair again."

"So you are working. I saw you talk to the people running the rides."

"I *was* working. Sorry. I'm done now." Though she wondered if she should instead be in the office, puzzling over Samuel Silver and his collection of guns. She'd told Nang she was working a murder in addition to the fair tragedy, but she didn't provide any specifics about Samuel Silver, and he hadn't pressed.

Besides, she really was stymied on some aspects of the Silver investigation until the banks and county courthouse opened tomorrow morning. She, Basil, and Oren would hit it hard then. Specifics on the guns had been logged in, and hopefully within a few hours they'd know if the weapons had been stolen or legally purchased … and if it was the latter maybe the documentation was in a safe deposit box. And she needed the report from Indianapolis to better address the ride disaster.

So she could afford a few hours for the concert, to recharge, settle her whirling mind, and then take a couple hours' nap before going back in.

"Let's take your mind off death for a while." Nang directed her into the craft and culinary barn, where they'd been headed when disaster struck Friday. "I've got a surprise."

It was a nice idea, distracting her from *every bad thing*. Still, questions about Samuel Silver kept rotating in her brain. How could you hate someone enough to ice pick them to death? And if the killer was looking for something, what was that *something*? Had it been found? Did a New Jersey license plate have anything to do with it? Follow the money ... usually ... but there'd been plenty of money untouched in Silver's bedroom safe. So it was not money in this case. And where the heck was Lloyd Ebersole?

"I'm good at savory, don't do much sweet," Nang explained, snapping her attention back. "But this year I entered three baking contests." He pointed out his entries in different cases, large blue ribbons attached to each one. "I was going to enter my peach cobbler. I didn't like the crust. It was tasty, though."

"Wow, Nang, this is a surprise. Three blue ribbons. Congrats."

She eyed the displays and his wins:

- Dough Sculpting, where he'd rendered a curled dragon that covered a big platter.
- Blue Star Yeast, his offering in the Ethnic Bread subcategory a Vietnamese Baguette, Banh Mi recipe.
- Cocoa Classics, a double-chocolate cake that had a larger ribbon noting Judges' Choice.

"Impressive," Piper admitted. "You won everything you entered?"

"Yes, my total winnings of twelve dollars will buy us a couple more corn dogs. They took my picture. It's supposed to be in the paper."

She remembered from her years in 4-H that the monetary prize attached to a fair ribbon was low. But it wasn't about the money. It was always about the ribbon. Piper glanced at the other entries, feeling hungry again: apple and cherry pies, brownies, cookies, macaroons, and muffins. Next came the gardeners' entries—early beans, peas, and carrots.

"But that's not the surprise I mentioned."

"Oh?"

"So ... I've been thinking..." He laced his fingers with hers and started out of the barn and toward the grandstand. "There are cooking contests on television."

"Reality shows. I've seen Gordon Ramsay commercials."

"Yes, I watch a few of those programs. Fun, you know. Sometimes I learn something, or get an idea for a recipe."

"Sheriff Blackwell!" A familiar-looking woman Piper couldn't name darted in front of them. She carried a stuffed purple duck in one hand and a bag of popcorn in the other. "Sheriff Blackwell! What about that accident? Friday? Me and Marge were here with Durinda. Heard you arrested someone who made that ride fall apart, killed those kids. What about that?" Another woman joined her, both mid-forties, SIC ME ANOTHER t-shirts in matching sky blue.

"It's been on the news out of Evansville and Owensboro," the other woman put in. "The arrest. How many charges of murder? Who did it?"

"It's an on-going investigation," Piper said. "So I can't talk about it. But no one was arrested for breaking the ride. No one was arrested for killing anyone."

"Told you it was an accident," the second woman said. "But I know someone's gonna sue."

Nang politely steered Piper around them.

"So there are auditions for one of those cooking shows in Indianapolis in August, and I sent in a video," Nang said.

"Really?" Piper noticed the two women following them. "Hope you get—"

"And Friday I got a call that I'm invited to the audition. The top finishers in Indianapolis go to New York for a televised cooking contest. If I'm lucky ..." He let that thought dangle. "Anyway, that's my surprise, an audition. I would have told you before, on Friday, but all the bad things happened. And Saturday you were busy."

Every bad thing, Piper remembered a teenager saying.

"Serious congratulations." Piper leaned in, rubbing her cheek against his. The warmth was good, and his face smooth. She thought he smelled of sandalwood. "An audition, eh? You'll nail it."

"We'll see. I thought maybe you could take a few days off, come with me in August. Indianapolis has a wonderful zoo. And there is this steak house I've been wanting to try. We could—"

"Which steak house?"

"St. Elmo. I had wanted to try Don Shula's, but it closed. Shula used to manage the Miami Dolphins. Supposedly one of the top ten steak restaurants in the country, football theme. I waited too late for that one. But St. Elmo is still open. Expensive, apparently, but it's a special occasion, this audition. I thought we could—"

They got in the short line at the grandstands, the one for reserved seats.

"I would love to take a few days off with you. It's been a long time since I've had anything like a vacation. And I've never been to the Indy zoo."

Nang smiled wide and she swore his eyes sparkled.

"Sheriff Blackwell!"

Piper drew in a deep breath and prepared to go into the "under investigation" reply.

"Sheriff Blackwell, wait a minute."

Piper dropped Nang's hand, turned, and saw a gangly man on the far side of middle-age skid to a stop so close she could smell his sweat. She recognized him: Chris Hagee. She hadn't pegged Chris for the county fair type. They didn't serve alcohol here.

"Sheriff Blackwell, what are you going to do about those Buddhists across the road from me?"

"Excuse me?"

"The Buddhists. Well, what are you going to do? I've complained to the county board and they won't do nothing. Talked to Oren about it a few times. Oren just blows me off. Oren's Jewish, you'd think he'd understand. Them Buddhists ... they've started up a retreat! I've been leaving messages for you—"

Piper recalled Oren and Sylvia D mentioning complaints about the Buddhists. It wasn't much of a retreat. Conrad Delaney, the previous owner of the big saltbox house Hagee referred to, had been discovered murdered early New Year's Day—her first case and first day with the department. Conrad's son, a Buddhist monk who had been living in Thailand, had inherited the house. Nice man, the Bhikkhu, Piper thought. The young monk was polite. A lot more polite than the man wagging his finger at her. She'd expected the Bhikkhu to sell the house and return to Thailand. Instead, he was turning it into a Buddhist Cultural Center, which was not against zoning on that county road.

"Well, what are you going to do about it? Arrest him?"

"Nothing, Mr. Hagee," she answered. "I'm going to do nothing about it. I'm not aware Bhikkhu Anthony Delaney has broken any laws."

"That's beside the point! They're Buddhists. And you can't be certain, not really, that he hasn't broken a law. We don't need a Buddhist retreat—" Hagee noticed Nang. "Oh, not that I've anything against the Chinese or their religion." He straightened. "It's not a proper place, my road, for something like that. I don't want it there."

"Look, Mr. Hagee, since you have complained about it, I will go out in the next few days and see if there are any infractions. I'll—"

"Next few days," Chris sputtered. "What about now? Or first thing in the morning? It's not like you're all that damn busy."

"I will check out your complaint as soon as possible, Mr. Hagee. Personally."

He squared his shoulders and glared. Piper recalled that he'd complained about the previous owner because of the lights from his Christmas display. She doubted Bhikkhu Delaney would put up any Christmas decorations.

"I suppose that'll do," he returned reluctantly.

"You could always move, Mr. Hagee," Piper added. "Surely there are houses for sale in Spencer County that are not across from

145

Buddhist Cultural Centers. Now, if you'll excuse me, I'm going to enjoy this concert."

Three more people stopped her before she and Nang got to their seats, these asking about the Cosmic Odyssey, who had been arrested, and if the boy on the hay bales was going to live. The last report she'd heard about the teen was hopeful. That was something else she needed to do: visit him in the hospital, or delegate that one of her deputies go.

"Wish I'd changed clothes," Piper told Nang. "Except for Chris Hagee, they probably would have left me alone if I wasn't wearing my uniform. Hell, probably wouldn't have known who I was."

"You shine," Nang said. "You are very good at dealing with assholes."

Piper saw Oren and Millie, four rows down and closer to the center. There was an empty seat next to them. Millie had mentioned that she'd bought three tickets, hoping her grandmother would join them. "She hates country music," Millie had said. "Thought I'd try anyway." Piper figured she should make it a point to meet Oren's wife, maybe have them out for dinner.

Oren wore a green baseball hat and had a lemonade in his hand. He nodded to Piper and then looked back to the stage.

"He thought to go to Batter Up!" Piper said.

Nang raised an eyebrow at her comment.

"A pancake place." She lowered her voice. "Oren found some surveillance video I would have missed because he wanted to go to Batter Up! I often think he should have won the race."

Nang leaned close. "Oren? Your chief deputy?"

"Yeah. He would've been a better sheriff."

Nang scowled. "He would have been a *different* sheriff. One with old eyes."

"Age doesn't—"

"Not old eyes because of his age. Old because he's been here so long. Seen it all. Knows everyone. Too close to the county. Your eyes are fresh, Piper. Your eyes are not old and you look at things with a new point of view. It's why I voted for you. New blood."

"He's more experienced."

"I will give you that." He plucked her Lemon Shakeup cup. "I have time to refill this before it starts. May I?"

"Thank you."

Piper pulled out her phone as soon as he left.

Basil had managed to email his notes before he took his wife out for her birthday dinner. She scanned them quickly.

It was mostly a list of what he still hadn't found:

- No bank records, though there was an empty envelope with Spencer County Bank as the return address. They'd go there in the morning with their search warrant.
- No personal records. None. Zippo. Perhaps Samuel Silver kept all of that in a safe deposit box, but the lack of *any* records at the house seemed odd.
- On Silver's desk was a warranty for roof work that had been completed in April.
- No personal correspondence, not even a Christmas or Hanukkah card he'd saved.
- No paperwork or licenses for any of the firearms they'd discovered. And what the hell did a comic store owner need with that much firepower?
- A bill marked paid from a physician in Rockport, treatment for a sprained knee from slipping on the ice in January. Found behind a file cabinet.
- Folder filled with CGC—Certified Guaranty Company— evaluations on comic books. The higher the number on a scale of one to ten, the better shape a comic was in and the more it was worth.
- Folder containing veterinarian records for the monkeys and the two African Greys.
- Folder thick with brochures on attractions along Route 66, as if he had vacationed there or was planning a trip.
- Envelope filled with appliance warranties and specifications.

147

- No photos.
- No address book.
- No Christmas card list.
- No telephone book. Probably used White Pages Online, if he used that type of thing at all.
- No college or high school yearbook.

Will be in early tomorrow to go through interviews conducted with neighbors once more, Basil wrote. *Then we'll go to the bank.*

She texted Zeke. *You still going out with your girlfriend tonight?*

Zeke must have been on his phone. He answered immediately: *Hdng ovr n 60 2 her hse. And she's not my grlfrd. Jst frd.*

No luck getting her phone. Please ask her for it tonight. Piper preferred to text whole words, not the abbreviations you had to sometimes puzzle over.

Zeke: *K.*

Piper knew that wasn't protocol. A deputy should secure the phone, and that hadn't happened yet because a deputy hadn't found Aggie at home, nor had she returned their phone calls. But Piper wanted to see the pictures. Screw protocol.

Drop her phone in my office tonight, please.

Zeke: *K.*

Piper replaced her cell phone just as Nang came back with a refill, beads of condensation glistening on the plastic. She wrapped her hands around it and felt the coolness. Took a sip. More heaven.

"I don't deserve you," Piper said.

"Maybe not." He kissed her forehead.

Nang said something else, but it was lost as the crowd cheered and an electric bass guitar growled.

"Welcome Spencer County's own!" a man at the microphone shouted. "Direct from Nashville—Clint Holster!"

The music competed with the cheers of the people in the stands as Holster ran up the stairs and onto the stage. Someone passed him a guitar, and he started strumming and singing, all his words swallowed by the wave of excited noise that enveloped the grandstand.

The twisted wreckage of the Cosmic Odyssey, the panic, the terrified screams from Friday night, all of it muted in Piper's mind by the joyous country cacophony. She smiled, noting all the exuberance, seeing Oren raise his free hand in the air and rock in time with Millie.

Nang grinned and swayed, too, the crowd moving with Holster, as he led them in the summer slow dance.

It was a treat, someone with Holster's talent and success spending a night in tiny Spencer County. For a moment she entertained the notion of going down to the stage after the concert, her uniform ought to get her there. Talk to him. Get a picture with him. Mention they'd gone to high school together.

His name was Clint Hollister then. He was the sort of soul you couldn't *not* remember. But back then he sang rock with a little garage band.

Tonight he sang about pickup trucks, old dogs, dirt roads, cold beer, and sunshine. Piper had heard some of the songs before on the radio. They sounded better live.

Holster wore tattered jeans and a SIC ME ANOTHER t-shirt. Piper had seen him with long hair on the posters in town, but if he still had those curls, they were piled up under an ivory hat that would do George Strait proud. During high school he'd practically had a buzz cut.

He used to sing the National Anthem at football and basketball games her freshman year. He'd been a senior then. And he'd been good, had all the teenage girls staring and dreaming. In the years after, he'd only gotten better, and maybe even more handsome.

She joined the crowd on its feet, the image of the ice-picked body pushed from her thoughts as she swayed.

Holster performed an hour more than the concert had been scheduled to run, and toward the end his voice was raspy ... a good sound, but one engendered from singing so long. It had been a mix of his top tunes, old favorites, and a few requests. Maybe Holster was feeling nostalgic, as he lingered after the band picked up and moved through the crowd pressed against the stage, signing autographs and posing for pictures.

Piper elected not to join the fans. She tugged Nang from the grandstands. Time to go home so she could get up early and delve into the Silver case before the bank opened.

"Can I get you a t-shirt?" Nang asked. "A Sic Me—"

"Yeah, I'd like a t-shirt, but I'll buy it," Piper returned. "I've got money with me." There was a t-shirt vendor on the way out.

"This is a date," Nang corrected. "I'm old fashioned." He bought one for himself, too.

And Piper got one more refill on her Lemon Shakeup.

Glancing over her shoulder she saw the neon lights of the rides, spinning, rising, people on board.

"I'll take you home." Nang draped an arm around her shoulders.

She leaned into him as they walked past the fried Twinkies hawker and games of chance.

"Do you want to stay tonight?" she asked. "Not that it'll be a long what's-left-of-the-night. I have to go in early early early."

"Definitely. For whatever's left of the night."

Piper thought she was liking Nang too much. On the other hand, she thought a little romance would help keep every bad thing away for a little while longer.

"Definitely," she parroted. Then her cell phone rang, Teegan, and she noticed she'd missed a few calls while she'd been swaying to the goat roping tunes. "Or definitely not."

CHAPTER EIGHTEEN

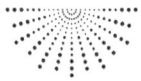

6 P.M.

Serilda made a *thunking* sound when Zeke turned too fast into the driveway and rode up over the curb. Aggie's parents lived on North Fifth, three blocks up from Main, and Zeke had visited enough times before to know you could see Kentucky across the river if you stood on a rise behind a flower bed in the front yard. It was a brick and vinyl-sided house, a split level with an attached garage, dated, in need of some updating like they do on those home remodeling reality shows. It had a nice backyard with a massive weeping willow in the center. He'd helped Aggie bury her favorite dog one summer beneath that tree, carved the dog's name in the trunk —Penny.

He should have asked Aggie out on a real date before now.

This was one of those last-minute-in-life opportunities, her going into the Coast Guard and leaving Spencer County behind. He might never see her again. She might find some fellow Coast Guard geek to fall in love with and move down to Florida. Should have made a romantic move on her before now. Zeke figured this was like one of those Hallmark Christmas movies, where the guy doesn't realize that the perfect woman had been right in front of him all this time.

Shouldn't have waited until now. That was a regret he wasn't going to shake off anytime soon.

Another regret ... having a big hole in the passenger side of Serilda's floorboard. He wanted Aggie to sit up front with him. He smiled slyly. Maybe if dinner and pinball went well, they'd both be sitting in the backseat before the date was over. Maybe the Coast Guard wouldn't pan out and there would be other dates. Aggie was little, short legs, and she might not be able to keep up in the basic training. But a part of him knew Aggie would make it through.

He didn't need to be getting serious about someone anyway. Did he?

Zeke checked his teeth and hair in the rearview mirror, smoothed a wrinkle out of his new Rebel Alliance logo shirt, got out, and hurried to the front door. He hoped Aggie answered, and they could swoop out of here without dealing with her mother ... who always wanted to talk about everything and throw forty questions his way ... and that had been when he and Aggie were just friends. Tonight, maybe they'd be more than just friends.

Too damn bad he hadn't gotten the courage for this before she signed on with Coast Guard. Too damn bad he hadn't given himself the option of getting serious.

Maybe, Zeke thought sadly, he'd gotten the courage to ask her out for a date *because* she'd signed on. Aggie heading out of state, there'd be no pressure for a follow-up date, no commitment, no future expectations. If the date tanked she wouldn't be around to make him feel bad about it. But if the date was awesome he'd be kicking himself.

Maybe he should have brought her flowers. But maybe that would've been over the top.

He hoped she wouldn't ask him about Sam. He'd promised Piper not to discuss the case with her. But he would ask for her cell phone, "sheriff's business," he'd say. He'd tried to call her to say he was coming over, but she didn't answer, probably talking to someone else.

Zeke rang the doorbell, knocked, waited, then after a few minutes went around to the back and knocked there.

"Shit. Must've gone out with her parents. She could've texted me.

Would've been polite." Then he remembered that her parents were at some family reunion thing up north.

He'd texted Aggie to say he was on his way, and she hadn't replied to that either.

"Shit and double rotten."

Zeke shuffled back to Serilda and leaned against the hood. Maybe he should wait a while. Aggie could be out on some Sunday errand, maybe a church thing that had extended into the late afternoon. She might be on her way back right now, and he just needed to cool his heels a little while. He texted her again.

He'd really been looking forward to the date.

"Young man!"

Zeke saw the vague shape of someone standing behind a screen window next door, the mesh distorting the image so he couldn't make out details. But the voice sounded sort of feminine.

"Yeah?"

"The Browns aren't home."

Zeke had figured that out. "I'm just waiting for Aggie to get back."

The shape tapped on the screen, making a *wukka wukka* sound. "Mr. and Mrs. are at a family reunion, Fort Wayne I think. The girl didn't want to go. She's home ... well, not at the moment, but I know she didn't go to the reunion with them. People have been here on and off all day looking for her."

Zeke moved up to the window. He could see the speaker better now, a doughy-faced woman with gray hair so tightly curled it looked like a swim cap. "What people have been looking?"

"Well, you. Are you a boyfriend or something?"

"Or something," Zeke replied.

"Somebody with the sheriff's department has been here a few times. She in trouble, the girl?"

"No trouble." He went back to his car and waited, texted Aggie again. "Shit."

"Young man!"

Zeke looked at the doughy woman.

"I don't think she's going to be back anytime soon. Just saying."

153

"Why do you think that?" Zeke was trying to be civil to the nosey neighbor.

"She came back home about five. I heard her 'cause of that damn little scooter she rides. I was fixing dinner and it *chink-a-chugged chink-a-chugged* up the drive. I watched her. She had a sack, like she'd been grocery shopping. Went in the back. Came out all in a hurry wearing a jean jacket and cowboy hat, took off *chink-a-chugging* again. Off to that county fair concert, I'm sure. She was gonna be late. Real hurry, she was in."

"Shit."

Zeke waited another few minutes, debating whether to put a note on the door, since texting wasn't working. Then he gave up and left, brooding, drove up to Sycamore, and then turned on Lincoln. He thought about going out to eat by himself, maybe across the river, cruise by Silver Age Sam's and see if his boss and Oren were still there. No, they wouldn't be. He remembered that they'd gone to the country concert too.

"Shit." He bet that someone had called Aggie and asked her to the concert, and she'd considered that a better option than pinball with him. No wonder she wasn't returning his calls or texts.

Dejected, he stopped at the grocery store, grabbed a couple of frozen pizzas, some tomatoes, and a twelve-pack of Mountain Dew and went home. He'd play some Path of Exile or Hearthstone, turn in early. Maybe call Aggie tomorrow and see why she'd stood him up.

Zeke lived in a furnished third-floor studio in Grandview, about six miles from the sheriff's department. It usually took him ten minutes to get to work. It was in a big Victorian that had been subdivided, which he counted himself ultra-lucky to have found it. The higher the apartment, the lower the rent. There weren't many apartment buildings in the county, so people either rented or bought houses, or rented apartments in Owensboro across the river where there were a lot more to pick from. He could have kept living at his parents' house, but he liked the independence, and the low cost: four hundred and twenty a month, all utilities and wifi included. His parents were going to charge him rent anyway.

The Victorian's long driveway snaked around to a three-bay garage. Zeke had to park on the gravel next to the garage as the bays were hooked to the first floor one-bedroom apartments.

He grabbed his groceries and went inside, trundled up the stairs that creaked with each step.

Four hundred and eighty square feet, plenty big enough right now because he didn't have all that much stuff. Good thing he didn't have a lot, he'd have hated lugging boxes upon boxes up those creaking stairs. He'd brought his clothes, a box of comic books, a tub of Loot the Castle cards, his laptop, and a few plates and pans he'd picked up at a garage sale. His folks were good to let him keep boxes of books, comics, and other crap in their basement—some of it stuff he'd go through before summer was out and likely toss or sell on eBay. He was into his Kindle now, downloading books because they didn't take up space.

Piper told him she'd "lived lean" until she inherited her house.

Zeke hoped to have a house someday, too, but figured that was years off ... after he made deputy and pulled in a bigger salary, could save more, sell a restored Serilda for serious cash. He'd have a computer room, man cave with a big screen television, and one of those refrigerators that dispensed ice and water from the door.

He put his groceries in his fridge—small, but a step up from what college kids had in their dorms, preheated the oven, and slid in a Tombstone pepperoni.

He paced, waiting for it to bake.

"Stood up. Great. Stood up."

Fitting, he figured, since he'd waited until the last minute to ask her out on a date. He should've thought to ask her to the county fair tonight. Country music—they could've got grandstand nosebleed seats if they'd gone early enough, corn dogs, deep-fried candy bars, a Ferris wheel ride where he might have kissed her at the top.

"Shit."

The timer dinged, he took out the pizza, and cut it into pieces, plopping half of it on a big plate, and letting the other half sit on top of the stove. Maybe he'd eat the whole thing if he was still hungry and still brooding. Maybe he'd put the other half in the fridge for tomorrow. Zeke was a champion of cold pizza for breakfast.

The pepperoni was good, just the right amount of grease and spice. He held a bite in his mouth to let all the juices soak in while he pulled out his cell phone. Nope, she hadn't returned a text. He started to send her another when his phone died.

"Shit." He should've noticed the charge was low. He stuffed the phone back in his pocket, would put it on the charger when he was done eating. Halfway through his third slice, he nearly choked when someone pounded on his door, heavy, fast.

Zeke dropped the half-eaten piece onto his plate and went to the door, put his ear to it. The door didn't have one of those little peepholes—not that he ever got the kind of visitors you needed to check out before opening it.

"Who's there?"

"Aggie. Open up. Now!"

The door hadn't been locked. But he locked it behind her when she burst in, panting. Just like the neighbor said, she had on a jean jacket— that looked a dozen sizes too large. The cowboy hat, also too big, fell off when she rushed at him and hugged him fiercely.

"Oh, Dear God. Oh, Dear God. Oh, Dear God," Aggie gushed. "Where the hell have you been? I've been by your apartment must have been ten times today."

"Among other things, I was at your house."

"Oh." She released her grip. "I just ... I just..." She hugged him again. "God, Zeke, I was scared and angry and not thinking straight and didn't know what to do or where to go. But I kept coming back here." She relaxed her grip again.

Zeke extricated himself. "You hungry?"

"Yeah. Starving."

"Sit." He went to the stove and brought over the other half of the pizza, leaving it on the cardboard to serve as a plate. He handed it to her and she sat on the couch. "Thirsty?"

"Yeah. Whatever you have. Soda. Or water's fine." Aggie started stuffing her face. "Anything. Starving, really."

Zeke looked in the fridge and popped open the pack of Dew that took up half the interior. He pulled out two cans, feeling that they weren't very cold. They'd do. He thought the water that came through his old pipes tasted a little funky. He needed to get one of those big water dispensers, like Culligan or something.

He handed her one of the Dews as he sat, keeping a respectable foot between them.

"I wish I would have been here earlier," he told her. Couldn't mention that he was at Sam's house for a chunk of the day, then had gone to a movie over in Owensboro, a double-feature, and had slept through the second one, something about a massive prehistoric shark.

"I was afraid to stay home."

"Went over to your place to pick you up. Like I said I would. Like we'd arranged. A date, you know." Zeke realized his voice had an edge to it, and also realized that Aggie didn't seem to care. She wolfed the pizza down. "What the hell were you afraid of at your house?"

"Sorry," she said, coming up for air and popping the tab on the Dew. She took a deep swallow. "There've been these deputies coming to the house. I was home, saw 'em out the window. Pretended I wasn't home in the morning. I don't know, I don't know, ya know. I'm going in the Coast Guard. I can't let anything screw that up. Thought maybe I was in trouble. Don't know what the hell I did to—"

"You didn't do anything wrong." Zeke opened his soda, took a sip, wished it was colder. He hadn't refilled his ice tray, so that wasn't an option. "The deputies—"

"Yeah, I avoided them. And when they disappeared I left the house, rode around on my scooter, went to the park, came back and saw another sheriff's car pulling in the driveway. Crap, eh? Like I need trouble. Should've called you, asked what the sheriff's department wanted with me, what I'd done wrong, who I'd pissed off. But I knew you weren't working this weekend, so you wouldn't know. Anyway, I kept riding, went back to the park. Then I saw them. Oh, Dear God. I saw *them*."

Zeke shivered when he saw Aggie's eyes—wide and not blinking.

Her hand shook and the soda wobbled, and he snatched it up and set it on the coffee table.

"Them? More sheriff's deputies? They only want your phone, Aggie. They want to see the pics you took at—"

"*Them.* The guys from behind Sam's store. Well, I think it was them. Same car. Dark gray car. The tall guy was wearing the same clothes from the picture I took." She breathed fast, hyperventilating. Zeke took the pizza cardboard and set it on the coffee table, tried to take her hands, but they were like little agitated birds, fingers fluttering.

"I was on a bench, in the park. The bluff park. The one where that boy was found buried last month. That park. On a bench. I saw the car, the gray one, pull into a spot, one of the angle ones. Didn't think anything about it at first. I was just sitting, thinking, about the Coast Guard, stuff. Thinking about you." She sucked in a deep breath and let it out in a *whoosh.* "And the tall guy got out of the car and walked toward me. Took me a minute to figure out he was familiar. Wasn't sure, so I pulled out my phone, pulled up the pictures from Sam's store, was pretty sure it was him. The car, the man. I had a real bad feeling, started to press 9-1-1, got as far as the 9-1 when he was on me. Oh, Dear God, Zeke. He grabbed my arm and took my phone, started pulling me toward his car."

"Aggie!"

"Broad daylight, Zekester. There were people in the park, and he was taking me. I screamed. There were some kids near the bluff, and they saw me. I screamed and screamed and the kids ran toward me and the guy let me go. He high-tailed it to the car, and then it took off. He's got my phone." She sagged against the back of the couch and closed her eyes. "I know I should've gone to the cops, the sheriff's. I know I should've. Well, I know that now. But I kept thinking about the sheriff's cars coming to my house. Didn't want trouble. Hell, Zeke, I didn't know what to do."

Zeke reached over and touched her shoulder. "I'll call the sheriff, she'll know what—"

"I don't want trouble. I don't want anything to screw with my getting in the Coast Guard."

Zeke gently squeezed her shoulder. "I don't think you heard me. You're not in trouble. The deputies were at your house to get your cell phone. I told them you'd got some pictures of the car, the guy behind Sam's. The sheriff wanted to see the pictures."

"Well, the sheriff could have called me, told me that. You could've told me that. What the hell was I supposed to think? Deputies showing up? All persistent? I figured I'd been speeding again or had some parking tickets I'd forgot to pay, played my music too loud with my folks gone. Disturbing my crappy neighbor's crappy peace or something. She yells at me when I'm out in the yard, tells me to keep my music down. I just didn't want trouble. I just didn't think." She leaned forward and picked up the soda, held it between her hands and then drank some more. "So after the park I got on my scooter and came by here ... several times. Finally I went home, grabbed my dad's jacket and hat—figured it was a little disguise in case that weird guy came after me, and I took off again. Just riding around. Just riding. On all the little side streets, just in case."

"You could've called me, Aggie."

"No phone. The dude took it. Weren't you listening to me? He stole my phone."

"Another phone somewhere. You could have called me."

"Don't have a landline at home. We ditched those for cells. And there's not a payphone to be seen anywhere in Rockport. I know. I looked." She eyed the pizza, pulled off a piece of pepperoni and put it in her mouth. "Finally finally finally you were home."

Zeke put his phone on the charger. He watched her finish the pizza and the soda. Her hands empty, her fingers were little birds again in constant motion. He went to the window and looked out, then he shuffled to the refrigerator.

"Another soda?"

"Yeah. Sure. Thanks," Aggie said. She held this one a while before she opened it.

Zeke cleaned up the empty cans and the pizza cardboard. He was still hungry and looked through the cabinet, finding a pack of Oreos he hadn't opened yet.

"Dessert?"

"Awesome," she said.

He put the cookies and a stack of napkins on the coffee table and looked at the charger. The phone probably had enough juice now for a call or two. He patted Aggie's knee, and then retrieved his cell.

"Who are you calling?" Aggie was still wide-eyed.

"My boss, but she's not answering." Zeke frowned. "The concert. She's at the concert, probably too loud to hear the phone." It went to voicemail, and Zeke left a brief message.

"Who you calling now?"

"Teegan. She'll know what to do. Teegan knows pretty much everything."

Zeke managed a few sentences before the phone went dead and he put it back on the charger.

CHAPTER NINETEEN

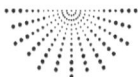

10 P.M.

Piper sent a BOLO—be on the lookout—to law enforcement agencies in nearby counties in Indiana and across the river in Kentucky, in hopes the gray Mazda with swiped New Jersey plates might be spotted and stopped. "Driver is a person of interest in an assault, attempted kidnapping, and theft case in Spencer County," she included. "Person is dangerous, could be armed, and is described as a middle-aged man, tall, wearing dark clothes. A more detailed description will follow." Then she requested a list of stolen late model gray Mazdas on the NCIC site—National Crime Information Center —attaching a report of the cell phone theft and attempted kidnapping. She hoped to hear something on both counts soon.

"Teegan, holler if anything comes in."

Piper returned to the break room, where she'd left Aggie and Zeke. She'd nearly called Basil to join them, but instead opted to videotape Aggie and record the conversation. Basil could talk to the girl when he came in tomorrow.

"So, yeah, I should've not hid from the deputies you sent over," Aggie repeated. "They just rattled me, you know. I'm going in the Coast Guard and I didn't want any trouble. I thought maybe ... well, I

161

dunno what I thought. I guess I wasn't thinking. Maybe I still have some parking tickets or something."

Piper settled in the chair across from her.

"Not thinking. Not thinking," Aggie went on. "If I'd talked to the deputies I'd still have my phone. Or you'd have my phone. The pock-marked thug wouldn't have it."

"Pock-marked." Piper made a note of that. Initially Aggie said she didn't get a look at the man's face. "So you remember a little more about the man."

Aggie shrugged and bobbed her head. "I guess. God, I wasn't thinking. I am so so so sorry I didn't come downstairs and talk to your deputies, give them my phone. I wasn't thinking."

Zeke opened his mouth to say something, but a glance from Piper shut him down. She told him he could sit in only because he'd seen the men and the car behind Sam's and because she needed his computer expertise. He sat behind a department laptop.

Piper had purchased FACES 3.0, a law enforcement software package she found on eBay for a mere hundred dollars. It was only one version out of date; the most recent being way beyond her budget. She hadn't used it yet, but Zeke had installed it on a few computers and had been practicing in his spare time. He'd taught Diego, and she was certain Basil was proficient. Piper put mastering it on her to-do list. But for the moment, she'd rely on Zeke.

"I guess I did get a little bit of a look," Aggie went on. "But just of the one guys. There were two. Guys. Probably the same two that were in the car behind Sam's shop. Hey, have you asked Sam if—"

Piper waved off the question. She was sure Sam's death would hit the news in the morning; despite her trying to keep it quiet there'd been chatter on police radios, and the coroner would conduct an autopsy in the morning and release her findings, which would be public. Maybe she'd tell Aggie, but she'd stew on that thought for a while.

"Let's go over again what happened in the park," Piper said. "Close your eyes and picture yourself there." It wasn't a technique she'd learned with the MPs at Fort Campbell, it was something she saw the

162

characters use on the television series *Criminal Minds*. Maybe the show's writers had gotten it from established police methods.

"Okay, I'm there," Aggie said, doing as she was told. "I'd parked my scooter on the west side, was walking around, picked a bench, I thought about that boy who was dug up in the park a month or so back. Made me shiver. Then I thought about the kids killed at the fair Friday night, how I'm only eighteen and I'm not guaranteed nineteen. No one's guaranteed anything."

"So you noticed the gray car."

"Yeah. At first I didn't think anything about it." She poked out her bottom lip and Piper was struck by how small the girl was and how young she looked. The Coast Guard could be good for her, but Piper knew that any branch of the service had a rigorous boot camp, and no concessions were granted for short people. "Really wasn't thinking today, was I?"

Piper didn't reply.

"I mean, there are other gray cars around, and silver ones. A lot of silver ones. So I didn't think anything about it. But then I saw the guys get out and I opened my phone, scrolling through the pics. I wanted to see if the license plate was the same, and if it was, then the guy we saw behind Sam's might be the same."

"The men—" Piper prompted.

"Yeah, well, I'd only seen the one Friday night, leaning in the car window. He had the same build as one of the guys coming toward me, same jacket, too, I think. Oh, and he had gloves on. I thought that was kinda odd, since it was warm out. I tried to get out of there, but the tall one was fast and grabbed my phone with one hand and my wrist with the other." She held out her wrist. "You can't tell it now, but it was red for a little while."

"Go on. The one who grabbed you."

"I looked up at him, I guess. I saw that his face was pock-marked. Like he'd had a bad case of acne and picked at it when he was a kid, little moon craters all over. Or maybe he'd had one of those skin diseases. I thought it made him look ugly. I know, judgmental, right? Not nice of me. But he wasn't nice." Aggie touched the sides of her

163

face. "Here and here he was pockmarked, and he had a little hair on his chin, like he hadn't shaved. Not like he was trying to grow a beard or anything, just like he hadn't shaved today."

"What color was—"

"They were both white, their skin. White men. The guy who grabbed me was a little darker, though. Ruddy, you know what I mean? Maybe he spent a lot of time out in the sun. Tanned, but a white man. And he had black eyes, or really dark brown ones. His eyebrows were sorta bushy and almost met in the middle."

"Describe the shape of his face."

Zeke was working feverishly on the laptop as Aggie chatted, but Piper couldn't tell from where she was sitting what he was coming up with.

"Long. A long face. It sort of fit him, being tall, you know. Long and thin, the cheeks were kinda sunken so the jaw looked sharper. His nose was long, too, and a little crooked at the end. It had a bump higher up like maybe he'd had to wear glasses when he was a kid and it put a knob there. He didn't have glasses on, though. The other guy did. His face was round and paler, like raw bread dough. So this guy, the tall one, his eyebrows were mostly black, but there were some grays in there. I figure he had to be forty, right, to have gray hair? You don't get gray hair before forty. I didn't get a look at the hair on his head, not really. He was wearing a hat with a little brim all the way around, but some stuck out. Black hair stuck out, kinda curly, maybe a little gray in it. The hat was dark plaid. I thought it was old and something you might get at a resale shop."

Piper smiled. The girl originally had said she didn't get a look at them, yet she was providing a good description now.

"Anything else you can remember?"

"The tall guy had shoulders that seemed too wide for his body. The other guy, the shorter one, was a little bit tubby. Not much tubby, and maybe not really tubby at all. Maybe he was normal but looked tubby because the other one was so thin. And though he was shorter, he wasn't a whole lot shorter, not a Bert and Ernie thing going on."

"I understand. Any scars on either of them? Tattoos? Earrings?"

Aggie scrunched her face. "The short guy had gold ball earrings. Geeze, Sheriff Blackwell, I guess I got a better look at them than I'd realized. The tall guy, the thin one, he didn't have earrings, but he had a tattoo on the right side of his neck. Don't know what it was, just some blue and red design through a whitish blob. No, a whitish lightning bolt through a blue and red blob. There were black eyes in the tat."

Zeke typed furiously. "Wait a minute," he said. "Wait, wait, wait."

Piper scowled, having told him not to speak during the interview.

"Like this?" Zeke keyed something on the laptop, switching out the screen from the FACES 3.0 program. "Was the tattoo like this?"

"Holy crap!" Aggie said when she opened her eyes. "Yeah, that's the tattoo. How'd you know, Zekester? You said you didn't see him."

"I didn't. I just like old music."

Piper liked old music, too, having acquired a taste for it in the Army. One of the guys in her unit played the moldy oldies all the time, usually Chicago, sometimes the Grateful Dead. The image on the laptop screen was the Dead logo, a stylized skull with a red and blue circle on the cranium bisected by a white lightning bolt.

"That's the tattoo," Aggie repeated.

Zeke swiveled the laptop back and kept at it. "Almost there," he told Piper. Give me a few more minutes and I'll have a couple of composites to show you." He looked up. "This program, this is more fun than the MUD I play."

Piper raised an eyebrow.

"Multi-User Dungeon."

Piper tapped the table. "Want something to drink, Aggie?"

"Any kind of soda would be awesome," she said. "Regular, diet, cola, not-cola. Anything cold. I'm thirsty. Something with caffeine if you can."

Piper noticed that Aggie was more relaxed now, having finally realized she wasn't in trouble for anything and that she was safe inside the sheriff's department.

"Zeke?"

"Yeah, I'll take anything, too. Thanks, Sheriff Blackwell."

Nothing yet on the BOLO, Piper returned with a six pack of Dr. Pepper she'd put in her mini-fridge. "Help yourself." She set the sodas in the center of the table, then walked around to stand behind Zeke.

It was breakthrough software, she knew; used by the military, police agencies, even the FBI. It had been around more than a dozen years, but it was new to her department. Spencer County didn't even have access to a sketch artist. She was determined to drag her office into modern times. Body cameras were coming in at the end of the week. She had a Belgian Malinois undergoing training. And a drone was on order. The latter three additions were curtesy of money gifted from the same man who had bequeathed her the beautiful ranch house and vehicles.

"Four thousand facial features to pick from," Zeke said of the program. "It's a matter of matching some of them to Aggie's description. It lets you add moles, scars, tattoos. I'm using pimples instead of pock-marks. I haven't found pock-marks. Maybe you should get the 4.0 version."

At least we have a version, Piper thought.

"Real easy to use," Zeke said, pausing to grab one of the sodas. He popped the top and drank greedily for a moment. "Maybe not quite as good as a real sketch artist, but hey, wait. Hats. Look at all the hats."

"A little brim," Aggie said. "All the way around. Dark plaid." She'd wrapped her hands around the soda can and brought it to her face, running the cool aluminum over her cheeks and forehead.

"Wow. I can make the hat plaid," Zeke said. "I could add feathers if I wanted."

"We can search databases against this." Piper pointed to the image on his screen. "Turn it around. Let Aggie see it."

"Oh, God," she said, nearly losing the soda. "That is so him. Well, really close to so him. Even the tattoo, but that was more on the side of the neck, the tat."

Zeke adjusted the image.

"Yeah, that's better. Make the nose a little bigger on the end. No, that's too much. He's not Rudolf. Better. Yeah, that's better." Aggie shivered and tucked in on herself like a turtle withdrawing into its shell.

"Send that to the printer," Piper said. "And email it to me, j-peg and PDF."

"Done," Zeke said. He tipped the soda back and finished it. "Let me work on the other guy."

"I didn't see him as well," Aggie said. "He's not the one who grabbed me."

Piper studied her. Aggie was the same age as Zeke, graduated in the same class. They were both geeks and gamers. But Aggie wasn't as mature, definitely not as sure of herself. The Coast Guard could be good for her, Piper thought again. Or it could crush her. She retreated to her office to resend the BOLO accompanied by the computer-generated image of the man in the plaid fedora. She added the image to the NCIC report, and then set up a search to see if any mugshots in the NCIC database matched.

When she returned to the break room, Zeke had another image ready that Aggie pronounced: "As close as it's gonna get. Really, I didn't pay much attention to him." Piper repeated the process with this face.

"Now we wait," she told Aggie.

"I'm not going home," Aggie said. "My folks are gone, and I—" She rested her chin against her chest and her words came muffled. "They got my phone, so they know where I live. Heck, they know where Zeke lives, probably, or can figure it out from my phone. Zeke saw them behind Sam's. And what about Sam? Someone should tell—"

Piper gestured with her head and Zeke got the message. He picked up the laptop and left the room, closing the door behind him.

"About Samuel Silver," Piper began. And Lucky Ducky, she thought. "Aggie, Mr. Silver is dead."

Aggie wailed like a squeezed cat.

167

CHAPTER TWENTY

7 A.M. MONDAY, JUNE 17TH

Basil talked to Aggie in his office. Piper hoped he was gaining even more details. She looked in on them, waved, and then ventured to the break room for Italian Dark Roast coffee.

Zeke and Aggie had stayed with Piper last night, and she fixed them breakfast before bringing them back in. Zeke was at the desk, taking his dispatcher shift and closely monitoring radio chatter.

Piper settled in her office, opened her laptop, and frowned that nothing substantial had come in from the BOLOs she'd sent out or from the NCIC query. There'd been a few reports from Rockport and Santa Claus police departments about sightings of the gray car, but the driver was crafty and lost them.

So they were still in the county. Somewhere.

And that meant that whatever the men had looked for at Samuel Silver's was still eluding them.

She'd had a deputy cruising between Zeke's and Aggie's residences, and zilch had turned up on the Mazda. The two men Aggie described had to be involved in the Samuel Silver case, maybe were his killers. Probably his killers, she thought, that notion cemented because they'd stolen Aggie's phone and had tried to grab her. Piper pictured Lucky

Ducky dead in the trunk of the Bronco. Would the men have killed Aggie?

No witnesses.

Where was Benzo—Lloyd Ebersole?

"Who are you?" She asked, tapping the printouts of the men's faces. "Just who the hell are you? And where are you? And did you kill Sam *and* Lucky Ducky? What are you looking for?"

There was a message from a Virginia State Police officer, confirming she would be arriving late tomorrow to take custody of Vernon T. Milgrew, who continued to moan, "I'm not gonna burn for this."

Nothing yet from Dr. Neufeld, the coroner. But Piper didn't expect an autopsy report on Samuel Silver until deep in the afternoon.

A report on the Cosmic Odyssey wasn't likely to come in before tomorrow from the Indiana Department of Homeland Security. She hoped to get that report before the State Police officer showed up for Vernon.

The banks and courthouse—those were at the forefront of her mind. It was two hours before they could delve into Samuel Silver's records at either place. Piper was anxious, though her father had ingrained in her not to wish for time to speed up, as it goes by too quickly on its own.

She Googled "ice pick deaths," finding a link to: BIBLE DIES BY LETHAL INJECTION. She clicked on the story. Danny Paul Bible, sixty-six, known as the "ice pick killer" was executed in the summer of 2018. He had been convicted of a series of rapes and murders throughout Texas.

Another article referenced Russian Marxist revolutionary Leon Trotsky, who was killed with an ice pick in 1940 in Mexico.

An article dated 2012 from the New York Times detailed that ice picks were still being used as weapons, even though they were no longer common household tools. It harkened back to the 1930s and 40s when a Brooklyn syndicate called Murder Incorporated used the picks in a string of slayings.

A man in Utah was arrested in December 2018 for hammering an ice pick through his roommate's genitals.

Piper turned off the computer, finished her coffee, and stood when Oren walked in her office.

"Zeke caught me up," Oren said, easing into one of the chairs across from her desk. "You could have called me in last night."

"Could have," Piper said. "But I needed somebody alert this morning." She knew she looked ragged, the circles prominent under her eyes, and the little makeup she'd put on hadn't wholly camouflaged it. Her run this morning had been brief.

"A lot of things to deal with," Oren said. "Awful things."

But his eyes shone, and Piper realized that while Samuel Silver's death was horrifying, as was the disaster from the fair, they were interesting and sadly exciting cases. There was an energy to the "awful things" that animated her, and clearly Oren too.

Basil joined them several minutes later to announce nothing more from Aggie. An hour melted as they discussed the Silver murder and the mystery men in the gray Mazda.

So much to do, Piper thought, and she wanted to be in on all of it —searching bank accounts and safe deposit boxes, delving into records at the courthouse, going back to the comic shop for another look around, and visiting the ride survivor in the Owensboro hospital. Zeke had announced to her that while the teen was still in ICU, he was now conscious.

"Dinner was good last night," Basil said. "Wife's happy."

"Concert was good," Oren added. "Wife's happy she didn't have to go. Hates country music."

"I agree with her," Basil said. "I missed the Chicago Blues Festival this year. It'll be next summer's vacation."

Piper couldn't be in on all aspects of the investigation, too many things had to be addressed at the same time. She had to delegate if she wanted matters covered quickly. They'd share their findings.

"Diego's in Africa this morning." She interrupted their banter. "He's trying to catch the neighbors we missed the other day. Then he's stopping in to visit the Buddhists in Fulda, and their nemesis."

"You're not going to satisfy Chris Hagee unless you go out there yourself," Oren said. "Chris needs to chill. Stop drinking. Find a hobby that doesn't include bitching about his Buddhist neighbors. About any of his neighbors. Even if you did shut down the Buddhists, he'd find something wrong with whoever moved in next. The previous owner wasn't Buddhist, and Chris objected to his Christmas display. At least the Buddhists won't put up Christmas lights to vex Chris."

Piper smiled at that. "Too bad," she said softly. "They ought to set that big sleigh in the front yard and put a spotlight on it to shine in the Hagee's bedroom window. They could find a Buddha statue to set in it. That'd give Chris a double whammy."

She took a deep breath and turned the printouts of the two mystery men around. "Nothing on these men yet."

"Sometimes it takes a while," Basil said.

She so wanted to be in on all of it. Piper tossed a keyring for Silver's comic shop to Oren.

"Head to Evansville and see what Dr. Neufeld comes up with on the Silver autopsy. We shouldn't wait for her to send us the report. Then swing back through Owensboro, take another pass through the comic shop, talk to the business neighbors, check with Owensboro police and see if they've located Benzo—Lloyd Ebersole." Piper thought it would give her Chief Deputy an opportunity to visit his dad in the nursing home. "After lunch run by the hospital and talk to the ride survivor. I know that's a lot—"

"He awake, the kid?" Oren leaned forward.

She nodded.

"I'm on it. I'm out of here." Oren stretched for the keys to Silver Age Sam's. "I better move. Annie sometimes starts her autopsies early."

"Basil, you've got the courthouse. I'll take the bank. We'll meet back here and put the pieces together. Stay in touch with cell phones. I'd still like this off the radio for a while."

"Getting records on Silver will be fast work. I can catch you at the bank afterwards, walk back here." Basil pointed to the printouts of the

171

two men. "I've some friends in Chicago. I'm going to email these pics to them."

Piper tipped her head in curiosity.

"Chicago's got an extensive facial recognition program, maybe the best in the nation, a perpetual virtual lineup, really." Basil stood. "About half of the residents in this country—legals and illegals—have their mugs in law enforcement facial-recognition databases. A couple of the techs at CPD have mastered linking cities' databases, spelunking they call it. Big controversy about it a couple of years ago when the *Trib* did a story. San Francisco, Oakland, someplace in Connecticut, have bans on the government using facial recognition software, calls it intrusive. Illinois and Indiana aren't to that point yet, thankfully for us. CPD and other departments scan photos and track people who have no criminal records. Some folks don't like the meddling, but it's out there, the tech and the photos, surveillance cameras everywhere, social media, no real safeguards involved. Privacy isn't so private anymore."

Piper whistled softly. "Intrusive and yet a gold mine."

"Anyway, I'll see if they can help with an ID, I'll call in a favor." He paused. "Because I think one or both of these men killed Samuel Silver."

"And Lucky Ducky," Piper added.

"Naming them will help us find them."

"Spencer County's not big. We're going to find these men, Basil, and find out why they ice picked a comic shop owner to death."

The county population was about twenty-one thousand, but the land covered more than four hundred square miles. There were a lot of places for the men to hide—if they knew law enforcement was looking for them. But they were still here as of yesterday, grabbing Aggie's phone and trying to grab her.

"Samuel Silver's killers didn't get what they were looking for," Piper said. "At least, I don't think they did."

"Yeah," Basil agreed. "Otherwise they'd be gone. They're still here."

"Somewhere," she said. "We'll find them."

CHAPTER TWENTY-ONE

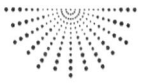

9 A.M.

Piper sat with the bank manager, Reginald Schwartz, a pale man in his late-thirties who wore a suit she thought intended for an earlier era—dark brown tweed, the shirt stark white, and the bowtie of forest green with tiny yellow dots. He had a shock of curly blond hair and silver wire-rim glasses perched toward the end of his nose. She noted no wedding ring. If Reginald had been married his wife might have helped him pick more modern attire.

"I don't recall ever seeing him in the bank," Reginald said.

She studied him while he read the search warrant twice and then stared at a photograph of Samuel Silver.

"No. I don't believe I've ever seen this man, Sheriff Blackwell."

Piper had pulled the picture from Zeke's phone and printed it out. The dispatcher had found one he'd taken from a Loot the Castle night a year ago.

"I mean, he must have been here, right? He has two accounts and a safe deposit box. He would have had to come in to set them up. A safe deposit box isn't something you can do online. One of his accounts goes back twenty years, and the other ... looks like a month short of twelve, and I had just started around then, twelve and a half years for me. So he's been here, when I've been here. I've just never seen him.

173

Not that I recall. But I probably couldn't recognize all of our investors anyway. I'll ask Jill."

He waved a hand and motioned to someone. "She's been here the longest, from teller to senior loan officer. She might have known him." Reginald sat back and pushed the search warrant toward Piper. "So how did he die? It wasn't of natural causes, was it? Otherwise you wouldn't be here with these warrants so soon after his passing. You said he died Friday or Saturday, right? Was he on that ride at the fair?"

"I don't have the coroner's report yet." Piper didn't want to discuss the murder. She was just hopeful someone at the bank actually knew Samuel Silver and could provide more insight into the man.

A brief chat with Jill yielded nothing significant, though she admitted Silver had been at the bank before and that she'd dealt with him on several occasions. Their conversations had been brief; he always seemed in a hurry. Jill added that he'd conducted the bulk of his banking online.

Piper glanced at the readouts the bank provided. The twenty-year-old account was a personal one, with a balance of a little more than a quarter-million dollars. The other was a business account for the comic book shop, with assets about half of that. She noted that shop expenses and salaries were about equal to income, like it was a break-even operation. But he had to be pulling a reasonable profit from something. The business account's set up coincided with his opening the comic shop. Maybe he had other investments, stocks and bonds.

"If Mr. Silver had a money market or other investments, it wasn't with us," Reginald said. "With that much in a savings account, though, he should've had a money market. The interest is a little better. Not really any interest to speak of these days with a regular account. Better than sticking it under your mattress, though."

On the personal account readout she noticed multiple transactions back and forth from PayPal, an online banking entity frequently used by people who bought and sold on the internet.

"How do I find out what's in that PayPal account?" Piper honestly didn't know. How do you serve a search warrant on something like the internet? There was a way to do it, she was certain, but it had never been part of her police training in the Army. She could ask Oren, but doubted he would know. Zeke might be the better option. Or Reginald. Hopefully the banker could help. That PayPal account was probably also tied to Silver's personal email address, and maybe she could gain a way into his messages that way.

"I have to admit I've never needed to dig into something like this. And maybe it's not important," Piper admitted. "But I need a full financial picture as part of my investigation."

"Because Mr. Silver was killed, right?" Reginald asked. "You wouldn't be asking about all of this otherwise. Not if he'd just up and died in his sleep."

"I don't have the coroner's report yet," Piper repeated.

"His account from this bank is linked to his PayPal account, that's why you see the withdrawals here to PayPal, and the deposits. But I can't give you access to those actual PayPal records because *I* don't have access." Reginald gave her a perturbed look. "It's not all that hard, really, to get copies of those things. I found out how to do it as part of a three-day banking seminar I attended in Indianapolis in the fall. You have to make your request over the internet. There's something called PayPal Holdings, and there's a web form that bank officials, government agencies, and law enforcement can fill out to gain access. There's some authentication process you have to pass, and it can take a few weeks. There's a little more to it than that, but that's what I remember from the seminar. Wait ... you have to use an official letterhead of your department." He paused. "Your department does have a letterhead, right? And it must be signed by you and some court officer, like a search warrant I'd imagine."

"A few weeks." Indeed. She'd include a search warrant to be safe. The Spencer County Prosecutor—DA Scales as he was known—would help get the warrant, and she'd stop by his office in a little while. In fact, he probably knew all about getting these kinds of records and might point her to some other online financial entities to check. She needed to talk to Scales anyway, bring him up to date on the Samuel Silver case. It was common practice for the sheriff's department and the county prosecutor to work together; it was how the system was set up. She didn't always agree with Scales, but she considered him on the same team. She probably should have called him as soon as she'd seen Silver's body. But Piper was still learning all the proverbial ropes of this job, hadn't even hit the six-month mark yet.

"Two weeks at the earliest, I'd think." Reginald gave a tight smile as he interrupted her thoughts. "Maybe you can hurry it up if you explain it is urgent and a murder is involved. It is a murder, isn't it?"

"The safe deposit box?" Piper wanted to be on her way so she could check other banks in town, go after more search warrants if needed, and then go back to the office to follow through on that PayPal records request. She remembered Silver had sold on eBay, likely why he had a PayPal account. She probably wouldn't need a formal request or warrant for his eBay records. Zeke could help—just find his seller's account and look at past sales; that was all public information. See what he was buying and selling, how much money was involved. Maybe he used other online auction sites. Did he buy and sell guns via the internet? Again, she pictured the weapons she and Basil had found. It was going to be a while before ballistics tests were finished and they learned if any of Silver's guns had been used in a reported crime.

"The safe deposit box. Sure thing." Reginald glanced one more time at the search warrant. "This way, please. It's one of our largest boxes. And if you take anything—"

"I will provide a form that shows what, if anything, I'm taking."

It was a large box, but not particularly heavy. She placed it on the table in the vault room, opened the lid, and took out her cell phone so she could get pictures of the contents as she removed them. There was the deed to his house on top, purchased twenty years ago for forty-one thousand dollars, along with a copy of the real estate listing. The house had been white then, the yard scabrous, no garage. He'd made considerable improvements, and she suspected the value of it had at least tripled. She found bills of sale for the monkeys, exotic cats, and African Grey parrots. The Department of Fish and Wildlife might be interested in some of these, she decided. A copy of *Amazing Fantasy*

#15, the first appearance of Spiderman, came next. It was signed on the front in thick marker: Stan Lee. Piper didn't know much about comics, but she recognized that this was a serious treasure.

Next came a birth certificate.

THIS CERTIFIES THAT
SAMUEL JEROME SILVER
WEIGHT: 8 LBS. 8 OZ. WAS BORN
ON THE FOURTH DAY OF OCTOBER
TO EMILY AND OSWALD SILVER
IN THE YEAR OF 1967
SEX: MALE
PLACE OF BIRTH: BELL COUNTY, TEXAS

Helpful. She'd start her search for relatives in Texas.

There was a six-page will, notarized a dozen years ago by a teller at this bank. She took a picture of each page. It designated everything going to Big Brothers & Big Sisters of New York City. The executor was Daniel McGuire, an attorney from a law office in the Bronx. Piper took a close-up of that and would call McGuire later today. Perhaps McGuire knew if Silver had other assets. Might be important, the root of the murder. The key could be Silver's money.

It was always money, right? Her dad used to say that when he was sheriff. So did Basil.

"Or am I just grasping at the notion?" Piper blew out a breath, fluttering her bangs. "No motive. No clues. No—"

At the bottom of the box sat two thin photo albums, roughly six by eight inches, one a little thicker. She held her breath and opened the cover of the first one to a black-and-white with yellowed edges of a young couple holding a baby between them. "Doyle at three weeks," the caption read. The next few pages showed more of baby Doyle, the mother in frayed jeans, the father in bell bottoms, hippie attire, Piper thought. In the background of one was a sleek looking car, a Volkswagen by the logo, but none she was familiar with. A quick Google brought up a Volkswagen K70, a four-door sedan marketed from

1970-75. So at least some of the black-and-white photos dated1970 or later. Whoever took the pictures or images maybe preferred working in monochrome. They were well-composed, looked professional. The car, the clothes, Piper guessed these were all taken in the early seventies.

A few pages later color photos started, though not as artistic. The first was of the same couple with a boy standing in front of them, all of them dressed up. "Margo, Walter, and Doyle at St. Ignatius of Antioch Episcopal Church."

Another Google delve yielded that St. Ignatius of Antioch, built in 1903, was a historic church in the Upper West Side neighborhood of Manhattan. A second picture on the church steps showed Margo holding Doyle's hand, and the caption: "First Communion." Piper figured that made Doyle seven. Who were these people to Samuel Silver?

Piper lost herself in the photos, some of which had been taken by an instant Polaroid, the captions written on the thick white strip at the bottom. Most of them were of Margo and Doyle, and by the second photo album the boy had grown to be a teenager. He was shown in baseball uniforms, theatrical costumes, and at St. Ignatius— in three-piece suits.

In a photo that seemed out of place in the timeline he was smaller and in altar boy robes. The final picture in the book was a high school picture, and Doyle had some resemblance to Silver, the face thinner, the hair longer and curly.

Piper stared at it. The eyes were the same, the jaw.

Were Doyle and Sam brothers?

She'd brought evidence bags and put the photo albums inside. She didn't need the will or birth certificate, she'd taken pictures of them, and they'd be secure in the safe deposit box, along with the special comic book. But she wanted to show Oren and Basil the photos, pieces of the puzzle that she hoped to assemble.

CHAPTER TWENTY-TWO

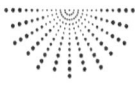

9 A.M.

Basil had never been in such a small courthouse. Quaint, he thought. Like a set from one of those Hallmark romance movies his wife frequently coerced him to watch, a building where the tiny-town characters get married in front of the justice of the peace. Cue the woodwind ensemble.

This should be easy and fast, the courthouse, the county so small. He'd go through the records then catch up with Sheriff Blackwell while she was still at the bank.

But it took only a handful of minutes to learn it was neither going to be easy nor fast, as not everything Basil wanted to look through was on the computer.

Too quaint.

Too rural.

Frustrating.

And yet the Silver case was curious and interesting and worth spending as much time as necessary.

Basil was going to be here a while, if he intended to be thorough about it—and he most certainly would. He texted Piper to tell her his record search would run longer than he had expected and that they should meet for lunch to share their finds.

179

Court records could reveal family relationships, property, and occupation history. He searched through various categories looking for Samuel Silver: divorce, adoption, licenses, taxes, property disputes, debt, naturalization, civil and criminal lawsuits, public office appointments, and probate. He didn't consider the files well-indexed—at least not what he was used to—and he cross-referenced records because he noted some of the jurisdictions changed. Basil considered himself fortunate that he didn't need a law dictionary to interpret the files.

He found a copy of Silver's birth certificate. He'd ask Zeke if Sam had talked with a drawl, could point to how long he'd lived in Texas. The Cook County Clerk's office in Chicago kept copies of birth certificates of everyone born in the county. Why would this office have a copy of Silver's? He wasn't even born in Indiana. Odd that a birth certificate copy would be on file here, and when he questioned a clerk, she just shrugged. Maybe Silver had needed it to prove he was a U.S. citizen for some court-related matter, she said when he persisted.

An hour's search through court files revealed that thirteen years ago a drunk operating a piece of farm equipment ran Silver off the road and totaled a new Buick LaCrosse he'd been driving. Silver had brought a civil suit seeking damages to replace the car—and won. Maybe the court had required the birth certificate.

Basil dug deeper into the traffic case, deciding he'd go to the DMV later to see if they had more information on the incident and anything else relating to Silver.

Two hours later and he uncovered other property listings. In addition to the house in Africa, Silver owned eighty acres of farmland in Carter Township. The township, Basil Googled, was thirty-six square miles, and Silver's stretch was near the unincorporated burg of Mariah Hill. Santa Claus, where Basil and Oren lived, was also in Carter Township. Basil figured he'd probably driven by Silver's land before. He'd make a point of doing it today. He made note of the neighbors.

He asked the clerk about Mariah Hill and she passed him an overlarge book filled with plat maps. Basil found Silver's property, the map showing tract orientation, property lines, and easements.

"German," the clerk told him as he looked. "Was originally called Maria Hilf, laid out in 1860."

"Hilf?"

"A nod to *Maria Hilfe der Christen*, which meant Mary Help of Christians. When they put up a post office in 1862 they anglicized the name. Postal service did that. The Hill produced some athletes. Did you know that?"

"I did not," Basil said.

"Ken Dilger, pro bowl tight end who played with the Indianapolis Colts and the Tampa Bay Buccaneers. King, too. Bruce King, a running back for the Kansas City Chiefs and the Buffalo Bills. You live in Santa Claus, right, detective?"

Basil was only mildly surprised she would know where he lived. Small place like this, and him a recent hire, the records of his home purchase would have come through here.

"Yes, I live in Santa Claus."

"So does Oren Rosenberg. Oren's been with the sheriff's a long time. Oren's come in to go through records before. Surprised he didn't come in this time."

Basil didn't say anything.

"Anyway, Santa Claus is where Jay Cutler was born. He played quarterback for the Broncos, the Chicago Bears, and one season with the Dolphins. He shouldn't have played for the Dolphins, he had a lousy year. And I should have known better. I drafted him in my fantasy football league, came in almost last place."

"I don't really follow football. I like basketball and baseball."

"Hmm. Too bad. You finished with this plat book?"

"Not yet." Basil wondered if the clerk was a member of the county genealogical society, or The Old Fart's Club as Sheriff Blackwell called it. The clerk was likely in her sixties and was well-versed in trivia about Mariah Hill.

Silver had another chunk of land in Huff Township, and he turned to that map. The fifty-two acre section was near the unincorporated town of Maxville, down from 64 in the north part of Spencer County. Probably farmland, maybe rented to someone who owned property adjacent. He jotted down the names of nearby landowners.

The final piece of property was in Luce Township.

"Luce Township," he said.

"You're pronouncing it wrong. It's not loo-chey, it's loose."

"Thanks. Luce Township." Basil found the plat map.

"Big township," she said. "Twenty-five hundred souls. Named for a pioneer who settled in 1820, David Luce. A young township. Median age of the folks who live there is thirty-five. My little sister Lucille lives in Hatfield. She just had a birthday. She's fifty-nine."

Basil knew that Sheriff Blackwell lived in Hatfield, too, and so she'd probably driven by Silver's forty-eight acres there. It probably wasn't far from her house.

"That's at the edge of Richland City," he said. "Right? Just past Hatfield? Just before Richland City?"

"In between, yeah." The clerk rubbed her temple. "Richland. Set down in ... in ... ah, 1861. Named for its fertile soil. City has a population of more than four hundred, if I remember the last census. A little more than a decade back, they all voted to incorporate. Silly for them to do, I think. They don't have their own police, have to rely on the sheriff. Maybe four-fifty. Yeah, I think four hundred and fifty. Has a library, and a post office that's been in operation for more than a hundred and fifty years." She smiled. "I'm the vice president of the genealogy club."

"Do you know Samuel Silver?"

She shook her head. "Not personally, but I've seen his name a few times, and two nice gentlemen were in here Thursday asking about him, wanted to see where his house was. I helped them find it. In Africa ... what's left of Africa, anyway. Only a dozen houses out on that road. That place was named in long ago years, Detective Meredith. Before people knew better. Prejudice was pretty thick back then. The two men asking about Silver? They said it fit that he lived in Africa, said they should've known that. They said they were old friends trying to get back in touch, had lost his phone number. I should've pointed out to them that Silver owned three more pieces of land, huh? But they just wanted to know where his house was. Guess none of that matters now, Mr. Silver being dead."

"Those men." Basil pulled out his phone and showed the artist renderings he'd scanned in.

"Yeah, that's them. Didn't think to ask their names. Figured it wasn't my business. They were polite, though. Didn't like the tall fellow's tattoo."

"Wonder how much this land is worth." Basil was talking to himself, but the clerk answered.

"Well, it's all farmland, don't know how good it is. But even average farmland goes for five thousand an acre, more depending on the quality, maybe up to seven or eight thousand. So that's a good bit of value there. He bought the land, according to the records, almost twenty years ago. Wouldn't have been as expensive, probably around fifteen hundred an acre then."

Basil did the math in his head. The land was likely worth between $800,000 and $960,000. So Silver had been a soul who invested in real estate in different areas of the county. Why spread out? Why not get the land in all one location? Maybe these pieces were all that was available when he was shopping. Did he also own land in other Indiana counties? Maybe over in Owensboro, too, Daviess County, Kentucky across the river. And Texas, where he grew up, maybe he owned some real estate there. He got the names of the people Silver bought the land and his Africa house from … not likely he'd need the information, but better to get a complete picture. In any event, it showed that Silver's investments had increased dramatically in value in the past two decades.

"I'm done with the book now." Basil's phone chirped: the favor he called in had turned up something. He walked out to the hall and perched on an uncomfortable wooden bench.

"Talk to me, Tug." It was good to hear a former partner's voice. "Yeah, I've settled down here just fine. Weather's good. I got a big backyard. Seriously big backyard. Wife and kids like it. Thinking about putting in a goldfish pond. You'll have to come visit." He meant the invitation, but he knew Tug wouldn't take him up on it because he wouldn't leave the city.

"But do you like it, Sherlock?" Tug asked.

Basil hadn't been called Sherlock since leaving Chicago. He missed Chicago, the bigness of it, the excitement, the endless entertainment options, the professional sports teams—particularly the Chicago Bulls-- the museums. His superiors were older than him, not like in Spencer County where his boss was several years younger and with less experience. He'd hoped to get the Santa Claus police chief job, which he'd interviewed for the same day as he did for the Spencer County Sheriff's detective role. He'd have been in charge. He probably would have liked that better.

"Do I like it?" He liked some of it: the large backyard, the house—which in Chicago would have cost a hell of a lot more, the neighborhood. He liked that it was a safer place to raise his kids and that his wife said it was more conducive to her writing. He liked that the gun violence—save Lucky Ducky getting plugged and stuffed in a car trunk—was non-existent. He liked the sheriff, despite her young age, and the chief deputy, though he often came across as a crusty old curmudgeon. Basil had thought he could adjust quickly, and hearing Tug's voice he wondered if he ever wholly would. Chicago's population was two-point-seven million, and Santa Claus, where his house and big backyard were, had twenty four hundred. No movie theaters. No real selection of grocery stores. No diversity.

"The air smells good," he told Tug. "Real good. Got nice neighbors. Some folks don't lock their doors."

"But do you *like* it?" Tug persisted. "You can't be making much, small as that place is. Sheriff's department over CPD? You like that, Sherlock?"

"It's an adjustment," Basil admitted.

"Got to be an adjustment for them two perps, too," Tug went on. "Those two mugs you sent me, found 'em in the system. Took a little bit. The one with the scar on his chin—"

Basil pulled out his phone and called up the two pictures he'd scanned in, focusing on the one that Aggie had said was taller and had grabbed her. The scar was faint and ran from the center of the chin to halfway along the right jawline.

"The one with the scar and the Grateful Dead tat is Ethan 'Bloodshot' Caine, forty-nine, Newark, New Jersey. The other one's Ashe Williams, fifty, aka The Barbarian, so-called because he beat a homeless man to death in the Bronx a dozen years ago. Record says the homeless man was begging, and The Barbarian didn't appreciate the guy's tenacity. Williams is also from Newark, but both of their records stem from crimes in New York City, mostly the Bronx. Looks like low-level mobsters with ties to the dying mafia. A couple of toughs, basically, reputed gangsters, a mix of minor and more egregious things on their rap sheets ... both doing time on and off. Bloodshot spent about two decades locked up, spread out over his ne'er do well life."

"Interesting," Basil noted. "Such as?"

"The Barbarian should've got longer than eight years on the homeless murder, but probably had a good attorney. He was out in four-and-a-half. Previously served seven months for criminal possession of a weapon, and there's long list of some petty stuff. He and Bloodshot share arrests for street fighting, public intoxication, bookmaking, stealing cars. The Barbarian boosted a Maserati on Long Island right after high school graduation. Want the full files, or just some links?"

"The full files. Email them to me."

"Sure, man. I'll put them together and get them right out. So they're in your bitty city, huh?"

"Spencer County," Basil corrected. "We think they're here in the county."

"So what do you think they did?"

"Murder," Basil replied. He'd give his old friend that for the rapid return on information. "We think they killed a man here, don't have a motive yet. Think they also tried to abduct someone." He paused. He would read the files in full soon, but there was something he wanted an answer on immediately. "These rap sheets ... did you come across anything about an ice pick?"

"Yeah. That popped out at me when I was skimming. Bloodshot

did five at Rykers for aggravated assault of a dry cleaner owner. Nearly ice-picked her to death in '95 in Bedford Park. Should've got at least a dime for it, should've been attempted murder." He paused. "Ice pick, eh? So you've an ice pick murder in the bitty city? These two perps of yours are dangerous, Sherlock. And they wouldn't be so far from home unless they're working for someone."

"Yeah, I'm thinking that."

"You got a gang problem in Hootersville?"

Basil laughed. "Don't know yet, Tug. I'll catch you up on it when we get it figured out. Thanks for the help, man. Really, thanks."

"Sure. Sure, Sherlock. Enjoy that clean air, and come back up for a visit, hear me?"

"The Blues Festival," Basil said. "I'm not going to miss the next one."

"Don't wait that long."

New Jersey gangsters. New Jersey plate on the gray car. The two men were serious felons with ties to the east coast. Whatever they'd wanted from Samuel Silver was likely—somehow—tied to the east coast, too. And that they'd killed Duckworth and tried to abduct a teenager who'd taken pictures of them proved they didn't want witnesses.

What the hell was this about?

And how did those two felons tie in to a comic book store owner who'd lived the past twenty years in Africa and had been born in Texas? The BOLO would have to get updated ASAP.

"This is weird shit," Basil muttered. "Esme ought to write a book about this."

After he solved it.

CHAPTER TWENTY-THREE

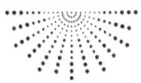

9 A.M.

"I started early," Annie said.

The coroner wore a pair of hospital scrubs, the green pants cropped to show her ankles, the top a wild paisley print of blue, red, and orange that Oren hadn't seen her wear before. Maybe the top was new, but he thought it garish, thought she should go back to the solid colored ones. He supposed the paisley helped hide blood spots.

She'd tucked her hair under something like a shower cap that matched the pants. Sans makeup, the dark circles under her eyes were conspicuous. To him, Annie always looked tired. She had little gold hoop earrings set with a few red stones—maybe rubies. Annie liked the real stuff.

"Figured you would," Oren said. "You usually start early." And here he'd driven fast from the sheriff's department to get in at the beginning of the autopsy.

"Should've let me know you were coming, Oren, and I would've waited. Maybe I would have."

"I doubt that." Oren was glad for this task, considering it more interesting than delving through the courthouse and bank records of the man on the slab. Besides, he and Annie were best friends,

187

stretching back to grade school. He always enjoyed spending time with her, even if in the presence of a corpse.

"So how far are you?" He saw that Silver had been cut down the middle.

Annie had a mask on, but he could tell she was smiling by the deepening creases around her eyes.

"Not terribly far," she returned. "I started early, but not *that* early, only about twenty minutes ago, I'd guess. Going to be a busy day, Oren. I'm taking young Mr. Duckworth next. Then I'm finishing my day with the cotton candy man, Mario Karalis. His son flew out, wants to take the body back tomorrow. I almost took Karalis first to accommodate the son, but knew you'd want the Silver results." She shook her head. "I've got the kids from the ride tomorrow, and I'm getting help with them. Way too young to die."

The Silver autopsy was indeed the priority, and Duckworth's death was tied to it. Oren also understood why there'd be an autopsy for the unfortunate man who'd been in the cotton candy wagon—the death hadn't been in a medical facility like a hospital or nursing home, so a formal autopsy was required by law. But he thought it wholly unnecessary, a waste of Annie's time: Karalis died because part of an amusement ride smashed into him and broke open his head. COA: the Cosmic Odyssey. The teenagers' autopsies would yield similar: death by being catapulted from a county fair ride.

He also knew what Duckworth's autopsy would reveal; that the young man had died from a bullet to the brain. But that autopsy might yield additional interesting information, especially if Annie could come up with DNA evidence from the killers.

Samuel Silver on the slab right now? That's where Annie's time and taxpayer money should really go. She said she'd started twenty minutes ago. Nah, she'd started before that. Oren could tell.

She spoke into a microphone that dangled from the ceiling, recording her observations, all clinical, professional, and delivered emotionlessly. He wondered if dissecting the dead still bothered her. In the early months of her first term she'd admitted it was depressing. A former pediatrician, Annie had been all about new life.

As Oren had long ago become inured to attending autopsies, he stood back against the counter and watched her work. He hoped his death came years from now so Annie was no longer the coroner. He didn't like the idea of his longtime friend slicing into him.

"Want to go to lunch after?" Annie raised an eyebrow. "Cork'n Cleaver opens at eleven, and I'd go for one of their prime and cheddar sandwiches before I start Duckworth."

"Can't today." He'd planned to grab some sandwiches in Owensboro and stop at his dad's nursing home. Ritzy's Grill came to mind as his dad loved their chicken salad that was generous on the diced pecans. He was partial to the grilled cheese on Texas toast. Maybe he'd be able to do that, order sandwiches and eat with his dad, if Annie was quick with Silver. A standard autopsy usually took two or three hours. If she finished in two, counting the driving time, he'd still make it with plenty to spare to "picnic" with his dad.

At ten-thirty Annie looked up, stepped away, and tugged down her mask. "I'm not quite done, but I might be for your purposes. Samuel Silver was most definitely tortured—but you know that, obviously. I haven't double-checked the count on the ice pick marks. Got one hundred and twenty-one on my first pass, all of them relatively superficial and carefully placed. I'd say that they were meant to cause pain, not death, though there was some internal bleeding. Your torturer knew what he was doing, and I doubt he wanted to kill the victim. Or at least not kill him with an ice pick. Samuel Silver suffered a sudden cardiac death."

"The ice pick didn't do it?" Oren was surprised.

"Indirectly you could say. A cardiac incident like he had is usually caused by ventricular fibrillation, an erratic firing of impulses from the heart's lower chambers."

"Because he was tortured," Oren said. "He couldn't take the stress of the torture. Scared to death."

"Basically." Annie nodded. "Emotional and physical stress can cause severe and usually temporary heart muscle failure. But in this case it wasn't temporary."

"So *because* of the ice pick, but not directly due to an ice pick jab."

189

She nodded again. "I'll do a full report. There are labs to run, a lot of things I'll triple-check."

"It's murder regardless," Oren said. "Scaring someone to death because you've made a pin-cushion out of their body is still murder."

"That's for you and the courts to hammer out," Annie added. "Have you caught the sucker?"

Oren scowled. "Haven't. Nope. Don't even know who yet ... other than I'm damn sure there are two of them and they're driving a car with New Jersey license plates."

"Those are two sickos who laid into the victim. Very sick. You get them, Oren."

"That's the plan. Send over that report as soon as you can," he said. "And Duckworth's. That's all part of it. I'll join you for lunch some other time."

"Your treat," she said. "Bibi'll join us."

He took IN 66 and 161 to Owensboro and made good time at forty-five minutes. He could have shaved a few minutes off that if he'd taken Henderson Road and US 60, but he liked this route better. It took him closer to the hospital where he could check on the surviving Odyssey accident victim.

He called the nursing home on the way—memory care center, he mentally corrected himself—to let them know not to take his father down to lunch, that he would be bringing it.

It wasn't a bad facility, but Oren didn't like it. Rather, he didn't like that his ninety-three-year-old father had to live in it. Dementia, Alzheimer's, hardening of the arteries they used to label it. His dad had been living at the place for the past three years because his mind was shot. Some days he didn't recognize Oren. Other days were good and he'd talk about past cases when he was with the Rockport police, and dispense wisdom about law enforcement that Oren found useful. The farther back the memory, the clearer it seemed.

Oren stopped by at least twice a week, once on either Saturday or Sunday and once during some random weekday depending on his mood and work schedule. He usually called ahead to see if his dad was having a good day or a bad one, sometimes avoiding a visit if it was the latter. He never brought food on the bad days because his father either wouldn't eat it or would throw it at him.

He hadn't asked if today was a good or bad one.

Oren had a sack with the sandwiches, sodas, and chips, and stopped at the nurse's station so he could warm up the grilled cheese in their microwave. Just twenty-five seconds so the cheese wouldn't ooze out. He borrowed a tray.

"Hey, Dad." Oren frowned when he saw his father propped up in the recliner, in pajama pants and a gray long-sleeve t-shirt with WKU HILLTOPPERS printed in red on it. The Hilltoppers were Western Kentucky University men's basketball team. It was in Bowling Green, about seventy miles to the south. Oren had never known his father to like basketball, let alone college basketball. He wondered where the shirt had come from and wondered more why the attendants had left his father in pajama bottoms. The room smelled of antiseptic, a little harsher than usual; maybe his father had an accident today and they'd scrubbed up.

"How you doin' Dad?"

The elder Rosenberg stared blankly, mouth working. Oren opened the wrapper and placed the chicken salad sandwich on a tray and pushed it in front of him. He put the can of Coke within reach, but didn't pop the tab. It didn't look like his father was going to eat anything. Not a good day.

"One of your favorites, Dad. Chicken salad. I asked them to put extra pecans in it."

Oren settled into a chair nearby and started on his grilled cheese. Cheddar, provolone, and pepper jack. Delicious, the only bright spot to being in this depressing place. He decided to save the chips for later; he'd drink his soda in the car.

"Try to eat some of it, please."

The elder Rosenberg dropped his gaze to the sandwich, but made no move to touch it. Outside a medicine cart rattled by and a woman in heels *click-click-clicked* past carrying a pizza box. Someone else sharing lunch with an inmate. Oren often thought of his father as a prisoner here. He'd take him home with him, set him up in the spare bedroom, which would be nicer—had thought about that several times. His dad could look out across the lake, maybe go out in the boat with him once in a while, fish. But in his heart, Oren knew his father required more care, and from professionals. The doctors said that when he first broached the subject of keeping the old man at home.

He accepted that his dad would die in this disinfected cell, and he worried that time was coming closer; a nurse had hinted such last week.

"So, Dad," Oren said as he finished the grilled cheese. "I saw Annie today. Always good to see Annie. You remember her, right? I used to go to school with her, one of my old fishing buddies."

The elder Rosenberg pulled off a piece of sandwich and appeared to scrutinize it before putting it in his mouth. It looked like he swallowed it without chewing.

"And after I visited with Annie I went to the hospital to meet a young man named Pete Chapman. Pete's a teenager who was injured at the county fair Friday. He's in pretty sad shape, but he'll be all right. Eventually. Pete would be in Annie's morgue if he hadn't fallen on a hay bale."

Oren watched his father pull off another small piece of sandwich.

"Pete's going to need some rehab. Probably a lot of rehab. He told me about the Cosmic Odyssey, this big ride at the fair that broke. Pete has me thinking that I need to look at all the footage from the fair. He's got me questioning some things. So I can't stay today, Dad. Busy day. But I wanted to stop, bring you lunch."

The elder Rosenberg said something that sounded like: "Dubba dubba."

"I've some more business in Owensboro, too. Have to check in with the police about a case we're working. And I have to run by a comic book shop for another look-see. I think I'll go to the comic shop first, it's on the way to the police station. Then I've got to get back to the office to watch that Odyssey video. A busy busy day, Dad."

Oren liked active days like this, stimulating and challenging. They proved he'd made the right choice by not retiring. Sheriff Blackwell had assigned him these tasks today because she wanted to delve into bank records. Hell, she probably wanted to be involved in everything … he wanted that, too. At least she was savvy enough to delegate the work so information could be culled faster. He would have divided things up a little different if he was the sheriff, but he still would have given himself the Silver autopsy.

Oren's father put the sandwich bit in his mouth and swallowed, then proceeded to break apart the rest of the sandwich into dime-sized bits that he arranged into a pattern. Oren reached over and popped the top on the Coke and nudged it closer.

"Your favorite soda, Dad."

Oren smiled when his father wrapped a hand around the soda can, tipped it up and drank, some of it running down his chin and onto his Kentucky shirt. Then the elder Rosenberg ate the sandwich piece by piece. Oren stayed until he was finished, wanting to make sure he didn't choke.

"I'll be back in a few days, Dad."

"Dubba dubba. You're a good boy. Catch the bad guy, Oren. Dubba."

It was turning out to be a better day, Oren thought, as he hurried from the room and set off for Silver Age Sam's. He'd take a pass through the comic shop, two or three, be thorough. Then head over to chat with the Owensboro cops.

Then he'd get to all that county fair video. He was really looking forward to more closely examining the video of the ride.

Complicated, the department working two big cases at the same time. The county, the resources, too small for it, really. The two events had been tragic, but at the same time exciting from a law enforcement perspective. And the county fair disaster was prominent in Oren's mind right now.

Pete Chapman had said something that had made Oren shudder.

CHAPTER TWENTY-FOUR

11 A.M.

Piper settled at her desk with the printouts of Samuel Silver's accounts from the bank. She opened her laptop, loading in the photos she'd taken of items in the safe deposit box, saving everything so Basil and Oren could access them easily. Zeke had left her a short stack of phone messages. She thumbed through them and grimaced.

Two were from Chris Hagee, who was apparently not satisfied with Diego's visit earlier this morning regarding the Buddhists. Piper shouldn't have put the angry man off on a deputy. "The Buddhists must go now," one message said. "An unholy blight," read the other. Chris had probably also emailed the department. She hadn't checked those messages yet. Piper would force herself to stop by Hagee's sometime today and calm the man down. It wasn't about finding the time to handle Hagee. Her drill sergeant at Fort Campbell had lectured about time. "If you try to *find* the time to do something," he'd said, "that 'thing' you want to do will always go undone. But if you *make* the time, it will happen. Be a wizard and make the time."

Piper would be a wizard before she went home tonight.

One message, only minutes old, was from Vanessa Wolfe at the Indiana Department of Homeland Security, reporting that official

194

results from the Cosmic Odyssey study would not be available until the end of the week at the earliest, but they had a preliminary ruling. Piper called, and learned Vanessa was in a meeting. She'd call her again in a little while and ask about the results. Her curiosity demanded to be sated.

A note from Dr. Hunter Carlisle, dated an hour ago, claimed one of Silver's Black-footed cats had FIP, feline infectious peritonitis, and was being treated before relocation to a sanctuary. A note from Nang said: trying a new duck dish, will save you and your father some.

The other messages came from news reporters—Indianapolis, Evansville, Owensboro, Louisville, the AP, and some online services, all regarding the county fair disaster and investigation. One Evansville Courier reporter had left three messages; persistent soul. She would divide them up between herself, Oren, and Basil and get them called back before the shift change. She thought calling the reporters back, even if she provided nothing more than "the investigation is ongoing," was necessary and courteous.

No message relating to the Silver case had come in except about the cat with FIP.

Piper signed onto eBay and went to the seller section, searching for Samuel Silver and discovering he didn't have a seller ID to match his name. She nearly called Zeke in for help, but took a deep breath and stared at the screen with all its blank search fields.

"Figure it out. Figure it out."

An eBay seller didn't have to use his or her name, just an identity they'd established. She tried Silverage ... nothing. Then Silveragesam came up with a seller's store linked to Sam's comic book shop.

Victory!

It looked like he sold comics and individual Loot the Castle cards, and featured a picture of his storefront. She scrolled through the transactions, whistling at the ones that went for a few hundred dollars ... all that money for playing cards basically. Many of the listed items sold for ten bucks or less. She compared the bank printout and discovered a few of the deposits matched his monthly eBay sales. Some of the auctions were on-going and had bids. It appeared Mr.

195

Silver had listed them two or three days before his death. Those would have to be closed.

There had to be a personal eBay account in addition to his store. Even she had an account—piperblack—though she rarely bid on anything. Until she'd been willed a house, Piper hadn't been into accumulating possessions. She sometimes picked up an old movie on DVD or an Ed McBain mystery book since she'd acquired a taste for the author and preferred paper to e-readers. Sam had to have a personal account, too. Maybe it wasn't important, but Piper was hell-bent on discovering all financial aspects of his life. It was always about the money, Lennie Briscoe on *Law & Order* used to say.

She tried Silversam. Nope. Silverysam. Samuelsilver. Sammysilver. Corkyandsam. Corkyandkesha. Keshaandcorky. Samandcorky. Samuelandcorky. Samsilverandcorky. Phewphew. And on and on and ...Junglesam. Samjungle. Africasam. Africansam.

"Whoa!"

Africansam was an eBay ID, the sales history showed comic books —and the seller shipped from Indiana. Had to be the same Sam, right? The comics that had been sold—none were currently listed on auction —included a mix of jungle titles:

Ka-zar #3-#13 NM-M sold for $60

Black Panther #1 FINE: $115

Jungle Action #1 "best offer" of $120 accepted

Jungle Adventures #3-#8: $55

Rulah Jungle Goddess #17, M: $2,300

Sheena Queen of the Jungle: $33

Congo Bill #4 for a "best offer" of $189

Burne Hogarth original art Tarzan Sunday comic strip 1949: $21,000

Burne Hogarth original hand-colored Tarzan comic strip 1941: $29,000

Seemed like an excessive amount of money for comic strips, but she understood that original art could be pricey. It wasn't any kind of art she'd spend money on, though judging from the attached photos she had to admit the artist's talent was impressive.

Four more auction items on a ten-day sale were set to end tomorrow, showing Silver had put them up a few days before his death:

Rulah #21, CGC graded 9.0, minimum bid $2,000

Congo Bill #2, NM, minimum bid $350

Jo Jo Congo King #7, G, rusty staples, minimum bid $100

Tegra Jungle Empress #5, MINT, bright white pages, minimum bid $500

Earlier, Silver had put up other comic-related items for smaller amounts of money, most of them comic books, but there were action figures and superhero bobble heads, too. Why would he sell these things here and not with his Silver Age Sam store listings? Because these were his personal comics, likely, not folded in with the store inventory, she guessed, meaning he had to keep them separate.

She looked at his buying history, which included acquiring jungle comics, aquarium supplies, and Hawaiian print shirts, one of which was a "1938 silk Aloha shirt by Chung" he'd spent more than four thousand dollars on.

"All of my clothes are worth less than that one shirt." She wondered if she'd seen it in his closet. Had his killers taken it? Were more of his Hawaiian shirts that valuable? Why the hell would you pay more than four thousand dollars for a shirt?

Piper devoted nearly an hour to poking through all the screens. Noon, Basil had just texted her that he'd be another "thirty minutes or so."

"Coffee. I need a lot of coffee." Piper slid back from the desk and rolled her shoulders. The department had an exceptional coffeemaker, courtesy of being willed money for it—from the same kind soul who had gifted Piper with her house. She'd bought a good supply of Italian Dark Roast from Nang's store that would ease her caffeine craving. She grabbed her mug and headed for the break room just as Zeke hollered.

"Sheriff Blackwell, over the radio. Right now. A Rockport squad spotted that gray car on Sycamore turning onto North Fifth. They're—"

Piper planted her foot and spun, racing down the hall and pulling the keys from her pocket. That was a handful of blocks from here. She wasn't going to sit in the office to see if Rockport Police could pull the car over. She slammed her palm against the back door. It banged open and she darted into the parking lot and was at her Explorer in a half-dozen steps. She slid in, dropped her empty coffee mug on the passenger seat, gunned the engine, turned on her lights, and left the siren silent. She hadn't heard a siren when she came out here, so maybe Rockport officers were trying not to rattle the driver and prevent a high-speed chase through a residential district.

"I am going to get you, you son of a bitch," Piper cursed.

CHAPTER TWENTY-FIVE

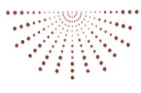

NOON

Piper sped out of the lot and onto the street, pressed the accelerator and breathed in relief when she caught the green light at the first intersection.

"Zeke," she said into the radio. "I'm joining in on this." Then she radioed Jake and Diego, who were patrolling somewhere in the county. "We need to stop this car," she told them. "The men are armed and certainly dangerous. And somehow they're involved in the Silver case." She hadn't really needed to add the armed and dangerous part; Piper had been thorough in her BOLO. Oren was either in Evansville or Owensboro and would be no help. Basil was still at the courthouse; she'd catch them up later. Right now, she focused on the street and drove faster. The few cars pulled over.

She took Main to Fifth, expecting to see the gray Mazda coming in her direction. The parked and stopped cars were a blur of color separated by the asphalt gaps of empty spaces. It seemed like there were always places to park in the small town. The few pedestrians out and about stayed on the sidewalks against the old brick buildings, heads swiveling and cell phones in hand as Piper sped out of the business district and into a residential stretch.

The chatter on the radio guided her, and she jinked left onto

Washington, then right onto North Seventh, catching sight of the bouncing lights of a Rockport police car ahead. She kept her speed steady, resisting the urge to press the pedal harder. A sedan pulled away from the curb, the driver oblivious to her lights, and she almost struck it. She leaned on the horn and swerved around. Out of the corner of her eye she saw a woman come out onto her front porch, cell phone up and likely videoing before she was zoomed past the house and closed in on the Rockport squad, which made a quick turn onto Vine.

Kids in a wide front yard stopped their game of croquet to watch the action. Nearby, a big brown dog barked loudly. This wasn't the place for a chase, too many variables—children, pets, unwary motorists. Piper had to absorb the surroundings and process it all at once. She turned on her siren.

Diego radioed that he was back in Rockport, on Lincoln.

"Straight north," she said. "Head up to Vine."

She couldn't see around the Rockport squad until it veered to avoid a car edging out into the intersection. The squad turned on its siren, too. The lights and racket bounced off clapboard houses. Piper stuck her head out the window, hoping to see beyond the squad and catch a glimpse of the Mazda. There!

"Cutting through the alley," someone in the squad car reported. "One in the car, won't pull over. Can't force it over here. No room."

Forcing the Mazda over along this stretch could be disastrous with more kids in yards and cars parked against the curb.

Zeke and Aggie had claimed they had seen two men in the car behind Sam's, and two when someone had tried to grab Aggie. Piper saw only one. Maybe one was hunkered down.

The chase continued east onto Sycamore as Diego radioed in that he spotted Piper's Explorer. The street was wider here, and busier. Cars that had been traveling on it pulled over, respecting the lights and sirens.

Piper navigated through them and was two car lengths back from the Rockport squad. The radio chatter continued:

"Fast for an old car," someone in the squad reported. "Driver's crazy or good. If he takes it out on to 66, we'll have room to force him off."

As if to accommodate them, a moment later the gray car swung left onto 66 and gunned it, opening up the distance. It shot well ahead of the Rockport squad and increased its lead.

"Sonofabitch," Piper cursed. "You're not getting away."

State Route 66 curved parallel to the Ohio River. Also known as the Ohio River Scenic Parkway, it provided a beautiful stretch of road both locals and tourists enjoyed. A sunny summer day like this, it had traffic. The other cars pulled over, though some did so at a snail's pace. The Mazda's driver put even more distance between his car and the squad. Piper saw Diego in her rearview mirror as they passed 231. Jake reported in, and she directed him to Grandview, where it looked like this was heading.

Grandview, one of the county's bitty burgs, had less than eight hundred souls; its claim to fame being children's book illustrator Bill Peet, who once worked for Disney. Piper prayed to get the suspect car stopped before it reached the town with its narrow streets. People would be out, and kids would be in the park. It was not a good place for a chase. Was any place in the county good for something like this?

The Rockport squad slowed and Piper passed it. Yet the Mazda sped up. What sort of engine did it have? She coaxed more speed from the Explorer, and seemingly by will closed the distance to her quarry. It had been a courtesy that the Rockport cops gave her the lead, she guessed, since they were past Rockport's city limits and in her domain. Or perhaps they backed off because Grandview was coming up and they didn't want a chase through a small town; it could be dangerous. No matter, the squad stayed right behind her, and she radioed asking for their assist with the stop ... which she was going to make in moments. Her ire was thick and her patience thin.

The Mazda's driver had skill, but Piper had more horsepower and wasn't about to let him escape. She'd driven military vehicles during down range assignments, weaving when shells went off all around her. This was easy in comparison, she told herself. She came up behind the four-door car and turned on her speaker.

"Pull over!" she demanded. "Pull the hell over now!"

But the car kept going, staying a few lengths ahead, and she took a new approach, coming up on the left-hand side of it, going faster still until she was even with the Mazda. A glance out her passenger window gave her a glimpse of the man alone in the car. The tinted windows made it too difficult to discern any more details.

"Game over," Piper muttered.

She floored it and edged ahead, weaving directly in front of the car and prepared to be rear ended by it. The Rockport squad closed behind, so the two effectively sandwiched their target. When the gray car tried to pull out into the opposite lane to get away, they mirrored it, essentially trapping the vehicle. Back and forth. Back and forth.

"I said game over." Piper slowed and continued to dance with the Mazda, glancing ahead and seeing the Grandview sign.

Between her, the Rockport squad car, and Diego, they boxed their quarry in and forced it onto the shoulder at the edge of the town limits. The driver couldn't go around them on the open side, as it was almost a straight drop to the river. He rolled the window down and leaned his head out, twisting and meeting her gaze as she jumped out of the Explorer.

Piper pulled her gun in the same motion. She heard car doors open behind her, saw that cars had stopped in the other lane, people watching and thankfully staying put, some videoing with their cell phones.

"Hands out the window!" she shouted. "Put your hands out the window now!"

Footsteps coming behind her.

"Sheriff Blackwell." It was Diego.

"Other side. There should be two of them in the car," she returned. Piper didn't have to look to see if Diego was approaching from the shoulder side; she trusted her deputy. In the distance she heard another siren.

"I said put your hands out the window now!"

The driver slowly complied and Piper slipped closer. The man's fingers were big and stubby like breakfast sausages. He had two rings on each hand, clunky things set with large stones that caught the sunlight. Gun in her right hand, she reached with her left to open his door.

"I didn't see any speed limit sign," the man said, his lip quirked up as he got out. He wasn't the tall one that Aggie had described grabbing her. He had a round face, but it wasn't fleshy-fat, just big. His black eyes looked hard, like marbles.

"Keep your hands up."

"Sure thing, officer," he returned. "Always cooperate with the police."

"Turn around, hands on the—"

She didn't have to finish her instructions. He pivoted, spread his legs, and leaned toward the car, placing his hands flat against the roof, waiting to be frisked. He looked linebacker muscular, the seams of his green polo shirt straining at the shoulders. His arms looked as big as tree trunks. Thick cords stood out in his neck.

"No guns on me, no needles, officer. Like I said, I just hadn't realized I was speeding."

Or that multiple cars with lights and sirens were pursing you, she thought. *Or that you can't tell the difference between the sheriff and a police officer.* Piper patted him down and drew his hands behind his back, attempting to cuff him.

Diego opened the door and looked in. He stretched to the console and pulled the lever that popped the trunk. Two Rockport police officers stood behind the car. Piper had seen them before, but they'd never met and she didn't know their names.

"Trunk's empty," one of them said.

The man's wrists were so big her cuffs couldn't properly fit them. She made a note to add "monster cuffs" to the Explorer, basically leg irons she'd heard some cops used as handcuffs for large prisoners.

"I've got zip ties," Diego volunteered. "I'll get them."

Ahead, a sheriff's department car coming from Grandview pulled to the side. Jake got out. Piper reached her free hand up to her radio and tapped it on.

"Zeke, I have the driver in custody." She listened to background chatter. "Jake and Diego are here."

"Arresting me for speeding? Can't you just write me a ticket? Really?"

Piper didn't have any evidence to connect him to the Silver murder—not yet, and Aggie had said it was the tall one who'd grabbed her in the park. But there were other charges she could bring that would keep him in custody until she sorted through the Silver case. Then she'd hopefully add even more charges.

"License," she said.

He kept one hand on the roof of his car and reached into his pocket pulling out his wallet, flipping it open, and passing it back.

"I have to get that renewed," he said. "I'll do that as soon as I get back home."

His accent was definitely east coast.

Diego came back with a big zip tie, and used it as cuffs, putting the man's hands behind his back.

"Ashe Williams, Newark," Piper read his license. "Expired four months ago."

"Yeah, well I said I need to get that renewed."

"Car registration," Piper said to Diego.

"Car's not mine," the man cut in. "I'm borrowing it."

"Are you borrowing the plates, too?"

"I don't know nothin' about that."

"Plates are from a pizza delivery vehicle in New Jersey," Piper said.

"Don't know nothin' about that, I told you," he repeated. "I was just borrowing the car. Why would I care about the plates?"

Piper saw Diego, gloves on, search the front seat and open the glove box.

"This is excessive," Williams continued, "for a speeding ticket."

"Charging you with speeding, reckless driving, and driving with an expired license."

"Just give me a damn ticket. And I wasn't driving recklessly."

"Going more than thirty miles above the speed limit in Indiana is automatically classed as reckless driving," Piper lectured. "Even if you're a first-time violator it's a Class B misdemeanor and you can face a thousand dollars in fines and up to six months in jail. I'd say you can also face a license suspension, but yours is already expired."

"Car's registered to Loretta Smalley of Trenton, New Jersey," Diego said.

"Radio it in," Piper said.

"Gun," Diego cut back. "Under the passenger seat."

"I don't know nothin' about that either," the man said. "I just borrowed the car, didn't look under the seat."

"Glock." Diego held it out in an evidence bag like it was a rat he didn't want to get near as he walked back to his car. "Calling in the car registration."

Jake looked in the back seat and made a sour face. "Lots of food wrappers."

"I want a thorough search," Piper told Jake. "Photos as you go. Call for a tow." To the Rockport police: "Thanks. We want him. Pretty sure this is connected to something we're working on." They could have argued for custody since the pursuit had started in Rockport, but they didn't.

"We're clear," one of the officers said. "We'll stay until your tow comes."

She noted the names on their shirts and would write thank you notes to them later ... something her father used to always do, a practice she'd also adopted.

"You have the right to remain silent," she told Williams. "Anything you say can and will be used against you in a court of law."

"I want a lawyer," he said.

"You have the right to an attorney."

"I said lawyer."

"If you cannot afford an attorney, one will be provided for you." She would repeat the charges to him back at the department, and then set him up in a cell next to Vernon Milgrew. They could keep each other company. "Do you understand—"

"Yeah. Yeah. I understand. Do you understand that I want a lawyer?"

"I'll get you the Yellow Pages from my office." She nudged him toward her Explorer, and put him in the back seat behind the divider. "Where's your friend, Mr. Williams? The tall man?" Williams asking for an attorney effectively ended her interrogation, and she shouldn't press it. But she risked the question anyway. She wanted to know if the other man was still in her county.

"Friend?" He cocked his head as if he didn't know what she was talking about.

"With the Grateful Dead tattoo," she added. "Where is he?"

"I don't have any friends," Williams replied. "I want a lawyer. I don't think I should talk to you anymore until I have a lawyer."

Piper slid into the driver's seat as Diego came up to her side. "Got a return on the car registration right away," he said. "Loretta Smalley reported it stolen from in front of her house. I'll stay with Jake through the tow."

She thumbed off her flashers and pulled away from the shoulder, turning around and heading back to Rockport.

"Borrowed the car," she said. Piper had not phrased it as a question.

"Yeah, from a friend. Didn't know nothin' about it being stolen."

"You said you didn't have any friends."

"Lawyer," Williams repeated. "Lawyer."

CHAPTER TWENTY-SIX

1 P.M.

"Can't talk to the sucker," Basil said. "Not without his attorney in the room."

Piper sat across from her detective in the break room, a steaming mug of Dark Italian roast in front of her. Basil sipped from a cup of pale green herbal tea. If it had an aroma, she couldn't smell it. She held her coffee close to her nose—its richness she could smell.

"Yeah, his attorney's not even in the state," she said.

Ashe Williams had made a call to an attorney immediately upon reaching the Spencer County Jail, said attorney being in New York City.

"Could be days before she gets here," Basil said.

"And we have to wait." Piper sipped her coffee, enjoying it. "A reasonable time anyway. I figure a few days before we re-engage Mr. Williams—unless he decides to change his mind. Scales is coming in to discuss it."

"Don't see that happening," Basil said, "Williams changing his mind and talking. He's got too much experience with the law."

Piper set down her mug and folded her fingers around it, the warmth seeping into her skin. It was a good sensation, as the air conditioning seemed cranked a little too high today.

207

"Scales is going to file initial charges tomorrow morning, I'm guessing. Grand theft—the car's worth more than five hundred, attempted kidnapping because Aggie identified him, and possession of a gun without a license."

"His record ... he can't legally have a gun," Basil said.

"There are certain provisions that allow for it," Piper pointed out.

Basil snorted. "Not in The Barbarian's case. I'd bet my house on it. Scales should tack on the traffic charges. Throw everything at Williams." He leaned back. "Should add murder."

"We need probable cause and—"

"More evidence. I know. Why the hell did a thug from New Jersey go after a comic book dealer?" Basil had shared the information he got from his former partner, the men's names and nicknames, record sheets. The BOLO had been updated while Piper was chasing Williams. "He's working for someone. *They're* working for someone. The Barbarian didn't come here on his own initiative. Who's he working for?"

"And why did he kill Samuel Silver?" Piper asked. "Had to be him ... or his buddy who went wild with an ice pick. We start with Scales' charges, which will keep Williams tied up in the county for a while. If Williams' attorney doesn't arrive from New York in what seems a reasonable time, the judge can force the case to go forward and can appoint someone local to represent him."

They sat quiet for a few minutes, Basil drinking tea and reading something on his phone, probably related to the case, Piper figured. She stewed and took a big gulp of the coffee, feeling it go down her throat and mollify her caffeine craving. Williams had to be their guy, she mused. They didn't have another suspect. And Duckworth ... why kill him too? What had Silver done to the New Jersey men—or their boss—to make them resort to murder? What had they wanted from Silver? They'd tossed his house searching for something, and they hadn't found it. If they had, they wouldn't still be in the county. At least, Williams still wouldn't be here.

"They did it," Piper said softly. "Or Williams did it alone."

"Killed Silver?"

Piper nodded.

"Of course they did. We just have to prove it."

Piper drained the mug. "Who was Samuel Silver to them?"

"The DA's here!" Zeke poked his head in the doorway, grinning, and Piper wondered if he'd been listening to their conversation. The break room's entrance was a half-dozen feet from the dispatcher's desk, and she knew Zeke had been following the Silver case closely. "Want him in your office or—"

County Prosecutor Scales stepped around Zeke and into the room. "Here's good," he said. "If I can get some of that coffee. Smells tasty."

Piper got up and retrieved a guest mug, filled it, and refilled hers.

"Two sugars," Scales said, as he picked a spot at the table. He hung his jacket on the back of his chair. "No. Three sugars today. Thanks."

He wore a charcoal gray suit, white shirt with faint maroon stripes, open at the collar. Probably had a tie in his pocket, Piper guessed. This is the first time she'd seen him without a tie. Scales was wiry, hair cut razor-close to his head, thin mustache, tortoiseshell glasses. He hadn't come in with a briefcase. Maybe he'd stopped here on his way back to the courthouse from lunch.

"So, what's this about?" Scales took the mug and stared at the surface before opening the three sugar packets and pouring them in. "The Silver matter, right? The young man up front told me you have a suspect in custody."

Young man; he'd meant Zeke, who was eighteen. Scales was probably a little more than twice that age. Young, but qualified, Piper thought.

Piper and Basil quickly caught Scales up on Ashe Williams sitting in the jail and the BOLO still out on Ethan "Bloodshot" Caine.

"Sounds like typical Jersey thugs," Scales mused. "Long rap sheets, lovely nicknames. I'll go before a judge with Williams tomorrow morning."

"That's fast," Basil said.

"I have forty-eight hours from his arrest, so technically I have until noon Wednesday, but let's get this done. The judge—and that'll be the Honorable Marjorie Saltzman—will set a bond on any felonies, like the attempted kidnapping charge. The misdemeanor charges you're talking about will carry probably between fifteen hundred and three thousand dollar bonds, and he only has to post ten percent of that to be released."

Basil scowled. "His ass is not being released."

"Of course not." Piper looked pointedly at Scales. "Right? I mean, we're also investigating him for Silver's murder. We just don't have enough evidence yet."

"Finding the ice pick would be good." Scales ran a thumb around the lip of the mug. "I get you. That's why I came by. Look, you're making it crystal clear this Williams character is probably worse than the current charges suggest."

"A lot worse," Piper said.

"So we'll ask for a higher bond—or no bond at all—because of the attempted kidnapping. I'll likely push for no bond, considering him a flight risk because of his past criminal record and he's from New Jersey."

"No bond. That's better," Piper said.

"So tomorrow I'll give a probable cause statement, covering what you've charged him with. An attorney will be appointed for him for the limited purpose of the hearing."

"Unless his New York lawyer gets here in time," Piper mused.

"Unless that," Scales agreed. "If not, Judge Saltzman will ask Williams if he intends to hire a private attorney, and since that's already the case, she'll schedule another hearing for the appearance of Williams and that attorney. There might be a continuance or two to give the counsel time to get here. But then there's the matter of a law license to practice in the state. This New York attorney ... do you have a name?"

Piper pulled out her notebook. "Yeah." She held it out to Scales.

"Not likely a lawyer from New York is licensed for Indiana. So she'll pick up a co-counsel, or maybe she'll try to get a special waiver to practice in Indiana for this specific case. In any event, if this drags out too long, getting attorneys set, the judge might push the case forward anyway. It's all up to what Saltzman is going to consider as reasonable time. Williams can't avoid a trial by dragging out the process of hiring an attorney."

"So at an arraignment," Basil cut in, "all the charges will be explained, possible penalties. Same as it was in Cook County."

Piper steepled her fingers over her coffee mug. "Williams going for this New York attorney, probably needing a continuance, this is going to work in our favor, actually. Gives us more time on the Silver murder. We can nail down probable cause. Find the ice pick." Her deputies had thoroughly searched Silver's house, yard, and ditches, but hadn't come up with the weapon. No ice pick in the Mazda either.

Scales gave a hint of a smile. "It will give me time, too. I have to put together a synopsis to file charges and argue for no bond." He drank the rest of his coffee and pushed the mug away. "You're doing the right thing, Sheriff Blackwell, not arresting him for murder now. Gotta have that probable cause. I really need that to file murder charges. Charge him for murder too early and hope for more evidence to trickle in doesn't typically end well. There has to be enough to convince a jury and get past reasonable doubt. Right now, you can't put him at the scene, can you?"

"We can put him at a pancake house," Basil said softly.

"We're checking his shoes," Piper said. They were being compared to the prints left in Silver's kitchen. "We're working on it."

"And let's talk public perception."

Basil's eyebrows rose at Scales' comment.

"Spencer County's small, public's going to follow this. It's exciting. We'll be under a ton of scrutiny and we can't let the public think we're filing charges willy-nilly. That's super-important regarding murder charges. Public perception is important."

Piper figured he was thinking voters. Scales had a political eye that she lacked.

"We can take our time on the murder end," Scales added. "Murder has no statute of limitations. You need the evidence, Sheriff Blackwell, before all of this swings into motion. Because once he's charged, he can demand a speedy trial, and that can be in as little as seventy days.

His fancy New York attorney could well push for that, hoping we don't yet have enough to convict."

Scales stood. "I have to get back to my office." He picked up his briefcase and breezed out of the room.

"And we have to get on that probable cause," Piper said.

"It's the ice pick," Basil said after Scales had left. "Williams' buddy—"

"Ethan Caine," Piper supplied.

"Ethan 'Bloodshot' Caine," Basil returned. "When you delve through his record you'll see he spent five years at Rykers because he ice-picked a dry cleaner owner, almost killed her. So maybe Williams wasn't wielding the pick on Silvers. Most likely Caine was. But Williams is still guilty because he was there." Basil growled from deep in his throat, and his eyes glimmered. "What did they want with Silver? Who are they working for?"

The million dollar question, Piper thought. Why were New Jersey thugs in Spencer County, her county, committing murder?

CHAPTER TWENTY-SEVEN

2 P.M.

Oren parked directly in front of the comic shop and grabbed his cell phone, taking pictures of the display spread along the sidewalk to the right of the door. The makeshift memorial had a dozen half-melted candles, like someone had held a ceremony; wilted bouquets of flowers; and stuffed animals with capes tied around their fuzzy necks. Signs with superheroes and monsters drawn on half-sheets of poster board hand-lettered sentiments, most of them in the comic sans font, made up the rest:

Be With God, Sam

My Heart Bleeds Silver

Loot Heaven's Castle, Sam

Sharing the Sadness

With Deepest Sympathy as We 'Member Sammy

I Will Miss You ... but my aim will get better

Mourning the Passing of the Jungle Man

Swing With Rulah and Tarzan and Sheena

Praying 4 You

In Caring Sympathy

Cards for Sorrow

213

There was a full six-pack of Pepsi placed amid the stuffed animals, like some sort of offering. A family-sized box of Cheez-It Snack Mix lay on its side.

Oren used the key and went in the front. He looked beyond the racks of comic books to the tables toward the back. It had provided a good place for young people to gather and play their fanciful card games ... without drinking and smoking, at least not on these premises. Maybe, he thought again, if the city was lucky someone would buy the business from whoever was named in Silver's will and keep it going. He took video as he walked.

The place felt eerie without customers. He pictured the tattooed girl managing here. They'd been thorough when they'd come in before, but without a computer and records there was no way to check inventory to see if there'd been a robbery. There was some virtual "cloud" where people stored a lot of information, and Piper had directed Zeke to dig into that, see if he could find Silver's shop records that way. It was all covered in the warrant she'd gotten. Oren was pleased he didn't know all that much about tech; he found that part of investigations tedious and uninteresting. He liked hands-on work, such as being here.

The shop smelled different without customers. Floor polish, glass polish, and mostly paper. There was a lot of paper, and some of the comics were old, which added a hint of musty funk that wasn't unpleasant, just fusty. He strolled past the Loot the Castle t-shirts, noticing that sizes ranged from L to XXXXL. Apparently small people either didn't play the game or didn't buy the shirts. He whistled; prices started at twenty-five dollars. Okay, kids probably couldn't afford them ... or the Loot the Castle cards for that matter. Oren got nice Fruit of the Loom pocket t-shirts in a variety of colors for four bucks each at Owensboro's Walmart.

In the office, nothing had changed. But he took video anyway. Nothing different about the bathroom or the hall except—

Oren stared at the floor by the back door. The rug was curled up on one edge, like someone had tripped on it or had caught the door on it. Hadn't been like that when they'd left Saturday. It was possible an employee with a key had come in. He took a picture and made a slow pass up and down the aisles. Maybe the Owensboro cops had come for a look.

There was something else a little different. Oren had perused the comics that were arrayed in bins on tables in the center, like the comics shown in the shop on *The Big Bang Theory*. The comics under "J" and "R" and "S" were pulled forward, like someone had shuffled through them. He remembered they'd all been sitting upright and proper Saturday. Again, it might have been an employee. And, again, Oren took pictures and decided he'd go get his kit and take some fingerprints ... just to be thorough. Maybe he'd call the tattooed girl and ask if any employees had not relinquished their keys.

The glass counters near the register looked the same, the items in plastic sleeves and marked with ridiculously high prices.

But something was off, he could feel it, and he spent an hour studying the store.

Someone had been in here after they'd closed it down and ushered everyone out. He'd ask at the Owensboro Police Department if some of the officers had been looking around—which he wouldn't be upset over. He just wanted to know. He had to go to the "cop shop" anyway to check in.

Oren was disturbed by the other possibility—that the men in the New Jersey car had come back, looking for something. Basil and Piper were convinced Silver's killers had been looking for something.

Had they found it here?

Oren locked up, took another glance at the tributes on the sidewalk, and left. He had other places to go.

One of those places was down by the river.

Oren thought this a younger soul's job, climbing down this steep, unfriendly bank to reach the river. But he only grumbled inwardly and grabbed onto thick branches and dug his heels in to keep from falling. Maybe there was an easier way to get down here, but he hadn't spotted it when he came from Triplett to East Second and parked in the drive of a house for sale. There were two Owensboro police cars nearby.

Maybe he should have looked harder for another route. But he was in a hurry, he didn't want to miss anything.

When he'd stopped in the police department they told him immediately there were officers and a detective on the scene of a one-eight-seven, code for murder. A fisherman had found a body and called it in not quite an hour ago.

"Might be Lloyd Ebersole," the desk sergeant had said, "the missing kid your sheriff was looking for. Heard on the radio it was him."

Oren figured an officer on the scene had found an ID. He rushed out of the station, a mix of disappointment and ire that Owensboro PD hadn't contacted the Spencer County Sheriff's Department immediately about the body. A call to Zeke while Oren drove confirmed the lack of notification. He made a second call, this to Sheriff Blackwell to let her know about the body and that he was handling things and likely wouldn't be back to the department until five or six. She told him that Ashe Williams was a suspect in Silver's and Duckworth's death and was in custody.

"And no doubt a suspect in this one, too," Oren mused.

Too bad the body was in such an inaccessible place.

The sand-mud mixture pulled at Oren's feet, making the way tricky. He slipped once and caught a pant leg on a spiky bush, but managed to stay upright and sucked a mouthful of river-scented air deep into his lungs. It smelled heavy here, redolent with earth and water, decaying foliage, and the fumes from Rockport's big power plant that drifted across the water.

At the bottom the odor changed and intensified—the unmistakable rot of a decomposing body. The first thing he noticed was garbage—several twisted beer cans, some discolored and moldy fast food bags, Styrofoam containers, and a plastic two-liter bottle of Orange Crush that looked about a third full. He hated litter, especially when it was left in hard-to-reach places like this so it likely would never be picked up. It ruined the pretty scape of the Ohio. Maybe the beer cans were the detritus of fishermen or teens who'd come down here to party, careless and unthinking and so lazy that they couldn't pick up after themselves. The garbage was too far to have been thrown from the bridge. He saw a rusted stringer caught on the roots of a red maple a few feet away. There had to be an easier way to get down here, he was certain. A fisherman himself, he wouldn't lug poles and a tackle box down this slope. And he wouldn't have left a stringer. He wouldn't have left any of this shit here.

Twenty yards away, four police officers and two men from the coroner's office circled a mound on the bank lying between the gnarled roots of a black gum. The ends of the roots disappeared in the water, like black snakes going for a swim. The mound was the source of the stench.

Several black gums grew on the banks above and down here, beautiful trees considered native to Kentucky, Oren knew, that could reach fifty feet high. The ones shading the police and the body measured probably thirty feet or so tall with thick plate-like bark and drooping branches. Stunning trees, they tolerated water well. Plenty of them on the Indiana side of the river, too. Funny how he always tried to find the "one pretty thing" to focus on when confronting a corpse.

The water beyond looked gray, the blue hid by banks of clouds that had thickened and darkened during his exploration of the comic shop. Could rain before the night was out, he thought.

The men talked, voices muted because their faces angled down.

"This is a bad one."

"I've seen worse."

"Pass the Vicks."

"Vicks ain't gonna help much."

"Cause will be easy. Bullet to the head."

"Hard to see that, Dean, skin all puffed like that."

"C'mon. That's clearly a bullet to the brain."

"Chief Rosenberg!" One of the police officers stepped away and acknowledged Oren. It was Alden Hopper, the detective that had ridden with him and Piper when they investigated the comic shop and stopped at the Pancake Palace. "I was just about to call you."

217

"I bet," Oren whispered. "I just bet you were going to call." Oren reached in his pocket and pulled out his cell phone, turned on the record function and walked forward, wanting to get all the grisly details to share back in the office.

"Fisherman called us," Alden said.

At a glance you couldn't tell the body had been a young man. The skin was gray, marbled, and had started to bloat and blister. The warm weather had aided the decomposition, and the flies were thick. Dead about seventy-two hours was Oren's guess, which fit in the same timeframe as Silver and Duckworth.

"Spotter said he was a regular down here, noticed the smell," Alden added. "Was fishing for channel cat."

Impossible not to notice the smell, Oren thought. He'd get the name of the fisherman, who was nowhere in sight, talk to him. Channel catfish? Oren wouldn't fish for them, not here.

"Might've been killed in Spencer County," Oren said. "Tossed off the bridge, drifted here. Should be ours, this murder, all part of the same case we're working."

"Hasn't been ruled a murder yet." Alden came over to Oren. "And you know he wasn't tossed off the bridge. Way the river flows, to the southwest, he would've been put in the water by the detention center or municipal utilities ... if he wasn't killed and dumped right here. He was put in on our side of the river."

If Oren didn't argue, Annie wouldn't have to deal with the putrid corpse. He might be doing her a favor, especially considering the bodies from the county fair accident. He stopped his cell phone from recording and called the Owensboro Police Department.

"I need to talk to the chief," he said. While he waited to be connected, he pointed at Alden. "I don't want to get into a pissing match with you, but this is our case."

Oren knew counties typically tried to work out jurisdiction issues, and usually the county where the murder occurred ended up with the case. But honestly, he couldn't say for certain that Duckworth and Ebersole were killed in Spencer County. They could have been shot shortly after leaving the pancake house, right here in Owensboro.

Silver, tortured to death in his living room, there was no arguing jurisdiction there. Duckworth had been stuffed into the back of Silver's car. Probably wasn't room for Duckworth and Ebersole. Or maybe the killers did Ebersole first, thinking that might get Silver and Duckworth to spill whatever it was that had been worth killing them all over.

Alden grimaced. "Even if Ebersole—and that's assuming this is Ebersole—"

"It's Ebersole. You pulled his ID." Oren noted a wallet in a plastic evidence bag near the body. "You opened his wallet to see who he was. He's got a t-shirt from Silver's shop on. Even if Ebersole was killed in Spencer County and transported here, we'd take it. We'd have jurisdiction on this case."

"Or the Feds would step in," Alden countered. "Across state lines, Feds might be interested."

The other men around the body had turned to watch the exchange between Oren and Alden, who was the ranking officer from Owensboro.

Oren's call was put through and he talked quickly, noting that Alden walked back to the body. "Yeah, I suppose we could form a Major Case Squad for this, but I'd have to clear that with the sheriff," Oren said. Three related murders fit the qualifications for a major case, and adding a police detective or two from Owensboro might be helpful to spread out the work. The chief talked for several more minutes.

"It's ours," Oren said after the discussion, holding the cell phone out to Alden, who reluctantly took it. "Talk to your chief, he'll confirm it's ours. We might form a joint squad over this, but that's an open issue right now. In the meantime, this is ours. We'll keep you up to date on everything. And I'll take the evidence with me."

Alden frowned, but accepted the judgment of his chief.

Oren took video of the body and its surroundings, collected the half-dozen evidence bags, and made another call to Sheriff Blackwell, confirming the death of Lloyd Ebersole. Then he called Annie to let her know she'd have one more body to cut into. Turning up his charm, he talked the Daviess County Coroner's men into transporting the body to Evansville's morgue.

As they were wrapping up, Oren glanced at the steep bank he'd climbed down, wondering how he was going to get back. Coming down had been difficult enough. Going up? This was indeed a younger soul's game. He'd worry over it in a little while since he'd stay put until the body was gone.

"There's a little path," Alden said, gesturing to the far side of the body, apparently noting Oren's dilemma. "Fishermen use it, the path."

Oren wished he would've spotted that path when he arrived. "Really, Alden, I'll keep you posted," he promised.

"I bet," Alden whispered. "I bet you will."

CHAPTER TWENTY-EIGHT

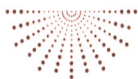

3:30 P.M.

Piper was stuck on Silver's collection of guns. Made her think of the news article she'd saved from when she campaigned. At the time she'd found it sadly interesting and certain it would never happen in Spencer County. More than one thousand guns, including assault weapons, had been found in a house in a ritzy California neighborhood. All the agencies—local police, FBI, and agents from the federal Bureau of Alcohol, Tobacco, Firearms and Explosives —had been involved in the recovery.

Granted, there weren't as many weapons hidden in Silver's residence, but she considered the find significant. Hidden in a concealed compartment of an animal cage, not meant to be found. Why had Silver owned them?

She believed the weapons linked him to the New Jersey thugs, and Basil had agreed. Basil was at the courthouse now, taking one more pass through the records. Then he said he was going to the DMV to go through Silver's records there before the office closed.

Her new detective was thorough and driven, making her incredibly happy he'd decided to leave Chicago for rural Spencer County. Plus, she was learning quite a bit from him. Basil had told her he wanted to get his family away from the gun violence.

Now look what they'd found. "Guns." And there'd been knives at the Silver place too.

Guns somehow tied Silver to Ashe "The Barbarian" Williams and the still-unaccounted-for Ethan "Bloodshot" Caine. Somehow. She'd read through Williams' and Caine's rap sheets and scoured links from New Jersey and New York. Basil insisted the men were working for someone, goons on a big boss's leash.

Who held the leash?

Piper contacted the Manhattan DA's office and the US Attorney's Office District of New Jersey, hoping to garner names of associates of Williams and Caine. People said they would get back to her.

"Teegan?" Piper hollered.

"Minute."

The dispatcher came to the doorway. Teegan had dressed surprisingly bright today. Normally she held to her usual Goth look, but today she'd braided her jet black-dyed hair and wore dainty earrings. She sported cornflower blue slacks and a short-sleeve ivory blouse, one of those thick stretchy bracelets around her wrist was covered with polymer clay daisies. Teegan was artsy and made jewelry she sold online and at area craft fairs. She'd probably made the bracelet. Piper hadn't seen Teegan come in and change shifts with Zeke, as she'd been too engrossed in her thug research.

"Teegan, you look—"

"Different. I know. I had a late lunch with my aunt. She's old and pretty much straight-laced and—"

"I was going to say you look summery."

Teegan smiled, and Piper noticed that the dispatcher had pierced her chin right below her lower lip with a shiny silver ball-stud. It was a new addition, hadn't been there yesterday. Teegan also had an eyebrow pierced and a stud in her nose, plus the piercings in her ears. Teegan was in her forties, but often acted more hip and young than Piper.

"Thanks, boss. Still nothing on the BOLO on Bloodshot Caine," Teegan said, visibly shuddering. "That's what you wanted to know, right? About the missing man?"

"Right. I was hoping."

"I'm hoping he's high-tailed it out of Spencer County. We don't need those kind of people here. We have our own home-grown nut jobs." Teegan fluttered a stack of messages in her hand for emphasis. "Case in point, I put nut job numero uno on top." With a flourish, she glided forward and passed the stack to Piper, swung around, and went back to her desk. Her phone had started to ring.

Piper looked at the stack and groaned.

Chris Hagee was on top. Teegan had scrawled under his name—*he won't give up about the Buddhists*. She'd underlined "won't."

"I'm a wizard," Piper growled. She'd make the time shortly to go deal with Hagee and try to cool him off. Silver's murder and the county fair disaster trumped Hagee, but she couldn't put it off any longer and risk something happening to whatever souls had gathered at the Buddhist retreat.

More messages from reporters. She'd called three of the reporters back from the previous stack, giving them all the same line that the Cosmic Odyssey was still under investigation. One of the reporters in this group, from the Owensboro daily, had left a message about Samuel Silver's death. Word was out. Piper was surprised it had taken this long. She'd received the coroner's report an hour ago that Silver had suffered a sudden cardiac death brought about by torture. She'd call all these reporters back—but later tonight.

Then came the messages Teegan had picked up through the department's email account and printed out.

Another two from Hagee. Piper had a headache, from stress, in part she thought from Hagee, but also because she hadn't eaten since breakfast. She'd been planning to take Zeke and Aggie out to dinner and then drop them at her house before returning to work. Piper didn't want them staying at Zeke's apartment or Aggie's house until Bloodshot Caine's whereabouts were known. And they couldn't stay in the sheriff's department twenty-four seven. Aggie's parents were coming back tomorrow, and a few days after that the girl was due to report for Coast Guard training. New plan: drive Zeke and Aggie to her house now and let them fend for themselves out of her refrigerator. She'd feed Marmalade and Camaro, and then go back to work.

Two more emailed messages from reporters about the fair.

One lengthy email from an old Army buddy who was returning to Fort Campbell from a long stint in Afghanistan and hoped to reconnect.

And one message from Gary Jefferson, deputy US Marshal. "I will arrive in Rockport, Indiana, late Tuesday regarding Samuel Silver."

"Oh." Piper stared at the Jefferson note, waited a beat, and then scrolled through her laptop to find the images she'd downloaded from Silver's safe deposit box.

It was the photographs she was interested in.

She found the one that niggled at her with the car and clothes from the seventies, then the color one of a youngish couple with a boy standing in front of them, all of them dressed up. "Margo, Walter, and Doyle at St. Ignatius of Antioch Episcopal Church," the photo was labeled.

A few clicks and she found a phone number for St. Ignatius on Manhattan's Upper West Side.

Piper counted herself lucky to find a secretary in the office; it was after five in New York. She explained who she was and described the photograph.

"I don't have last names, and this goes back a while, forty years at least. The boy's name is Doyle, and the parents are Margo and Walter. I need a last name." Piper listened. "Yes, I know, needles in a big haystack. But this is important." She waited. "Okay, I understand. It's a lot of years and names to look through. Please call me if you come up with anything. It's important," she repeated. Piper gave the department's number and her cell phone.

Then she found a number for the US Marshals Service in Indianapolis, guessing Gary Jefferson was assigned there. After being transferred three times Piper was told Jefferson was not available.

"Of course Gary Jefferson is not available," Piper grumbled after she disconnected. "That would be too easy if he was."

She called Basil, who was just arriving at the DMV.

"Samuel Silver," Piper said. "I think his real name is Doyle something or other. Working on the something or other. And I think he was in witness protection. I think that's why there were no photos at his house, no hint of family."

US Marshals were an enforcement arm of the Federal Court system. They served federal arrest warrants, captured fugitives, handle some prisoner transports, and oversaw the country's witness protection program.

Witness protection. Why else would a U.S. Marshal be coming to Spencer County regarding Samuel Silver? Because Samuel Silver really wasn't Samuel Silver. Because he was the boy in the photo in front of the church. Because it would explain a lot of things, like why her deputies had not found anything on Samuel Silver before his past twenty years in Spencer County, and why he had so many guns. The guns were part of his "real" persona, an arsenal he hadn't divested himself of when he set down roots here.

Maybe her theory seemed all too much of a leap, Piper thought, but she decided to embrace it anyway. It would explain why the man had hung onto vintage photos of people with no last names in a safe deposit box. If Samuel had been Doyle, he had an east coast connection—and so did Williams and "Bloodshot" Caine. It made some of the puzzle pieces fit a little better. But there were still a lot of gaping holes … like what, beyond guns, connected the three men. And after Samuel Silver had spent two decades in flyspeck-sized Africa, presumably hiding in witness protection, what had he done to draw the thugs' attention? What had he done in his previous identity to warrant witness protection? She looked at the US Marshal's note again—no contact information beyond an email address. Piper quickly typed him a note, asking for clarification and background on Silver, and hit send.

She'd check her email on her phone when she went out, hoping Deputy Gary Jefferson responded. Piper called Basil.

"I have to drop Zeke and Aggie at my house, feed my critters, and then I have to run out to Fulda. Yeah, the Buddhist thing. Shouldn't take long."

She listened. "Yes, I want to get a look at Silver's county farmland, too. I can take the acres not far from my house. I've probably passed them on my morning jogs, and—" She listened again. "Okay, meet at my house and we'll look at the land together, take one vehicle. Then we go to Fulda. I have to deal with Hagee. Silver has property between Fulda and Santa Claus, probably five miles from Hagee's place. After that, we'll find Silver's land in Luce. And we can talk about witness protection as we ride."

On her way out of the building, Piper called Oren and caught him up on the Silver case.

Thirty minutes later, with Zeke and Aggie tucked away, she and Basil stood on the side of a dirt road a mile from her house.

"Yep, I jog by here often," Piper said.

"Forty-eight acres." Basil had a printout from a picture he'd taken of the plat map. "Feels like a lot of land, but I guess not if you're a farmer. My old partner Tug, he got the IDs on Williams and Caine for me. I said I'd let him know how this turns out. I'm going to leave out this part. About walking in corn." He folded up the printout and put it in his pocket.

Silver's property was split by the road, and it looked like all of it was planted in field corn, the land leased for years to a local farmer. Basil had spoken to him; the older man had provided no interesting information.

"I'll take this side of the road," Piper said.

"I'm definitely leaving this part out." Basil took the other, and they kept in touch with their cell phones as they walked the dusty aisles between the rows.

The corn reached Piper's hips. She recalled the old saying her father had repeated when she was a child: knee-high by the fourth of July.

Basil said they should look for an old camper and a 1990 jade-green Chevrolet Lumina, a mini-van that had debuted that year. According to the DMV they were both still licensed to Samuel Silver, the sixteen-foot camper a vintage 1966 Shasta. They certainly hadn't been parked at Silver's house or at the comic store. Maybe they were long gone and he'd just kept the licenses up for … sentimental reasons? Or maybe they were stored in a barn, like the one farther back on this property.

Piper's mind churned. If the mini-van and camper were still around, did they hold more guns? Money? Something his torturers had been looking for? If Silver had been in witness protection, and Basil agreed it was an intriguing possibility, had he been a gun-runner?

"Who were you, Samuel Silver?" Piper walked quickly but carefully down the rows. From the road the ground had looked flat, all the acreage level. But between the rows it was uneven from where the equipment had churned it up for planting, and she stumbled several times. She mused that if she fell and died here, no one would find her body until harvest time.

"Nothing so far," Basil reported in at 5 p.m. "Called my wife and told her I'm not going to be home until late."

"You don't have to work this all night," Piper said, even though she intended to. "Go home to your family."

"Yeah, I do have to work late," Basil returned. Again, Piper felt lucky to have him on her team.

A half hour later, she searched a small barn in the field that tipped precariously to one side, the roof half gone. The whole thing was held together by peeling paint. It was empty save for a rusted harrow that weeds had twisted around. The farmer had told Basil he'd wanted to tear it down, but Silver said it needed to stay.

"Nothing in the barn," Piper reported, her voice thick with disappointment. "But it would be a great place to grow pot." Across the river Kentucky State Police regularly checked old barns. Marijuana growers planted their crops inside and relied on shoddy or missing roofs to let the rain in to water everything.

She walked the rest of her side of the property. It was simple, but beautiful land, all green, the stalks rustling in the breeze and the air fresh. Piper reflected again that this wasn't how she expected her life to turn out, being in rural southern Indiana. If things had gone according to plan, she'd still be in the Army, maybe on another down range assignment, maybe climbing the ladder toward another promotion. She wouldn't be here, in a cornfield chasing down leads in the murder of a comic shop owner. But she wasn't unhappy, and a small, rural county wasn't a bad place to settle.

They met back on the road a few minutes after six.

"Silver had a piece of land nearly twice as large over in Carter," Basil said, pulling out another printout. "Here. Stretches here, and across to here."

"That's past Santa Claus," Piper said. "It's about eight miles from Fulda. And I have to be a wizard in Fulda."

Basil cocked his head.

"I have to stop in at Chris Hagee's sometime tonight. I'd rather do it now, while there's a greater chance he's sober. So, we'll swing by his house in Fulda and then tackle Silver's Carter Township land."

"Your fellow Nang," Basil prompted.

"What about him?"

"He's got that restaurant in Fulda."

"It's sort of a restaurant."

"I'm more than sort of hungry," Basil said.

"Dinner, then Chris Hagee," Piper decided. She was more than sort of hungry, too. "If I talk to Hagee first, I might lose my appetite. With luck, we can walk the Carter farmland and head over to his Luce property while we still have some sun."

"I have flashlights," Basil said. The set of his jaw told her he wasn't going to quit on this tonight.

She called Nang and put in their order.

"Spencer County's version of fast food?" Basil joked.

"It'll be on the table when we get there."

"So the chef's sweet on you, huh Sheriff Blackwell?"

Piper wondered if maybe she was too sweet on Nang.

CHAPTER TWENTY-NINE

5 P.M.

"Not coming home for dinner, sorry. Still working." Oren called his wife. "The murder, yeah. I'm working that." He did not tell her about the body by the river, though he wanted to—that there were three murders, not one. They were all part of the same case. He would have enjoyed bragging that he'd handled this scene without Sheriff Blackwell being anywhere in sight. Maybe he'd tell her about it when he got home. "We're all working the murder. Extra hours. Whatever time I need to throw at it."

He listened to her lecture and suggest again that he consider retiring so he wouldn't have long days away from home covering grisly things. In all these decades he'd never been able to get her to understand that he found the grisly and unfortunate incidents exciting to work.

"I'm also dealing with the fair thing. Where the ride broke and the kids died. A lot of stuff on my plate." He paused and listened more, imagined that indeed the pot roast would be lovely. But it would taste even better warmed up. "I don't know, a while. An hour, two. Maybe longer. However long it takes." Another pause. "No, I am not too old for this. See you when I'm done."

He parked and went into the office, nodding to Teegan and disappointed Zeke was done with his shift at three. He would have liked Zeke's expertise and young eyes on the fair video. Ah! Zeke would still be here, right? In the break room with his little girlfriend.

"Zeke, you got a minute?" Oren poked his head in the doorway. It was empty. "Zeke?"

"Sheriff Blackwell took Zeke and Aggie to her place for safe-keeping," Teegan called.

"Piss," Oren muttered.

Oren stopped to pour a large cup of coffee. Good thing he hadn't eaten the chips at lunch with his dad. They'd make a suitable snack now, followed by a Hershey bar chaser ... he had one left in his bottom drawer.

"What's up?" Teegan followed Oren into the office.

The chief deputy's office was the same size as Piper's, but it was cramped because Oren had larger chairs, more file cabinets, and one of those dormitory-sized refrigerators on the floor because he preferred having his own than using the community one in the break room. Framed photos covered the walls—several of him in uniform through the years, being presented this or that award by the mayor or the previous Sheriff Blackwell. There was also a photo of his boat, with his granddaughter at the wheel. Next to it hung two collector edition Star Trek plates he'd received one birthday. His wife wasn't a science fiction fan, so he displayed them here. He couldn't consider himself a science fiction fan either, but he loved Star Trek. Zeke always ogled the plates whenever he came in.

"Video from the fair," Oren said. "Pete, the young man—"

Teegan bobbed her head and Oren noticed a new piercing.

"Why'd you have to do that? You have such a pretty face." He pointed to a spot below his lip. "I bet it hurt. Gonna get infected when you eat." If he wasn't tired, grumpy, and picturing that tattooed and pierced manager at the comic shop he would have kept those words inside.

Teegan scowled. "I like it. Been wanting another hole in my face for a while." She paused and leaned out into the hall, as if listening for the phone. It wasn't ringing. Oren could hear when the dispatcher's phone rang. He figured she was going to bolt because he'd insulted her.

"Well, at least it isn't one of those big hoops."

"Gee, thanks." She blew out a breath. "So what's up? What did you need Zeke the Geek for?"

"There's all this video from the fair. It's on all these chip things, and Zeke said he'd loaded it all onto a jump drive for us. I got one of the copies."

"And you want him to show you how to use a jump drive?"

Oren made a face. "I damn well know how to use a damn jump drive." He put it in his laptop to demonstrate. "I just—"

Teegan settled into a chair across from his desk, head cocked toward the open doorway. "Just what?"

The first video popped up, sound with it—screams, shouted questions, people yelling to call 9-1-1, music blaring from the ride speaker. He turned down the sound; he didn't need that.

Oren swiveled the laptop to the side so both he and Teegan could see it. "I'm going to get to some spots where I want to slow it down. Not stop it. I know how to do that, but slow motion. I don't know."

Teegan showed him what to do.

"Then I zoom in, like this?"

"You got it," Teegan said. "Mind if I stay and watch? Until the phone rings?"

Oren shrugged. "Fine."

Oren leaned in close and watched the first few clips, which were of the Cosmic Odyssey operating normally, riders waving their arms, mouths open. It was better without the sound to distract him. Vernon Milgrew in his dayglow shirt helped everyone on and off, never paying attention to the chart that read: "you must be –this– tall to ride." Many of the clips were confusing, the camera or cell phone not held still, colors blurring and angles changing as the image panned from ground level to the top of the ride.

Oren rubbed at his eyes.

"You're looking for something," Teegan said.

Obviously, Oren thought.

"What are you looking for? Maybe I can help."

"The kid at the hospital, the ride survivor. He said the operator didn't latch the basket they were riding in. Said he hollered at the operator as they started to rise, wanted him to stop, but the ride kept going. So I want to see if someone recorded that, Vernon Milgrew not clamping the basket closed."

"Holy shit," Teegan said. "You mean that guy we got in the jail—"

"—and that someone is coming to pick up tomorrow—"

"—is responsible for killing all those people."

Oren shook his head as he continued to go through the videos. "I don't think Vernon made the ride fall apart. There was some sort of equipment failure involved with that. But witnesses talked about two riders flying through the air *right as or right before* the ride broke apart. I think they were two separate awful things that happened at about the same time. Bizarre. Unreal. A million to one odds. But I think it happened. And I have to find some visual evidence of that. I think maybe Vernon Milgrew caused two boys to be ejected from the ride, one of them dying, and one trussed up in the hospital. And maybe they wouldn't have gone flying if the ride hadn't broke. You know, the jarring of it opening the boys' basket."

Teegan whistled low. "Every time I go back there to check on him, Milgrew, he shouts 'I ain't gonna burn for this.' But maybe—"

"Yeah, maybe he will burn."

"Gotta go. Phone."

An hour later, Oren found a video clip he went through frame by frame, and enlarged the image.

"Shit and two is four," Oren said. "Milgrew didn't lock the bar. Milgrew screwed up. He didn't break the ride, but he screwed up big."

Oren saved the video clip to a separate file on his laptop and printed out a dozen images. His stomach rumbled, the bag of chips and the chocolate bar coming to mind. His coffee was long-cold. The printed photos showed Milgrew correctly locking two baskets, but not catching the lock on another.

Oren retrieved his cell phone and made two calls. Then he went into the jail.

"One boy died because of you," Oren told Vernon. "And one boy's in the hospital because of you."

"I didn't do nothin' wrong," he returned. "I ain't burnin' for this."

"You have a right to remain silent—"

"I done got read my rights at the fair. I know what my rights are."

"That was for the drug charge you were wanted on," Oren said. "Anything you say can and will be used against you in a court of law. You have the right to an attorney. If you cannot—"

"I ain't burnin' for—"

"—afford an attorney, one will be provided for you." Oren stepped back and regarded the haggard-looking man. "Do you understand—"

"Damn right I understand. But I didn't do—"

Oren held up one of the printouts. "You didn't hook the lock on this basket. One boy died, another is pretty broken up. Going to be in the hospital a long time."

Vernon stared and gulped.

"Probably going to get charged with felony manslaughter," Oren said. "Wish it was something harsher, but manslaughter is appropriate. And some sort of serious assault charge regarding the injured boy. It'll be up to the county prosecutor and the grand jury to indict you."

Vernon sputtered, eyes wide and mouth working.

Oren went back to his office and detailed his notes, reviewed the video, and printed out additional pertinent images. He made a separate file for his notes on the discovery of Lloyd Ebersole's body.

Scales arrived a little while later, still dressed in his courthouse suit and tie.

Once more, Oren went through everything. He glowed inside, that he'd settled some aspect of the fair disaster and that justice could be found for two of the ride victims.

"Sharp work," Scales told him. "Seriously sharp, Oren. Not many people would notice that, and come up with the evidence. Incredible coincidence. Terrible coincidence. But—"

The county prosecutor tapped the images spread out on the conference table and shook his head.

"I'm sorry. Sharp work, but I really think it's for nothing," Scales pronounced. "Mr. Milgrew won't be found guilty of felony manslaughter because I don't think we can meet the 'beyond a reasonable doubt' level of proof. Negligence, sure, we could get him on that. He was negligent and sloppy, and it shouldn't have happened. But negligence isn't a criminal act. He wasn't trying to hurt anyone, was he?"

"Doubtful," Oren added. "No, I don't think he wanted to hurt anyone."

"He didn't purposefully not lock the ride. It looks like an accident to me," Scales said. "An unfortunate accident. An oversight. You can get him on negligence. Maybe recklessness or reckless disregard which in a perfect world could support manslaughter. But I honestly don't think so."

"Son of a bitch," Oren grumbled. "That's not right, Rob."

Scales frowned and shrugged with one shoulder. "Doesn't mean I like it. But that's the way it will go. You can't meet 'beyond a reasonable doubt.' There was great bodily harm, but not on purpose. Negligence, and that's not a criminal charge. That's a civil suit. And I'm sure there'll be plenty of civil suits flying over this whole thing. Supposedly one was filed today. No way you can prove he knowingly left it unhooked. Let him go. Get him on the east coast drug charge. That's something he's guilty of."

"Shit and two is four," Oren said.

CHAPTER THIRTY

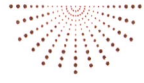

6:30 P.M.

Piper wondered if Basil was a vegetarian—not that it mattered. She was just curious. He avoided caffeine, pooh-poohed corn dogs, and in the office usually ate a salad and fruit he packed for lunch. At Nang's Quick Stop, sitting across a table from her, she watched him dive into a large plate of *Bún chả giò chay*, a mix of rice *bún* noodles and vegetable spring rolls. Piper had opted for Vietnamese caramel chicken, which she'd never tried before but found incredible, and a side of stir-fried oyster mushrooms.

"So is Phan a family name?" Basil asked.

The place was called Phan's Quick Mart, but from the day she'd met the proprietor, he'd told her to call him Nang.

"Yes."

Nang's was primarily a gas station, the only one in Fulda. It had four pumps, one for diesel, an automotive bay, and a three-thousand-square-foot convenience store stocked with a good variety of grocery items—bread, cereal, coffee, canned fruits and vegetables, soft drinks, and frozen goods such as pizza, ice cream, egg rolls, and chicken. In the back corner by the restroom three small tables gave diners a place to sit. Nang offered a sampling of Vietnamese dishes he made fresh every day, and claimed he was a better chef than an automotive mechanic, even though he had a degree for the latter.

Piper had stopped here in early January, putting gas in her Explorer and grabbing something to eat. She and Nang had hit it off and started dating soon after. He hovered around their table now, pouring tea, then serving the other two tables—a middle-aged man eating alone who probably was with the semi- parked to the side of the Quick Stop, and a mother with two young boys, one complaining that he wanted a cheeseburger.

"We're not going to walk all the rest of Silver's acres before dark," Piper said, looking out the store's big front window. Maybe we'll get through one of the properties, not both."

"I know," Basil admitted. "And as much as I want to, I know damn well my flashlight won't cut it."

"So we'll take the big chunk near Santa Claus today, and the other —Luce—in the morning."

"It's pronounced 'loose,' I'm told." Basil nodded. "And maybe I'll get home in time tonight to read to my kids. We're working through the first Harry Potter book."

As she ate, Piper watched a few cars pull up to the pumps, pay, and drive off. A mix of customers: a navy blue Volkswagen Beetle convertible she imagined would be fun to drive and thought the driver should have put the top down on this lovely day; a rusting Ford pickup, the bed filled with wooden chairs and bar stools tied down with cords; a shiny black Mustang with an orange stripe on the front panel—she knew it belonged to the volunteer fire chief; and a boxy white SUV that reminded her of Samuel Silver's vehicle. None of the drivers came inside.

"Pay at the pump is new," Nang said, returning to her table. "Got it put in one week ago. I'm not sure I like it. I made more grocery sales before I put it in."

"It's convenient," Piper said. Her eyes held his gaze. She reached for her wallet. "Gotta go, Nang. So friggin' busy."

"No charge," Nang said.

"Can't let you do that," Piper returned.

"Then you can let me take you to dinner tomorrow night, yes?"

She smiled. "I hope so."

"Maybe we will go back to the fair and get funnel cakes for desert."

Basil put a twenty on the table. "My treat, Sheriff." To Nang: "I'll bring my family next time and we'll get a lottery ticket. This is good food." Piper had told her detective that Nang purchased this place with the proceeds from a lottery ticket he'd bought from the station's previous owner. Often the customers who did come inside bought lottery tickets hoping to strike gold.

Several minutes later they pulled onto Hagee's long driveway, and Basil waited in the car, listening to the scanner. He reached for his cell phone.

Hagee's house mirrored the saltbox across the street, save this one had been painted battleship gray and had red shutters. The Buddhist retreat was a white saltbox with green shutters. A three-foot by three-foot sign in the middle of the front yard, roughly where a sleigh had sat at Christmas, had an artful black symbol on it—probably Taiwanese, Piper thought, though she had no idea what it meant. But she could read the words under it: REFLECTIONS SPIRITUAL RETREAT AND CULTURAL CENTER.

Piper's first day as sheriff—and first case—had taken her to that white saltbox. It was New Year's Day and the home's owner, Conrad Delaney, had been found dead and posed in the big sleigh, part of his Christmas display.

Delaney's son, Anthony, inherited the house. Piper found Anthony to be affable and competent, a Buddhist monk who'd returned to Spencer County from Thailand, where he'd been living.

Chris Hagee hadn't gotten along particularly well with Conrad Delaney, especially during the holidays because of Conrad's brightly lighted decorations. And now the dislike had transferred and magnified to Delaney's son.

Chris Hagee came to the door before Piper's fist hit it for a second series of knocks. She figured he'd probably heard the Explorer come up the driveway. Or saw her. A glance at the portico revealed a security camera aimed at the cracked cement stoop. Another camera on the front of the Hagee home pointed directly at the house across the street.

"Good afternoon, Mr. Hagee. I—"

"Wondered when the hell you'd get here." Hagee looked tired, the circles pronounced under his eyes, his hair a little disheveled, and his plaid sport shirt rumpled. Well behind him, Piper heard someone moving around, then came a call: "Who is it, dear?" Hagee glanced over his shoulder. "The little sheriff." He returned his attention to Piper.

"I know you've left several messages, Mr. Hagee. Deputy Diego came out here this—"

"I talked to him," Hagee returned, interrupting her. "But that Mexican isn't in charge of the sheriff's department. I wanted to talk to you. Oh, he was nice and all, polite, but he's got no real power. He can't do anything to fix this. You can."

Piper expected him to invite her inside, but he didn't. He just stood in the doorway, right hand against the frame, gaze focused past her on the saltbox across the street.

"What do I need to fix, Mr. Hagee?"

He sputtered. "I've been telling you, leaving messages. Told that deputy this morning. You need to make them Buddhists move. They got no right to—"

"Anthony Delaney owns that house, Mr. Hagee."

"He's a monk and he's operating some sort of church over there. But it's not a Christian one, and this county is Christian. Hell, it ain't even Jewish across the road. It's Buddhist, where they pray to some gold statue of a pot-bellied oriental man. It's a corrupting influence, and you know it. This sort of thing just ain't done around here."

Piper cringed. "Look, Mr. Hagee, Anthony Delaney seems like a reasonable man. Why don't you and I go over there and—"

"I ain't setting foot over at that place, haven't since his dad died. I see him out there, the boy, in orange robes, watering the bushes and flowers. I see him bringing people into that house. Conrad should have raised his boys different."

Piper heard the faint rattle of pans and plates, and she smelled garlic. She doubted the Hagees ate this late, so Chris' wife was probably cleaning up the kitchen.

"Has Anthony caused you any problems directly?" Piper asked. "Loud gatherings? Litter? Has he and his guests—"

Hagee speared the ball of his foot against the floor and made a grinding motion. "No, they're a quiet lot. Eerie in their quiet. Creepy. Always smiling, waving to me. That boy—"

"Anthony."

"Yeah. Anthony Delaney, but he calls himself something else, some religious title I think, he's come over a couple of times, inviting us to lunch or tea, trying to be all neighborly. I remember him from being a kid, growing up over there. Friendly. Won't have none of that. I want them out of here, Sheriff Blackwell. It just isn't right, Buddhists on this road. Let 'em go to the big cities like New York or Chicago or Philly. Indianapolis if they like this state so much. They're not supposed to be *here*." He paused and let out a long breath. "It's just not right. Why the hell didn't that boy go back to Thailand after his father's funeral? That boy wanted to be a Buddhist, let him be a Buddhist over there."

Hagee leveled a stare that gave her goosebumps. She thought there was meanness in his eyes, but sadness, too. He was clearly, painfully unhappy. Maybe Hagee needed to be unhappy about something. First Conrad's Christmas decorations, with the spotlight that shone toward the Hagee's bedroom window, now the Buddhist son's retreat.

Piper wondered if Hagee was capable of violence.

"They've not broken any laws, Mr. Hagee."

"They shouldn't be here." His voice was flat and his jaw was firm.

"Don't start trouble with Anthony Delaney," she warned.

"Thanks for coming by, Sheriff." Hagee stepped back into the house and closed the door.

Piper checked her phone for weather information. Sunset today would be 8:12, last light a half hour after that. She and Basil had an hour or more to walk some of Silver's land. Maybe going up and down some aisles of corn would keep her mind off the trouble brewing at Hagee's place.

CHAPTER THIRTY-ONE

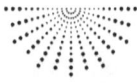

7:30 P.M.

Piper called her father on the way, and told him that she and Basil were walking acreage in Carter Township, near Santa Claus. Since Paul Blackwell was the chief of police, the notification was a professional courtesy. Paul volunteered to help.

"I'll take you up on that tomorrow, Dad," Piper said. "Especially if we don't get this section covered tonight."

Carter Township covered roughly three dozen square miles, with Silver's property only about a fraction of a square mile. She pulled to the side of the road just past Mariah Hill, which was about twice the size of Africa.

"Basil, I didn't think about a search warrant. We shouldn't have—"

"We're covered. That warrant I got for back at Silver's house, I included 'all properties in the county' in my wording. Just something I learned in Chicago. Cover your bases. I suppose I could've been a little more specific, and a court might tell us that, but I didn't have the coordinates for the farmland. Hell, I didn't know he had farmland until I poked around the courthouse."

"You're savvy," Piper said.

"Maybe." Basil gestured to the west side of the road. "Maybe just lucky. About twenty acres here, sixty on the other side that's planted in soybeans. When you were talking to Hagee I called the family who rents this land. They rent two other larger pieces from a retired farmer nearby. They know we're out here to look around. A lot of land Silver had."

Piper decided not to correct him. To a city-man like Basil eighty acres probably was a lot, but it was hobby-farm land around here. "The renters, how much are they farming total?"

"Total, a crapload, about four hundred acres. The largest farm around here. But like I said, they don't own all of it, they rent about half." He showed Piper on the printout what had belonged to Silver.

She elected not to tell him four hundred acres was not a big farm.

The twenty acres to the west was uneven, scrubby, and had a mix of dead, half-dead, and vibrant trees behind a stream that ran almost parallel to the road.

"We'll take this side first. Might be something hidden in the trees. Can pretty well see across the soybeans over there. Looks flat and empty. I don't see any buildings."

"Empty except for the soybeans," Basil said.

"Yeah, except for the beans." Piper radioed Teegan to tell her where they were, and listened to a quick recap of Oren's frustration over Scales and the Cosmic Odyssey. She didn't blame Oren for being pissed, but she understood where the DA was coming from. She took a deep breath; the air smelled good, clean, and was tinged with smoke, probably someone burning brush.

"Wish I'd thought to bring boots." Basil started down the slope to the ditch. "Walking this is not going to be a piece of cake."

No wonder this section of land wasn't being farmed, Piper thought. It was rutted, rocky, and near the road had the remains of a barn scattered amid clumps of weeds. It needed to be cleaned-up and leveled.

Piper watched a motorcycle, a large black Harley, approaching from the south. . She'd learned a lot about motorcycles after inheriting the vintage bikes in her garage. This was an expensive model. It slowed, and the rider flipped up the visor on her helmet.

"Sheriff," the rider acknowledged as she stopped. The rider, stocky and well into middle age, had on a blue and black leather vest with fringe. "Something wrong out here?"

"Probably not," Piper said.

"Tillman's goats get out again?"

"Not that I know of. We're just looking around. Do you live in the area?"

"Not exactly." The rider shook her head. "In Santa Claus, but I use this road to go home because I can ..." She paused and smiled. "Open up my bike if this stretch is empty. Not speeding today, though. You have a good evening, Sheriff Blackwell. Rain's coming. Hope you don't get caught in it."

Piper watched her leave and then waited as three cars drove past coming from the north—a dark blue VW Beetle with the convertible top up, a bright yellow Honda pickup missing its tailgate, and a green Ford Escape, similar to her department car, but smaller. All three slowed to gawk, the Escape driver stopping and the driver leaning out.

"Sheriff Blackwell!" The woman looked familiar, but Piper didn't know her name. She noticed Basil in the ditch, waiting for her. "What brings you out to Mariah Hill?" Before Piper could answer, the woman continued. "Hey, did you find out what happened to that big carnival ride? Gail here—" She tipped her head to indicate her passenger, who looked to be in her early teens. "Gail was out there, at the fair Friday night, said it was awful. What happened?"

"We're still investigating," Piper said.

The woman shook her head. "Awful thing. Have a good evening." Then she drove on her way.

"Losing light," Basil said as Piper joined him in the ditch.

"You're right about the light." She looked up, the sky was growing overcast. "And about the boots."

They picked their way through the rotted wood and crossed the stream, then started toward the trees. Piper doubted this land had ever been farmed, as rocky as it was. It could be, though, with work. Dividing it and using it for houses wouldn't be practical because of the stream, at least not along this section.

They put about twenty feet between them as they walked. Basil found the trailer soon after they reached the tree line and cut through the dead section, disturbing a family of ground squirrels. A large crow perched on the trailer's roof offered a scolding caw.

"Wonder how the hell Silver got this trailer back in here." Basil stood between two maples and scratched his head. "I don't see any way that man could have got this here without building it in place."

"Does it match?"

"With the records I found at the DMV? Probably. Looks like sixteen feet of 1960s to me. Says Shasta on the side. I'd call it a match … and a wreck." Basil put on his gloves. "And interesting. I'd call it that, too."

Basil took pictures with his cell phone.

The trailer was the kind you'd pull behind a truck or SUV, but as they got closer they noted the broken, rusted hitch, the flat tires, and the sky-blue and white surface pitted with dents and peeling.

"He might have pulled it in here twenty years ago," Piper said, "and the trees grew bigger around it."

"1966 model, according to the DMV registration," Basil said. He'd turned his cell phone to video mode and recorded his walk around it.

Piper had to work not to get her feet tangled in the thick overgrowth. She'd plodded through worse in some of her down range assignments, but she'd had boots then. Spiky vines sliced through her pants.

"Well, look at this, Sheriff."

She followed Basil around to the other side of the trailer. A path had been cut through the foliage. Beyond the copse a weed-dotted dirt lane snaked toward the county road on the far side.

"An easier way to get back here," Piper mused. "Too bad we took the difficult route."

"Don't know if that road over there is on my map."

"Not all of them are on the county map."

This side of the trailer wasn't in quite as bad shape even with the cinder block under the door serving as a step. The door handle had a padlock and a length of chain on it, along with a motion sensor that turned on an outside light as they stepped toward it.

"Windows are all small, a tight squeeze if we want in that way," Piper said. "Not like RVs today."

"Has solar panels," Basil observed. "So a piece of sixties junk modernized, tucked away and—" He nodded toward the front end. "There's a gas-powered generator, too, and it's in pretty good shape. I'd say this place got visited once in a while."

"I'm going back for bolt cutters," Piper said. "Keep videoing. I'm calling for another car with evidence boxes. Whatever's inside is important. Maybe we'll need another pair of hands."

She saw Basil's eyebrows crook up.

"You know it's important," Piper said as she turned to go. "Whatever's in there is important. I want extra people."

"I can go get the bolt—"

"You don't lock a rusting piece of crap and hide it in the trees if there isn't something important inside. Sit tight." Then she was trudging back to the road.

"Flashlights, too," Basil called after her. "Cell phone lights aren't good enough."

When Piper returned she drove in from around from the other side of the property, down the dirt path as far as she could go without running into trees. Her headlights revealed the ruts on the path, where a vehicle had driven in before, repeatedly judging how deep they were. The sky had domed with clouds and it had started to sprinkle by the time she shut off the engine. She saw Basil sitting on the cinder block, hunched in on himself, looking at his watch. It was a little after eight, but dark given the clouds and the thick trees. She slid out with bolt cutters and a big flashlight that she turned on and shined at the trailer.

"Millie's on her way with boxes and plastic garbage bags," Piper said. The latter because she knew rain was coming and she wanted any evidence kept dry. "She's finishing up a call, probably thirty minutes or so out. She should be able to find this easily with GPS."

"Smart you bringing the car back here," Basil said. "I want to get in that trailer. The mosquitos have declared war on me. Tried the windows, they're stuck or locked."

"And small." Piper handed over the bolt cutters. She put on gloves as he snapped the chain and lock. Basil opened the door and she went in first.

The trailer, though ragged on the outside from the years and weather, was dated but pristine on the inside. Part of the linoleum floor still shone, but the yellow-white-orange pattern was woefully old. It clashed with the olive green vinyl-covered benches that straddled a small table with a beige Formica top. Overhead oak storage bins had been heavily varnished. She aimed the flashlight beam around and saw a furnace, plus a small stove and refrigerator in matching yellow-gold. She glanced behind a shower curtain that served as a door to the tiny bathroom.

The whole place smelled like Lysol and lilacs, not overly strong but definitely noticeable. A pass with the flashlight showed floral air fresheners sitting on a ledge. They were reasonably fresh; Samuel Silver had been out here not too long ago.

Piper heard a thrumming sound.

"Try a light switch, Sheriff."

Basil had started the generator. Piper noticed a switch on the wall and thumbed it on.

"Works," she said. "Amazing." She meant both that this old trailer had electricity and what filled its interior.

At the far end a twin bed with a jungle-print coverlet and green toss pillows stretched under a light fixture decorated with dangling plastic vines. She didn't see any dirt or cobwebs, as if the place had been swept and dusted recently. She felt the trailer shift slightly as Basil came inside.

"Weird," he pronounced. "Like something you'd see in one of those horror films, a retro-trailer in the middle of nowhere." He had his cell phone out, videoing. "Definitely weird. Look how clean this dump is."

"I'm looking," Piper said. Two photos hung on a wall—one of Silver's African Grey parrots, the other of the man and woman she'd seen in stills in the safe deposit box.

She reached up and opened one of the storage bins, having to tug because the fastening was stubborn. "This is interesting." Ten ledger-style books had been crammed tight inside. She turned off the flashlight, set it on the table, and pulled the books down. The lights in the trailer were bright enough to read by.

With his free hand, Basil opened another bin. "Huh." There was a neat pile of comic books, each in a plastic sleeve. He left them there and opened more bins, all of them holding comics in plastic sleeves. One also held a small tin box.

"The man definitely collected," he said. "Comics at his house, comics here. Why the hell keep some here? Out in the middle of nowhere? Think he's got some of them early Supermans? If they're valuable, why not keep them in a safe deposit box?"

"They don't make a single safe deposit box big enough for all those comics." Piper sat on one of the benches and opened the top book, expecting to see business notes, and instead finding news clippings. Basil turned off the video recorder and sat opposite her, reaching for the second book in the stack.

"This one's like a scrapbook," Basil said, opening it. "But not family fun. These are all about arrests, murder reports. It's almost like a police murder book."

"This one, too. Here are articles about a trial." Piper reached for her phone. "Teegan, who's in the office? Jake? Put him on." She turned a few more pages. "Jake, do a search on Doyle Ricci. Mid-nineteen eighties to nineties, New York and New Jersey. Mob ties, crimes, that sort of stuff, warrants issued for him." She could do a Google search on her phone, but it wouldn't be as thorough as the law enforcement sites linked via the department computers, and she needed to spend her time right now going through these books, not surfing. "Call me when you get something, and email me files."

"Doyle Ricci," Basil said. "Sam Silver, right? Sam was Doyle."

"They have to be the same man. Look at the face. Well, look at the twenty-some-year younger face. And it doesn't look like he was a good soul back in the day."

Basil flipped through the pages of newspaper clippings. "Murder, gun dealing, drug running." He opened the tin box and showed Piper a vintage pair of diamond cufflinks and a worn-smooth Yale University ring set with a blue stone. "Someone he knew graduated from Yale sixty years ago."

Piper turned another page in the book. "If Doyle—Sam—was hiding in witness protection, he gave up enough valuable information to void all the criminal charges against him." She glanced to the small window when the bouncing glare of headlights cut through the thin curtain. "Millie made good time. We can take all this stuff back to the office with—"

Then a car door slammed and a spray of bullets ripped into the trailer.

CHAPTER THIRTY-TWO

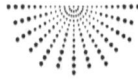

8:30 P.M.

"That's not Millie!" Piper slid off the bench, flat onto the linoleum, Basil a heartbeat after her. They drew their guns and listened. A second spray of bullets sounded staccato, some punching through the door and the shower curtain.

"Automatic," Basil said.

"Maybe two of them. Sounded like two shooters."

"Only one practical way out of here," Basil said, nodding toward the door.

"Stay low." Piper was on her feet as another spray came, jumping on the bench and opening the back window with her free hand. The window was narrow and she turned sideways as she vaulted out of it, scraping her shoulders and hips, momentum carrying her through. All the windows were small, and she doubted Basil's broad shoulders could fit through them. She thumbed her radio as she landed awkwardly in the weeds on the other side. "Teegan, we're under fire. Warn Millie. Send more backup. Now."

Diffuse light shown from the trailer window. Not enough to see well by, it cast the growth in a mass of twisting shadows. The rain that fell was soft, barely a drizzle, but it made the weeds slick as she pulled herself along. She could use the light on her cell phone, but that might be noticed, and she wasn't sure the shooters knew she'd gotten out, what with the racket from their gunfire on the other side. Keep to the shadows as long as possible, she thought. She gritted her teeth as more bullets pelted the trailer, then she heard a man shouting, but the words weren't clear, and it wasn't Basil.

She did a low crawl through the scrub, across rocks and branches, a piece of metal something, a shard of glass. Piper was sure she'd cut herself, but that was nothing to worry about. The threat was from the gunmen. They might come around the trailer at any moment. *They*— she was pretty sure there'd been two guns firing. She heard Basil return fire, maybe he'd opened the door, a risky move. Maybe the door had been shot to shit.

Piper crawled through a cloud of gnats and mosquitos, something stinging getting into her eyes. At the end of the trailer, she moved fast, listening, watching. The trailer's motion-sensor light, coupled with the headlights from the shooters' car, gleamed bright on this side. She made out a VW Beetle next to her Explorer. Not a coincidence she'd seen it at the pumps at Nang's and then later on the county road. It had followed her. Was it the same Beetle she'd seen on one of her morning jogs—across from one of Silver's farm properties? A dark silhouette of a tall man with a rifle stood near it, backlit by the headlights. Could be Ethan "Bloodshot" Caine. The rifle looked to be an M16. The second figure, a woman by her slight build, stood in the shadows, holding some sort of machine pistol, leveling it at the door and firing.

Piper slid like a snake under the wheel well then rocked back as a shot pinged inches away. More pings, bullets against metal, staccato sounds cutting through the once-quiet night.

"Drop the guns or I'll torch the comic books!" That was Basil.

Piper exhaled in relief that her detective was still alive.

"I'll burn them!" Basil threatened.

"Don't give a damn about the comics!" It was the woman. She fired again, and between bursts Piper heard the other shooter reload. "Burn 'em all. I want a ring! That's all I want!"

Piper pictured the Yale University ring. Certainly nothing to murder anyone over.

"You can have the ring. Drop your weapons!" Piper warned, trying to end this bloodlessly. "Drop your—"

The woman swung the gun down, shooting, bullets biting into the flattened tires and the earth, and chewing up rocks and dirt. Piper kept her head down and returned fire. The tall man shot in Piper's direction, too, then aimed higher at the trailer. Everything was a chaos of gunfire and approaching sirens.

Piper rolled under the middle of the trailer, using the cinder block step for partial cover. She fired twice more and the woman dropped her weapon. A moment later, she collapsed.

"Lulu!" the man shouted. "Son of a bitch. I'm gonna kill you." He shot repeatedly at Piper, who worked farther under the trailer, trying to escape the gunfire. Bullets chewed into the cinder block. "You're dead, hear me! Dead!"

He shot again and again. By the sound of it, Piper guessed he was alternating between trying to hit her and firing into the trailer. She heard return fire; had to be Basil. She crawled forward again, her shoulders scraping against the underside of the trailer, the light from the motion sensor and the Beetle's headlights making it almost impossible to see. She slammed her eyes shut, then opened them, squeezed farther to her left, picturing herself under the tiny kitchen, and then almost at the other end. Another foot and she'd be out from under the trailer, a proverbial sitting duck.

She avoided looking directly at the headlights here, everything still bright and hazy, the drizzle making it all seem like a mad impressionist's painting. There! She saw the body of the woman on the ground, not stirring, and next to it the legs of the man, spread wide in a firing stance. She heard another burst from the rifle, more return gunshots from Basil. Piper fired too, until her gun was empty.

Ballistics tests would determine whether Basil or she got the man. He fell half over the woman. Piper held her breath, listening, hearing sirens coming closer—two from the sound. No, three. She tried to hear if there was a third gunman. The trailer above her shifted a little, Basil stepping out of it.

"Sheriff Blackwell?"

"I'm okay. You?" She scrabbled out, still alert, and slammed another magazine in her gun.

"Yeah. I'm okay." Basil bent over the bodies, feeling for pulses.

"Nothing," he said. "Gone, both of them."

Piper saw that the trailer's door had been shot apart, all the small windows on this side broken. Bullet holes had made Swiss cheese of the trailer's shell.

A sedan bounced down the dirt path, lights flashing, siren keening. It was Millie. Piper got to her feet and batted at the cloud of insects that swarmed her face. The drizzle had done nothing to keep the pests away.

"The tall man's Caine." Basil holstered his gun and took pictures with his cell phone. "Those body cams coming in this week?"

"Yeah," Piper said, catching her breath. "Would've been nice to have them days ago. Would've been handy for this. The woman?"

"No clue who she is. But she looks hard. Got some prison tats on her arm."

Looking down on the bodies, putting the car headlights to her back, Piper made out the details. The woman, who'd fallen on her right side, Caine across her legs, looked to be in her mid- to late thirties, short hair, a multitude of earrings, the largest of which were skulls and daggers. She had big shiny scars on her gun hand, like she'd been burned. The tattoos were visible and numerous. Piper wondered if she'd seen her a few days past during a morning run. She might have been the woman putting on makeup while sitting in the bug across from the field that had belonged to Silver. If that had been her, maybe she'd been searching for Silver's property. Maybe she'd been one of the man's torturers.

Another car pulled in with lights and siren, an Explorer. Oren got out. One more car was driving in farther back. Oren padded forward, holstering his gun when he saw the threat had passed. They all stared

251

down at the bodies. And as if to better accommodate them, the rain stopped.

Piper glanced at the Beetle. It had New Jersey plates; maybe it had been stolen, too.

Oren reached for his cell phone and punched one button. After a moment, he said: "Annie, got two more for you. I'm going to send you directions, otherwise you'll never find this place. Wear boots. It's a little muddy." He paused. "Yep, lucky guess, give the woman a ribbon. It's connected to the Samuel Silver case."

"Except he wasn't Samuel Silver," Piper said softly. "He was Doyle Ricci."

"This is going to take a while," Basil said.

"I wonder if there are any more thugs from New Jersey in Spencer County," Piper mused. "I hope these two and the one in jail are it."

Basil shrugged and stepped on the cinder block. "I figured it was about the comic books. There are some really old ones in here."

"The woman mentioned a ring."

"Yeah, I heard. I showed you a ring. Maybe that was it. Hardly think it was worth all of this, an old ring. Anyway, maybe word'll get back to New Jersey that whatever they were sent to collect is evidence now, not worth sending any more goons for."

"Too bad no one's alive here to explain it," Piper said. She glanced at the bodies again.

"Somebody can." This from Oren. "Somebody can damn well explain why so many people are dead."

CHAPTER THIRTY-THREE

2 P.M. TUESDAY, JUNE 18TH

Piper rode her 1953 Ariel Square 4 motorcycle to work for the first time. The bike was vintage and valuable, but life was short—as proven by the county fair catastrophe Friday night —and so she'd taken it out of the garage. Her department Explorer was not useable. Its tires had been shot out by the New Jersey thugs, and bullets that went through the grill had caused some serious engine damage.

A good reason for the motorcycle and to be sluggish on getting a loaner vehicle.

She, Basil, and Oren had worked until early morning before going home for some needed sleep. She told Oren to take the day off, but suspected he wouldn't. In confirmation, she pulled into the department's lot and parked next to his car.

"Coffee," she said, going through the back door. "I need a lot of coffee."

"Vernon Milgrew is on his way to Virginia," Oren reported as she poked her head in his office. "It's not right, but it's what it is."

"Coffee?" Piper tipped her head toward the break room.

Oren got up and followed her.

"Hey Sheriff." Zeke leaned around the corner from his desk.

253

Aggie's parents had picked him and Aggie up from Piper's house when they got back into town. Piper hoped the threat had truly passed and that her dispatcher and his girlfriend were safe. "Got a stack of messages waiting for you."

"I'll get them in a little while." Piper headed to the coffee maker. "I need a lot of coffee."

"Annie told me last night she's thinking about quitting," Oren said, holding out his mug. Piper filled his first. "Said she's too old for this."

Piper didn't respond, not knowing what to say. She certainly wouldn't want to autopsy anyone, let alone the number of bodies that had crossed Dr. Neufeld's slab in the past handful of days. She filled her mug, took a sip, drank some more despite how hot it was, then topped it off before turning toward the evidence table.

The break room also served as work space. Boxes filled with the comics from the trailer were stacked at one end, the books filled with news clippings, eBay printouts, and other things—including Doyle Ricci's real birth certificate and original Social Security card—sat on the other end.

Piper and Oren perched in the middle where they could reach either pile.

"I don't like the outcome with Milgrew either," Piper told him. "His inattention caused one boy to die and another to end up in the hospital. But Scales is right. An accident. Probably couldn't pull a conviction for manslaughter."

"Doesn't mean Scales shouldn't have tried," Oren grumbled.

"It was good work, though," Piper cut in. "You finding those video clips, talking to the kid in the hospital. Impressive work."

"All of it was awful work," Oren corrected. "Lots of people hurt at the fair. I looked at that woman's preliminary report on the Odyssey that she emailed this morning, said that one of the main support beams was corroded inside, and that it wouldn't have shown up on an inspection. Hidden rust. Shit happens, eh? That's the saying, shit happens. Rust. People—kids and a guy selling cotton candy—died because of hidden rust." He shook his head.

"And two innocent young men were killed because they were with

Samuel Silver," Piper said. She held the coffee to her nose, but the enticing scent didn't make her feel better.

"They certainly weren't killed because of expensive Hawaiian shirts," Oren said. "What the hell was at the bottom of it? Not comic books. No comic book is worth the price of a human life."

"Williams' New York attorney isn't coming in until next week. Maybe we'll find out the whole picture then," Piper said.

"Or maybe we'll find out sooner." Oren gestured to the doorway.

Zeke stood there with a man in a US Marshal's uniform.

"Please, Dear God, let us find out sooner. I don't want to wait for the trial," Piper breathed.

"Sheriff Blackwell, Special Deputy Marshal Gary Jefferson," Zeke said as introduction. The phone rang behind him, and he spun to answer it.

Jefferson was tall, narrow, and had rounded shoulders. His shirt looked a size too big. Piper put him in his late fifties, his hair salt and pepper, set against a tanned, high forehead. Wire rim glasses poked out of his front pocket. He held a folded Spencer County map in his left hand, the glossy blue and white ones the Chamber of Commerce offered.

"Coffee?" Oren asked Jefferson.

"Chief Deputy Oren Rosenberg," Piper introduced him as she stood.

"Coffee would be good, thanks."

The coffee is very good, Piper thought. But it wasn't good enough to make things better today.

The conversation stretched the remainder of the afternoon, and Basil joined in when he arrived.

Piper learned it wasn't an expensive Aloha shirt or Congo Bill or Tarzan comics that led to Silver's—Ricci's—demise. It wasn't even the ring the woman had mentioned, though pursuit of the ring had led to the shootout at the old trailer.

It was vengeance.

"I remember putting Ricci down here twenty years ago," Jefferson said. "My partner at the time and I were assigned to him. We were handling witness relocation in Indiana and part of Kentucky and Ohio. Ricci hadn't wanted to be dropped into the Midwest; he'd told us he wanted to live in Hawaii or the Texas coast, that the weather would suit him better. But he got Indiana, Spencer County, though at the beginning he had a place across the river in Owensboro. Had minimal plastic surgery, and not to make him look different. He'd had his nose broke and jaw fractured in a prison fight. It was just to repair the damage. He mostly looked the same."

Piper recalled how similar Silver's face had looked to the pictures of Doyle in the older photos.

"I don't know how he got all those guns you found, or why he had them. No one needs that many guns for protection." Jefferson scratched his chin.

"Ballistics showed they'd not been fired for a long while," Basil said. "One had been linked to a killing in the Bronx twenty-four years ago."

Jefferson shook his head. "Somehow he'd managed to get the guns, his tools of the trade I'd call them. We knew he'd gotten the comic books he'd appropriated—stolen. He must have stayed in contact with someone from his past, despite the witness protection. That someone brought the guns to him."

"We went through his records, charges, dug through some trial reports," Piper said. Jake had found extensive files on Doyle Ricci, and Piper had read through everything into the early morning. "Wasn't a nice man."

Jefferson supplied an empty smile and folded his hands on the table. Piper noticed a pale stripe of flesh where a wedding ring had been. "Murder," he said. "Ricci was a hitman for Valentino Lombardi's mob, back when the mobs had more power and prominence. Fell in with them as a teenager. He admitted to killing six, but we always thought there were a few more. All rival mobsters that Lombardi considered troublesome. Ricci did a little gun-running too, was involved with Lombardi's drug operation."

"He had no business being on the outside," Oren said.

"Ah, but the government thought he did," Jefferson argued. "Ricci traded enough information to buy his freedom and land him in witness protection. He gave us enough evidence on Lombardi's deals to put the boss and a more than a dozen of his closest allies in prison for the rest of their lives. All of those fish were a helluva lot bigger than Ricci. His information shut down a massive drug distribution system, protection rackets, and solved a lot of open cases. Ricci was gold." He picked up the coffee mug and drank. "This is good. What is it?"

"Italian Dark," Piper said.

Jefferson laughed, drank again. "You know, the mobs are pretty much all gone now, replaced by gangs. It's a different culture, but the crimes are still there, the networking, drugs, prostitution. But for a while, things were better because of Ricci. So many of those mobsters locked up. I kept tabs on him—Samuel Silver was the name he picked out—came down and looked in on him once in a while. Seemed to have turned his soul around here in Indiana. Didn't seem like a bad sort. No one would have guessed he'd had a criminal past. He could have lived to be an old, old man here with his comics and jungle critters."

"But he was found out," Basil said. "Something he did."

"Something he put up for sale," Jefferson nodded. "See, Lombardi loved comic books and had an extensive collection. And Ricci stole crates of them before putting down roots here. We looked the other way because they were just comics, right? He'd served up Lombardi. So we just looked the other way. Jungle comics mostly from what I heard. Lombardi and Ricci shared a love of jungle comic books." Jefferson reached in a pocket and pulled out a notebook, flipping through it. "One comic book—*one*—brought the mob here and led to Ricci's murder."

"Care to elaborate?" Piper encouraged.

"Ricci put one up on eBay, and it sealed it, caught their attention like it was a blazing search light. Rulah the Jungle Queen, number twenty-one, graded at a 9.0 rating, practically perfect. Apparently it was the finest condition of that particular issue ever reported existing. Lombardi knew he'd had the only 9.0 in existence. He knew that

Rulah comic book had been his. And he knew Ricci had stolen it. Ricci had both ratted Lombardi out and stole comics from him. Ricci would still be breathing if he hadn't put that *one* comic book up for sale. I'm sure they used the eBay posting to find him. One comic. I don't know a lot about comics, but this condition-grading thing … it's all about that. The search light shining from Africa."

"So that comic—" Oren prompted.

"Lombardi was supposed to spend the rest of his life in prison. But two weeks ago he was given compassionate release. Pancreatic cancer. He's maybe got another week or two left. Maybe. All these years, Lombardi had searched for his comics with his network—hoping to find the rat with them, and one of his men saw that eBay listing for that particular Rulah. That *one* comic book. Word is Lombardi dispatched a crew the same day the listing had went live."

"It was all about revenge," Piper said.

"Lombardi would call it justice," Jefferson returned.

"Caine and Williams," Basil said. "Caine's dead. Williams is in a cell. We're waiting on his attorney. The woman shooter dead."

"The woman from last night," Piper said. "She was part of the Lombardi crew? We don't have an ID yet, none of them carried ID." They hadn't found the ice pick either, probably never would.

"She was Lombardi's granddaughter, Lulu. Don't know where she'd been hiding, but the FBI had been looking for her for several years. My director figured she was after her grandfather's college ring. He'd made it clear that he wanted to be buried with it, and that he'd given it a long time ago to Ricci. He wanted it back. So I'm pretty sure she was following her grandfather's orders to find that ring. Rulah the Jungle Queen led Lulu to Ricci's doorstep."

"Comic books," Oren grumbled.

"And I'm sure Lombardi would have liked his prized Rulah back, maybe have it buried with him, too," Jefferson said. "The heart of it, though, was about betrayal. Ricci betrayed Lombardi, and so Lombardi wanted Ricci—Silver—dead. And he won't be buried with the ring. That'll be locked up with all the evidence."

"Maybe Silver—Ricci—was due," Oren said, "for everything he'd done, people he'd murdered. But there were two young men executed just because they were with him. They didn't deserve death."

"Lombardi wasn't known for leaving witnesses behind," Jefferson said. "His mobsters would've kept with that."

Piper thought about Aggie, who would leave tomorrow for Coast Guard basic training. They'd tried to get her, too.

"So you think this matter is closed?" Piper asked.

"I do," Jefferson nodded. He finished the coffee. "You confiscated the comic books and that Yale ring."

"And the diamond cufflinks. Evidence," Piper said.

"I'll want it all, you realize. It's part of our over-arching case."

Piper thought good riddance, if the comics and ring were a mob magnet, get the magnet out of Spencer County. He'd probably want to take Williams, too, but she'd put up a fight for that. Williams was involved in the deaths of Silver, Duckworth, and Ebersole, and the attempted kidnapping of Aggie. Piper wanted him to stand trial here. No, he wasn't going to get Williams.

"Make sure Lombardi gets wind that you have his stuff," she said. "We don't want more of his thugs coming here looking for them."

"Sure. Sure. So I consider it closed," Jefferson said. "His granddaughter dead, Ricci dead, Lombardi soon to be dead, the comics and ring locked away. It's done. Just a matter of filing all the reports. Closed."

"Ricci had a nice comic shop across the river," Oren said softly. "A good place for kids to gather. That's closed now, too. And that's a shame."

CHAPTER THIRTY-FOUR

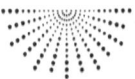

7 P.M.

Piper finished the corn dog and threw the stick in the trash. She reached for the funnel cake Nang held out.

"I'll be stuffed if I eat this," she said. "I'll have to run twice as far tomorrow morning to work it off."

Nang didn't reply. He was eating his own funnel cake.

She'd come out to the fair with Nang after Jefferson left for Indianapolis. Exhausted, she didn't think she could sleep, her mind too jittery with everything that had happened in the past handful of days.

There was a crowd, but it wasn't really *crowded*. The fair manager told her attendance was about half of previous years, that the Cosmic Odyssey had changed everything. "Hopefully things will be back to normal next summer," he'd told her. "We've two days left before it packs up. Maybe closing night will be better. Or next summer."

It will take longer than that, she thought.

Nang finished his treat first, wiped his hands on a napkin, then put his arm around Piper's shoulders.

"You shine," he said.

Mungo Jerry's *In the Summertime* blared through the nearest speaker.

"I'm stuffed," Piper said. "But now I'm thirsty."

"Share one of those big lemonades?"

She smiled as he steered her toward the Lemon Shakeup vendor. Nang selected the cup that would let them come back for refills.

"Owensboro, Daviess County, has a bigger fair," Nang said. "Used to go every summer when I lived there. But I like this one better."

Piper looked up at him. "Because—"

"Because you're here with me. That makes this fair the best."

She kissed him and decided she was fine with liking him a lot.

"Dare the Ferris wheel?" he asked.

"Absolutely." She hoped they'd get stopped at the very top.

THE END

ACKNOWLEDGMENTS

Many thanks to Robert Scales for his legal eyes; Bill Gilsdorf for teaching Piper how it's properly done; Donald J. Bingle, Vicki Steger, Christine Verstraete, and Janet Deaver-Pack for their review; Kelly Flanigan and Ursula Cutter for the amusement rides; Beth Terrell for the birds; Alan Goff with the Indiana Division of Weights and Measures for pointing me in the right direction; Amber Kent with the Indiana Department of Homeland Security's Elevators and Amusement Ride Safety Section for her expertise; and Wrinkles the Wonder Pug for keeping my feet toasty warm and my heart happy.

SPENCER COUNTY, INDIANA

It's a real place, about as far south in Indiana as you can go. The towns, roads, and some of the businesses I reference in this novel exist. There really is a Santa Claus—it is nestled between the Ohio River and Interstate 64. On my visit to the Christmas store there I picked up some walnut fudge and a Boston terrier ornament that I had personalized. Rockport is about twenty miles away from Santa Claus, and is where the real Sheriff's Department sits. I've fictionalized the county, taking considerable liberties. I used to live in Indiana —Evansville, during my newspaper reporter days. Spencer County isn't far from there. The place is a good home for Piper Blackwell and company.

ALSO BY JEAN RABE

From Boone Street Press

The Bone Shroud

The Dead of Winter

The Dead of Night

The Finest Creation

The Finest Choice

The Finest Challenge

From WordFire Press

The Cauldron

Pockets of Darkness

The Love-Haight Casefiles (with Donald J. Bingle)

Plus dozens more - find out more at www.jeanrabe.com!